Hawkwings

Also by Karen Lee Osborne

Carlyle Simpson

Hawkwings

Karen Lee Osborne

Chicago

Book design and production by Midge Stocker
Text set 11.5/13 ITC Clearface
Printed on recycled, acid-free paper in the United States of America.

Library of Congress Cataloging-in-Publication Data

Osborne, Karen Lee, 1954-
Hawkwings / Karen Lee Osborne. -- 1st ed.
p. cm.
ISBN 1-879427-00-1 (pbk. : alk. paper) : $9.95
I. Title.
PS3565.S43H39 1991
813'.54--dc20 91-11962
CIP

This book is available on tape to disabled women from the Womyn's Braille Press, P.O. Box 8475, Minneapolis, MN 55408.

Third Side Press
2250 W. Farragut
Chicago, IL 60625-1802

First edition, May 1991
10 9 8 7 6 5 4 3 2 1

for JoAnn
and to the memory of Peter
and for Abby,
who teaches us to remember
how we once loved flight

There was so much to love, I could not love it all;
I could not love it enough.

Louise Bogan, "After the Persian"

There are the lover and the beloved, but these two
come from different countries.

Carson McCullers, "The Ballad of the Sad Cafe"

He Always Called Me "Sweetie"

If I'm going to go, I'll have to make up my mind. Mango's no help. She purrs softly in my lap, her body stretched out, legs extended beyond my thighs, belly exposed. What have I done to deserve such trust? I could sit like this another hour stroking her, and then it would be too late to go to Fiona's party.

"Should I go?" I ask George. "After all, it's been two months since I've seen Fiona. It's nice of her to throw a party at the women's bar, inviting clients as well as family and friends. Other therapists are giving her flak for that."

I study his clear eyes, the rich mustache, the fine, strong jaw and sensitive lips.

"I guess by going I'd be announcing I'm past the grief, ready to face the world again. Maybe."

Ready to face other women? Ready to socialize? Smile, even laugh, make small talk?

I stand, forcing Mango to wake up and jump down.

"I miss you, George," I say to the photograph in its silver frame. "I miss having you to talk to. You always understood."

With George, I felt I had a home. I had stopped thinking of my small town in Virginia as home when I was 18 and left for the suburbs of D.C. with two of my high school friends. We worked in restaurants and went to the community college. Back in high school, before I was old enough to vote, I posted signs and handed out flyers supporting Shirley Chisholm for president. After she lost the primary, I started posting McGovern signs and stickers everywhere. I was an embarrassment to my family in that town. I was the only white face in the second largest black gospel choir. After the director, Brother Johnson, got tired of calling on the altos and hearing a shaky tenor polluting their clear tones, he moved me into the tenor section. But the men had beautiful tenors, and mine was decidedly second rate. When I left, everyone was relieved.

After community college, I couldn't get enough financial aid to see me through and gave up on transferring to Georgetown. One night after my shift at the restaurant, I went out drinking with a guy home on vacation from the School of the Art Institute in Chicago. He was driving back to Chicago in August and offered me a ride.

I stayed at Jim's for a few days. At his apartment was a painting with some of the palest blues I had ever seen. One shape looked like that of a man singing, with his head tilted back. Out of his mouth a miniature woman was flying, her long hair streaming behind her, all the way back to the source of the sound you couldn't hear. When I asked Jim if he had painted it, he laughed. A couple of days later, he introduced me to George. George was graduated from the Art Institute on a full scholarship, whereas Jim still had two years to go, but everyone there, it seemed, knew George. He had grown bored with painting, he said. After giving all his paintings away, he enrolled in graduate school at DePaul to study theater and music. He was an accomplished pianist and child actor before he left home in Michigan, and now he gave a few piano lessons every week to earn money. He had a big apartment, and he needed a roommate.

I moved in with George when he was still sleeping with women and I was still sleeping with men, but we never slept together. During the next ten years, even after George found Eric, we still lived together. There was plenty of room for Eric to stay whenever he wanted, and they never felt it necessary to live together. I was like his sister, George said. In Chicago, instead of restaurant jobs I got secretarial jobs, and then I went back to school and finished a degree at Roosevelt. After working temporary jobs for awhile, I was hired by a state agency to help teach city survival skills to recent immigrants, the differently abled, and those who had previously been in institutions. After a big budget cut, my job was changed to part-time. I stayed anyway because I liked working with people who had never learned how to use public transportation, how to handle money, how to drive. People who were afraid. Like me. I was afraid until I lived with George.

We talked. I had run out of things to say to my parents and brother in Virginia years ago, even before my father died. In most of what people call homes, there is speech, but people avoid talking with each other. Their talking masks a deeper silence, a refusal to hear or speak. George and I had a home where we could actually talk to each other. I learned that that is what a home is. The people in such a home can be talking to each other even when they are silent.

I loved it most when George sang. When he sang, the words didn't mean what you thought they'd meant before. He turned the words into pure air, pure sound, and then when you saw the words printed somewhere it wasn't the same at all; they were the wrong words entirely to describe what you'd heard. When he sang, you'd find yourself biting your nails. The words turned into air, and the air floated into your head and found its way into your throat and your heart.

He became a drama teacher and voice coach at a small college on the far north side, but he still kept the apartment in Newtown because he wanted to be close to theaters and everything else the city had to offer. He was a Chicagoan, intoxicated by all the different faces on the street.

George was someone who could touch and be touched, and not just physically. When he heard a particularly good recording of Brahms's "Alto Rhapsody," he was not ashamed to weep. All six feet of him, musclebound from gym workouts. His students knew they could tell him everything, and they often did. George always listened to me when I was upset or depressed or feeling rejected by this or that woman. "Emily, remember you're a hawk," he'd say. "Hawks should be proud." I needed George to remind me.

Then Bonnie came along. She was an irresistibly beautiful younger woman; her passion delighted and scared me at first. I had never been needed like that. George was happy for me. He loved the way Bonnie devoted herself to me. Put his long arms around both of us. He towered above us both, but he'd lean down and give us each a kiss on the cheek. "She's a gem," he'd say to me, and wink.

I remember his dazzling blue eyes. This photograph hasn't captured them. No photograph ever did. Only a few of us really remember him. With George you didn't have to pretend or be anything other than who you were. He loved me exactly as I was. He didn't care about my second-rate tenor and encouraged me to sing along with him, although I didn't. He never wanted anything from me. Just to have me near him was enough. We were comfortable with each other. Perhaps more comfortable with one another than two lovers can ever be. No imbalances, no unfulfilled desires. We understood one another completely in our separate forays into love affairs. He was a romantic, as I am. Both of us romantic to a fault.

If he were here, he'd tell me to go to the party. Why not? It would be good to see Fiona. She'll be happy to see how much better I'm feeling. How the grief really has abated somewhat. For George, dead a year ago at 35. And for Bonnie.

Bonnie showered me with love and affection, stayed with me through most of the grieving, and then left. She's been with another lover for more than eight months now. I've been alone. Celibate. At first I grieved almost constantly; then, gradually, something inside me changed.

Maybe I like my solitude too much. I should go to the party. Be around other people. Even other lesbians. It's been long enough since Bonnie. I can handle it. I can handle it very well. I am so attached to my solitude now that I can stand among a group of lesbians and not be attracted to anyone. Not feel any desire to ask anyone out, or to be asked. Not look at anyone and see halos. I've let George carry the illusion of halos out of my life for good. People are not divine, despite my romantic tendency to bestow divinity upon them. Most are not even especially interesting—certainly nothing to burden myself with desires for. They walk around, these ordinary, not very interesting creatures, oblivious to the absence of George. How can they live without this knowledge of difference? I used to wonder how I could live with it. How can they have missed the transformation of the world? The loss. The loss of that open heart, those loving eyes, that quick and ready smile, that reassuring voice. *Sweetie*, he always called me.

You should go, sweetie.

That's what he'd say. I blow a kiss at his picture, grab my jacket and keys, and close the door behind me.

On the street the parked cars are covered with ice. A woman in a red coat is scraping her windshield, both hands gripping the small plastic tool. Chipping away at the ice without success.

"You look like you could use some help there. Want to let me try?"

She looks me up and down, decides I'm OK, hands me the scraper. Her dark face is sweating. I jab the scraper into the ice, over and over, in one tiny spot. Finally I've reached the windshield. I dig under one edge of the tiny hole and rake upward. The ice is too thick and doesn't budge. I go back to jabbing and make the hole bigger. Finally it's big enough that I can slide the scraper well under one edge. I lift a piece off. Then I start hammering the ice in another concentric circle. I manage to get another big chunk loose.

"I see what you're doing," the woman says. Her breathing has quieted. "Here, I can get it now. Thanks."

"No problem." I hand her the scraper.

I take the Broadway bus up to Montrose. As I walk the few blocks to Paris, I feel the lightness in my step. I've felt it these last few weeks. Spring is coming.

Fiona's Party

"Emily," Fiona says, greeting me warmly just after I come in the door and sign the guest book. There are many names ahead of mine. I scan the room. Must be over a hundred people here. Her mother and some aunts and uncles and siblings, but also a good number of her women friends, straight and gay. And more women who are clients, like me. We won't know how to tell who is who. "I'm so glad you could come."

"Congratulations," I tell her. Fiona's just received the Silver Award for service to the community. Her work in a women's shelter was cited, along with several other accomplishments. She thanks me profusely for introducing her to my boss, Zee, who helped her get a grant for the shelter.

"It was nothing," I tell her. I leave her so that she can talk to a new crop of guests. At the bar I order decaffeinated coffee and drape my jacket across my lap.

"So, uh, how do you know Fiona?" The woman sitting next to me is about ten or fifteen years older than I am, I guess. She's drinking an imported beer.

I look at her evenly. "I used to be a regular client, for about a year."

"Wow, you just come right out with it, don't you? I like that. I mean, you don't care who knows, do you?"

"No, I don't. Fiona's wonderful. I can't imagine being ashamed to say I'm one of her clients."

"Ya know somethin'? You're right. Damn right. Well, hell, now that you've told me, I'll tell you. That's how I know her, too. Only you're the first person here I've told. Hey, can I buy you a drink?"

"No, thanks. I don't drink. I've got my coffee here."

I'd like to get down off the bar stool and slink away.

"Hey, Emily," a voice behind me says, and someone slaps my back. It's Jenny, another Fiona fan, and a friend of mine. I turn and smile. "Good to see you, Jenny."

"My name's Sherry," the woman tells us. "I was just about to tell your friend here why I think Fiona's a great therapist."

"Why?" Jenny asks innocently. I'm not sure I want to hear.

"Because when I had this spoiled young thing with me, I tell you, I'd give her gold bracelets, worth a thousand dollars, and she'd say things like, 'is this ALL?' Oh, what I wouldn't do for that woman, and boy did she take me around the block. Finally, after months of my dillydallying and getting hurt and asking for more and getting hurt again, finally Fiona said, 'fuck the bitch and let her starve!' Hell, anybody who'll say that to me ain't gonna let me get away with no bullshit."

I nudge Jenny away, mumble "Really," and head toward the front of the room. We both decide that Sherry has embroidered on Fiona's actual words. Fiona, who has spent several years working with homeless women so that, among other things, they don't starve. But it's a good story. And who knows? Even Fiona has her contradictions.

"Hey, Emily," Fiona comes up, putting her arms around Jenny and me. "Are you mingling? There's plenty of women here for you to meet."

"Yeah, Em, she's right. You never know when you might meet someone." Jenny's happy because she's in love. She recently fell head over heels for Lucinda.

"I'm not looking to meet someone." I half expect Fiona to snicker, "yeah, SURE," but she doesn't. She's too kind for that. "I came to celebrate with you, Fiona. But now that I've got you here, I would like to ask about the woman who helped you figure out your computer problem." Fiona almost didn't get the last grant application done in time because she couldn't adjust her printer parameters properly, or something like that. Some brilliant computer whiz solved the problem for her.

"There she is. The woman in the dark blue blouse with the gray sweater. Her name's Catherine." I follow Fiona's eyes and the nod of her head. I see a woman sitting at the bar.

She's turned sideways, away from me, talking to a woman on the other side of her.

I'm stunned. I can't say why. But suddenly, everything else at the party fades. I no longer see Fiona or Jenny. I hear nothing. I'm like Tony seeing Maria across the dance floor: the camera zooms in, and all the surrounding dancers are a blur. I have eyes only for Catherine. The rest of the world seems to be going on around me, as if no one has noticed that she is here. In our midst. *How can they not notice?* She wears her light brown hair a reasonable length, just past the chin, not quite to the shoulders. Not short and spiked like my own dark stuff. Charged with intensity, mine can curl up into tight little balls all on its own. I can't control it. This woman's hair falls along the sides of her face in soft, gentle layers. No curls.

When she turns to look straight ahead, and I see her face more fully, it takes my breath away. She has the broad, open expression of someone at once curious, reserved, yet passionate about life. It is not a pointed face, nor a perfectly oval one. Yet her high cheekbones give her the authority of an actress. Something regal is there, a confidence quite distinct from haughtiness. She's wearing little, if any, makeup. Her blouse looks like satin; indigo blue, loosely covered with a bulky, gray cardigan.

What she is, or what strikes me, seems neither specifically feminine nor specifically masculine. I can't tell whether she considers herself butch or femme, and it doesn't seem to matter. She has the authority, the commanding presence of butch, and the subtlety, the grace of femme. More than some evocative androgynous eroticism.

"Go on, Emily, introduce yourself." Jenny is nudging my arm. I can't move. Fiona has disappeared somewhere behind me.

I want to move. I want to stand next to her, to look into her eyes. I want to hear her voice. I want to know her. But how? How can I make my legs take me there, make my mouth tell her my name?

"Don't be chicken," Jenny urges.

"Bad joke," I say. But I start moving. What the hell. George would say, "go for it." I didn't believe him, especially when it came to women as beautiful as this, but then there was Bonnie. She persuaded me that a beautiful woman could find me attractive. I don't know. This one is *really* beautiful.

"Hi. I'm Emily Hawk," I hear myself saying. "Fiona tells me you're the one who helped her with her computer problems on the grant application."

"Oh, it was nothing, really. Glad to meet you. I'm Catherine Morris. You must be the one who helped put her in touch with the right person in the state office." Her wrists move when she speaks—not too fast, like the pace of her speech. Graceful. I think, maybe femme. Yet her hands and wrists, for all their grace of movement, are larger than mine by half. She lights a cigarette. She's careful to blow the smoke away from me. Everything about her seems considered. Nothing raw or indecorous could fit.

We talk about how wonderful Fiona is. Despite her reserved manner, Catherine has no hesitation about being both a client and a fan, like me.

"But this is the first time I've ever come to this bar."

"Oh?" I notice she's wearing a skirt. A dark print, folksy but dressy, well made like the blouse and sweater. The colors, the style, her manner of wearing them—all are neither butch nor femme.

"Fiona's been trying to get me to go to more lesbian events, but I've just been too nervous. I've known I'm a lesbian for years, but this is only the second or third time I've gone to something." She doesn't look nervous. She looks remarkably self-possessed. Her voice is breathy. Seductive without knowing it seduces. The ear hungers for a voice like this.

I don't tell Catherine I've gone to lesbian events for a few years now. I tell her a little about George and Bonnie. I tell her I almost didn't come today, but I'm glad I did. She smiles.

"I am, too." Then she blushes and looks down at her skirt. I like it that she blushes. I think, she is beautiful, proud, but vulnerable, too. Her voice, her words touch nerves, set off sparks. I feel as though I'm coming up out of a long sojourn in a silent country, and sounds shock me. These sounds. Hers.

I learn that Catherine manages the educational department of a computer software company. She and her staff design and produce manuals, brochures, textbooks. But her real life is going to shows and films, reading books. She began seeing Fiona more than a year ago when she realized that she was essentially in a lesbian relationship without sex. With a straight woman who would never change. The relationship lasted for ten years. Before that, she'd had one lesbian affair, a fling one summer in college.

"So I've known since college, but Fiona says I've been afraid to test the waters."

"Sounds like Fiona."

"Oh?"

"I mean, she says things she knows we'll take as outrageous. Shock value, sometimes."

"Maybe she's right. I've done pretty much what I want to do in my career, and I'm finally beginning to feel less guilty about my mother." Both Catherine and I are children of alcoholics. As are most people alive today, it seems. I scan the room for Jenny, but don't see her. She must have left. I turn back to Catherine. "Fiona said I can't just sit around and wait for somebody to come and throw me in the water." Catherine laughs. "She said I have to at least stand on the banks."

I laugh. "What? And get splashed?"

"Anything beyond my toes makes me panic." She laughs again.

She's talking to *me*. She's telling *me* these things. I am amazed. As I listen to her breathy voice making its witty comments, then its intelligent observations, and then its more personal revelations, I realize I've encountered something I've been looking for all my life but was not prepared to find. Am I ready to find it, to understand it, now? The necessary, the inevitable: the classic. Catherine is the classic, the principle that shapes all our patterns, our balances, our spirals and returns. To this all romantics must come at last, I think. Sitting on this bar stool in front of me, drinking what looks like a club soda, is the most elegant yet unpretentious woman I have ever seen. Her reserve seems to mask a deeper passion. She's here, after all, despite her nervousness. Is she ready to test the waters? Am I the one she'll choose?

When she leaves to meet her best friend Patrick, a gay man, for dinner and a movie, I forget to ask for her phone number. But I know her name. And she's told me she lives in Oak Park.

Piss and Vinegar

The next day at work I concentrate in order to keep my mind off of Catherine. I tell myself to wait at least a couple of days before trying to get her number.

When I finish helping my last client of the day fill out agency forms, I say goodbye to Zee and to Mark Berger, who shares my office. I head for home on the train and halfway there change my mind. I get off instead at the Sheridan stop, near where Paul lives. Paul was a year behind George at the Art Institute and kept painting. He had some success in competitions and kept it up until he got sick. His wicked sense of humor and devilish irony seems to keep him going. He's outlasted several of his doctors' predictions, and everyone says Paul's piss and vinegar keeps him alive. I used to visit Paul every week, but I haven't seen him in a while.

For a long time after George's death and after Bonnie left I was just tired, too tired to do anything more than show up for work and eat and sleep. I'd listen patiently to foreign clients struggling with English, but I had no energy left over to give to anyone, including me. For a few months I couldn't bear to visit anyone in the hospital, couldn't bear any more AIDS fundraisers, benefits, races, or auctions. I felt empty, as though I'd given everything I had to trying to save George. When my efforts hadn't worked I didn't know how to replenish the energy.

I ring Paul's buzzer in the lobby of his apartment building. No answer. Should have called first.

At home, I dial Eric's number. Eric so far is HIV-positive but symptom-negative. We saw so much of each other prior to George's death that we've kept a respectful distance since.

"Emily? How good to hear your voice."

"Sorry I haven't stayed in better touch. I don't know, I guess I was just hibernating this winter or something."

"Don't worry—I know exactly what you mean."

There's an awkward silence. Eric sure has had reason to hibernate. But he's been much better than I have about visiting his other sick friends.

"I'm calling because I stopped by Paul's and nobody was home. Just thought you'd know how he is."

"Oh. I guess you didn't know—he's been back in the hospital for almost a week now. Some kind of new infection. The doctor said he's lived so much longer than most AIDS patients that he's one of the first to get this particular infection. Something to do with birds. I can't remember the details, exactly."

"Can they treat it?"

"Yeah. They've got him on several prescriptions, and one of them seems to be helping now."

"Is it OK to visit him?"

"Sure. I bet he'd love to see you. In fact, you might be surprised. Paul still jokes around, but he's not like he used to be. Not so, well, cynical or something. He seems to have changed."

"Hmm."

Neither of us is sure whether this is a good thing.

After dinner and before visiting hours are officially over (although no one seems too picky about visiting hours with AIDS patients), I stop in at Paul's room.

"EM! What in the world have you been doing? You look like a new woman!"

"What?" I look around, as if to see another woman in the room. Then I look at Paul. He seems thinner and whiter than he did a month or so ago. A sharper outline of bones in his wrists and elbows.

I walk to the bed and take his hand.

"So, what's her name?" he asks, with a crooked grin.

Hands

A week later, I call information and get the number for a Catherine Morris in Oak Park. It's Tuesday night. I dial the number. She answers. Her voice on the phone sounds delighted, as if she had expected me to call and is glad I did. I suggest dinner, and we meet on Friday at a Thai restaurant downtown. I want to ask her to come home with me, but I don't. As I walk her to the train at State and Lake, I want to take her hand, but don't. Before she heads up the stairs she turns and looks at me with the eyes of someone who wants me very much. "Emily," she says, as though she's out of breath. "I've really enjoyed dinner. I wish I didn't have to leave, but I don't dare take a train any later than this."

The following Friday, we meet for dinner at an Italian restaurant in my neighborhood, and Catherine has driven her car. She flushes when she sees me come into the restaurant, and hardly takes her eyes off me during dinner. I can't look away, either. We have tickets to a play, a drama about the Nazi persecution of Jews and gays. After the play, we're in a somber, reflective mood, but still there is a charged tension. She drives me home, and I invite her to come up and meet my cat Mango. After we circle nearby blocks for twenty minutes, Catherine tells me, "half an hour is my limit." I'm sure we won't find a space, but we do.

Catherine sits at my dining table. Mango affectionately jumps into her lap and sits there while I make tea. We talk about Mango, about the play, about our coworkers, about being gay, about anything and everything except how much we want to touch each other. Finally, I can't stand it, and walk over to where she sits and wrap my arms around her. I can feel her fine, broad shoulders, her straight, solid spine. Her hair smells faintly of cinnamon and musk. I close my eyes. I could stand like this, inhaling this intoxicating, sweet smell, for an hour. She hugs me and gently runs her hands up and down my back. Eventually, I lean down and kiss her, tentatively at first. She kisses me back, and we keep kissing for several minutes.

"I'd like you to stay," I say. Before she can answer, I add, "It would be nice just to hold you." She is trembling in my arms. I am afraid of moving too fast for her. Bonnie, though a little younger, was experienced. Catherine, my own age, has very little experience. But she stays.

The next morning, over coffee, she seems reserved, but just before she leaves, she asks if I'd like to come to Oak Park next weekend.

I can hardly wait for Friday. Paul teases me at the hospital, Jenny calls and teases me, and almost everyone who sees me has to wave their hands in front of my face. I make sure to put in my time at the agency. When Friday comes, I run along the lakefront in the morning, do laundry, clean house, answer mail, and run errands. I pack a gym bag loosely with clothes and am on my way before three. First, I stop at my neighborhood florist's and buy a spring bouquet. I go to a hospital just a mile away to see my friend Mercedes. She's been diagnosed with cancer, has had surgery, and now is going through a series of chemotherapy treatments. The doctors opened her up to look at what they thought was an ulcer and found a tumor the size of a grapefruit wrapped around her spinal cord. Her partner Paula lost a breast to cancer two years ago.

"Hey, Em, what's up?" she says, trying to be cheerful, her dark hair limp, her once glowing olive skin now sallow.

"Not much," I say. I set the flowers in a vase and run water. I leave the gym bag on the floor and notice her noticing it. She and Paula used to run the Strongwomen gym, but they had to close it. My new gym is convenient and cheap, but grungy. Mercedes doesn't ask me about it. She knows we've all scattered to various second-rate places. Sometimes I miss the women who used to work out at Strongwomen.

"So where are you on your way to?"

"Well, tonight I have a date."

"With that new woman you mentioned?"

"Yeah. Catherine. She's invited me to her place."

Mercedes smiles. "Well, she must be pretty special, Emily. You're looking brighter than I've seen you in a while."

I don't know what to say. Mercedes changes the subject.

"Cass was in here yesterday. She asked how you were."

"Oh? How's Cass doing, anyway? She and Nora doing OK?" Cass was my workout buddy; now we go to different gyms.

"Yeah. I think those two are talking about moving in together."

"That's great!" I like Cass and Nora together. Cass is headstrong, like me, and Nora is, well, capable of handling just about anyone. Everyone likes Nora.

Mercedes closes her eyes. I can tell she's in pain. I touch her shoulder. I stay a few minutes more, then close the door softly behind me.

At a florist's near Northwestern Memorial, I buy a spring bouquet for Paul. He's looking just a little perkier today.

"My, my, flowers even. Whatever *has* gotten into you, Emily?"

"Just felt like it, that's all."

"Don't let me hold you too long, Em," he says, smiling. "It's written all over your face."

Downtown, a block from Catherine's office, I buy a dozen roses from a street vendor. I hide them as best I can in the gym bag, but part of their wrapping still pokes out. We go to an early show of one of those warm-hearted French films with Philippe Noiret, and then take the train to Oak Park. We stop for dinner at an old-fashioned family restaurant with plain but not greasy food, and walk to her apartment. Once inside, she turns on lights, checks messages, and reads mail, while I busy myself with a newspaper. Then, while Catherine's changing out of her work clothes, I find a vase in the kitchen and run water. When she comes out she sees the roses.

"Emily, you shouldn't have."

"Why not?"

"Just because." She blushes. I don't take her in my arms then, although I want to. She puts on a CD. "I hope you like Andrea Marcovicci," she says. I do. "Patrick and I go to hear her whenever she's in town. She sometimes recites poetry, too—Edna St. Vincent Millay, for example." Catherine loves torch songs and lyric poetry. We sit next to each other on the couch. Again, it is torture to sit in the same room and not to touch her.

"Why don't you come over here?" she asks. I sit closer. She puts her arm around me.

Later, she says she's tired and ready for bed. She shows me where everything is–towels, a nightshirt to sleep in, which side of the bed she prefers to sleep on. It is her house, and I am not sure of myself. I slide under the covers on my side of the bed, and Catherine reaches for me. She holds me as I rest my head on her chest and she kisses my hair. "I'm so glad you're here," she says. We lie like that for several minutes, and neither of us falls asleep. It is hard to know whether Catherine wants to make love: is she expecting me to take the initiative? Or is she glad I haven't? Finally, I start kissing her, start moving my hands slowly over her body, at first just caressing her over and over, gradually exploring her erotic responses. As I stroke her long limbs, I am worried that I won't do things beautifully enough: Bonnie knew exactly what to do when she seduced me, had no hesitation. Finally I ask Catherine if it is all right for me to be doing this, and she nods yes. Yes. Knowing this, I continue. My hands touch her with a joy they had forgotten existed. When I place my palm on her chest, I can feel her heart pounding like a drumstick about to burst through the taut skin. We keep touching each other, and if Catherine has had little experience I could not guess it tonight, for her large, tender hands are magnificent in expressing their regard for me. We sleep late the next morning, nestled snugly together, lovers.

Realism

That was a month ago. Now we see each other every week. Catherine works downtown, in a glass building on Michigan Avenue. On Fridays, if we're both free, we meet downtown for an early dinner or a movie. Then we take the train together, before it gets too late to travel safely, to Oak Park. Occasionally she will invite me to Oak Park on a Sunday, and we'll take the train together into the city on Monday morning, our backs to the sunrise, reading the newspaper.

Tonight is a Friday in May. I stopped off at Mercedes's room with some flowers. Mercedes was asleep and I didn't want to wake her, so I just left the flowers. I don't mention her to Catherine because there's nothing I want more than to temporarily forget how it felt to see her, with her once thick, muscular arms lying like toothpicks across the white sheet.

Catherine meets me in front of her building. We eat curry at a Thai restaurant on State Street and then walk to the train. The sky is a scrim of faded blue pierced with huge, charcoal gray thunderclouds. We sit on the train facing the sunset and watch the series of west side spectacles visible from every stop and between. Low-rise public housing projects with broken windows and ragged, billowing curtains are followed by high-rises with no windows at all, no curtains either. Along one external corridor, someone has hung laundry. Colorful rows of socks and shirts and underwear line the chain link fence. Turquoises and pinks and yellows. Next to the laundry, young children dance in a row up and down the corridor.

Catherine takes this train nearly every day, to and from work, with thousands of other commuters. She doesn't need me to point out what there is to see. She doesn't need my words spoken aloud, naming the obvious. I am a north-sider who has seen the west side, even from the distance of a train, only a few times. But it is a vast river, and Catherine and I both know this. When Soviet emigrés come to Chicago, this is what I want to show them. I want to take them on this train so they can see the price of our conveniences for the few. I want to take them out to Gary, Indiana, so they can see the rusty spines and belching smokestacks, our city's ugly body, its hidden tumors beneath the glowing complexion of its lakefront. But I don't take the emigrés there, because they have more pressing demands for school, clothing, housing, jobs. I take them where the agency says to take them.

"What are you thinking about?" Catherine asks. I have been unusually quiet. I am the nervous, chattering one, when I am with her. Only now, after a month, are we beginning to have some quiet times together, where I do not always rush to fill the silence.

"This." I nod toward the window.

She follows with her gaze.

"Oh." She nods. "Yes."

Her calm, slowly articulated "yes" tells me she knows what I am thinking, that she is not untouched.

We get off at Oak Park Avenue and walk a few blocks to the video rental store. Catherine has a VCR and a good color television. I have neither of these devices. "Pick out anything you'd like to see," Catherine tells me.

I read the titles. I want to see at least a dozen of them, all of which Catherine has seen already. Finally I pick *Madame Sousatzka.*

"Well, I'm not one of those people who just *loves* Shirley MacLaine, but–"she pivots, as though aware she's giving herself away–"I like her." As we leave the store, she explains, "I definitely like her. Some people wouldn't like this movie in particular, because she really overdoes her role, but I like it."

"I like Shirley for doing different roles, for risking things–in her roles and her books and her life," I say.

"Hmm."

"Talk about testing the waters. That's Shirley."

"Hmm."

Does Catherine remember our first conversation, when she mentioned Fiona's telling her to test the waters? Am I being disrespectful to mention it? I explain, "I mean, she's serious about some things, but she doesn't take herself too seriously."

By this time we are at Catherine's courtyard.

"Hmm. Right now, I'm serious about getting out of these clothes and into a bath." So she *did* remember, and she's having fun with it, I think. Or maybe not. Maybe it doesn't matter.

Later, wearing one of her tailored cotton sleepshirts, Catherine is nestled in my arms as we lie together on her sofa, watching the movie.

The movie has nothing to do with realism. Oh, it tells a real story, with real characters, and takes place more or less in the "real" world, but it doesn't care about realism. Madame Sousatzka, her atomizers spraying every other minute, doesn't care about realism. She knows that nothing has ever had anything to do with realism.

Catherine strokes my arm as I hold her.

"For ten years I loved Elaine but would never let myself touch her."

"Never?" I can hardly imagine it. I'm constantly petting and kissing my cat Mango, and when I have a lover it's hard for me not to express physical affection.

"Hardly ever. Oh, a quick hug every now and then, when we exchanged gifts at Christmas. Nothing more."

She continues to stroke my arm, my hair. I relax happily. I could lie like this forever in her arms and listen to her lovely voice as it punctuates the movie. As Catherine lets herself stroke me gently, I know she is convincing herself that I am real. I am real, and I am here with her, and she can have all she wants with me and from me.

"I don't think it was just Elaine's not wanting me to. Not that so much as my own fear. I was so afraid that if I even touched her a little I'd go wild—and be even more frustrated than I already was." She pauses. "It's hard to believe I wasted all those years."

I want to tell her she didn't waste them. For ten years she loved a woman who insisted she was not a lesbian, even though Catherine and she maintained a relationship that was primary in both of their lives. But those years were not wasted if they led Catherine to find me. That's how I like to think. Those years prepared Catherine to be able to see me when I appeared. To be ready to stroke me like this.

Catherine needs to touch, to learn to allow herself this joy. I need to learn the confidence that others will touch me and that I do not need to touch them to reassure myself that they are real.

Catherine snuggles closer, nibbles my ear.

"My heart is beating so loudly I'm embarrassed," she says.

I feel her chest against my back, the subtle but strong beating of her heart. I remember the first time I reached out to her and placed my hand on her chest, just there, and felt how fiercely her heart was pounding. I fell in love with the steady strength of those vibrations. Now, feeling the same vibrations pressed against my spine, I relax in the growing familiarity between us.

Catherine, although she is somewhat afraid of me–afraid of letting me see past her tailored clothes and polished manners–is drawn to me, her hidden passion seeking mine. She needs to press herself against me, just like this, to know that her powerful heartbeats will not carry her away into the chaos she fears. And as the movie and its music draw to an end, I gladly allow myself to be cradled in Catherine's arms, to be rocked gently, to trust the ancient, classic rhythms of our beating hearts.

A Request

A few days later, I run down the lakefront to the hospital, hoping to catch Paul awake. He'll sleep most of the afternoon, if he's lucky.

It's near eleven o'clock. I stop to buy cans of soda from a machine. The door to Paul's room is open, as usual, and I walk in, still sweating. He looks up and smiles weakly.

"So how's romance?" he asks.

I shrug and grin like a teenager.

"Good, huh?"

"So far, I guess," I say, as if I can hardly believe it myself. What is ironic, what Paul understands without my having to tell him, is that just when I've become comfortable with being alone, with waiting five, ten, or even fifteen years for my next lover to appear, someone suddenly appears who makes me want to be her lover very much. Just when I've told myself I know what I want in my next lover and won't settle for less, she appears. No need to settle for less. Or to wait forever. I pull a chair closer to his bed. Then I put the can of cola on the nightstand for him. "Here," I say. "Want me to open it?"

He nods and pushes the button to raise his bed. I open the can, put one of the straws scattered on the nightstand in it, and hand it to him. Then I open the other one for me. I sit and drink. There's an album, with a red leatherette cover, on the nightstand.

"What's this?"

"Just a photo album. I asked Eric to bring it Sunday. I don't read much these days, but I can still look at pictures." His voice trails off.

I wait for him. He looks bad today. His face seems whiter, his skin puffier than ever. The Hickman catheter in his chest keeps his arms free of I.V. needles, but the various drugs they're feeding into it don't seem to be helping much. They've got him on morphine now. When he's lucid he wants to talk, and right now he is. He doesn't seem to want to waste energy on jokes anymore.

"I mean, I thought I could look at pictures. I started to. I didn't get too far. Kind of like pouring salt, you know."

"Memories?"

"It's like they're there–my mom, my dad, my sister–in those pictures, but they're not *here*."

I know his parents haven't visited him. They had trouble accepting the knowledge that Paul is gay. His sister wants to come visit, but has to save up money and time.

"Go ahead, Emily–if you'd like to look through it, feel free. I think there might even be some of George."

I pick up the album and begin slowly turning pages. Mostly it's party snapshots—guys clowning for the camera. George is in one of them, the tallest of the bunch. The biggest smile, the brightest teeth. Then there are pages of photographs of paintings and drawings.

"Are all of these yours, Paul?"

"I think there's one or two of George's. Here." I hand him the album. "I don't even know who took all of these. Maybe Eric. He thinks it's a good idea to keep slides of the work. Maybe he thought I had slide film in the camera, or something." He pauses, staring intently at something.

"Do you see one of George's?"

He shakes his head and closes his eyes as if in pain.

"What is it, Paul? Is there anything I can get you?"

He shakes his head again and opens his eyes. Then he sighs one of the purest sighs I've heard. One single, even, long exhale. He hands me the album.

"It's David," he says, finally. "That drawing I did of David, oh, six years ago."

I scan the page, remembering that name as one of Paul's ex-lovers, before I knew Paul. Suddenly, I see what looks like a drawing of Catherine; something in the face, the cheekbones, the angularity, the arresting yet not exactly direct gaze.

"I should have asked George about it," Paul says, his face turned toward the wall, away from me. "But I didn't. And then I thought of asking Eric—I know he'd try to help, but I don't really want to put him through more than he's already been through."

I wait for Paul to warm himself up to the point where he can ask whatever it is.

"Did George know David?" Even though we were close, George had many acquaintances I never knew about.

Paul turns back toward me. He looks steadily at me.

"They met at least once, when David and I went to a show and wound up sitting next to George and someone else, I don't remember who now—it was before Eric. When I was still drinking. Before I found the program." The A.A. program. Paul and I are both in it, but we don't usually talk much about it.

"Anyway," Paul goes on, "I think George must have run into him again—maybe more than once—because later, after David left, I was telling George about it, and George told me he didn't think David wanted to leave me."

"And George didn't explain what he meant?"

"Not really. It might have just been George, trying to get me to look at things from more sides. You know, for someone who wasn't a program person, George was OK. He had his own program, I think—just spiritually alive, wise, like you always said. But I think maybe he knew something—something he didn't feel free to tell me."

"Something David told him, maybe?"

"Maybe. When I asked him why David would leave me if he didn't want to, all George would say was that maybe David was confused and needed to go figure things out, and that it probably didn't have anything to do with me."

"Sounds like George."

We pause. I'm conscious of my T-shirt sticking to my back, of my underwear, shorts, and socks all damp with sweat, beads of sweat still standing out on my legs, gradually drying in the air-conditioned room.

"What about Laura?" I ask. "Did you ask her if she knew what's happened to him?" Laura knew both George and Paul from the Art Institute. She's a successful painter, and one of the only straight women I've known who doesn't mind when lesbians fall in love with her.

"She didn't. Hadn't heard anything since he split five years ago."

I begin to wonder. Maybe Laura and George were both protecting Paul from something.

"Emily, I asked around later—after I got out of the hospital the last time—and nobody knew where he was. Nobody knew anything about him. I even dialed all the numbers of all the David Millers in the phone directory that I thought could by some chance be him, but none of them were."

"Maybe he's not in Chicago."

"Maybe not. Probably not, I guess."

"And probably George didn't know where he'd gone off to, either." I lean forward, take Paul's hand. "Don't be so hard on yourself, Paul."

He pulls his hand back, waves both of them as if to brush away the nonsense. This is a different Paul. No longer the fun-loving, totally irreverent guy who always talked as though he never took anything seriously, while drawing and printing picture after picture of dead-serious apocalyptic vision. Surrealistic landscapes, slightly distorted, detailed, eerie yet beautiful male nudes.

"I'm not being hard on myself about it anymore, Emily," he reassures me. "I was hard on myself for a long time, but now I've decided I have to do something—for my own peace of mind."

"What are you talking about? Are you sure that seeing him again would bring you peace of mind?"

Again he waves my question away. "No, it's not that, Emily. I haven't told you the worst. It's not David's leaving that bothers me anymore. It's the horrible things I said about him after he left. The horrible things I thought. Because I didn't understand why he left, I couldn't accept it. And I hated him for it. For hurting me."

He pauses. I look down. This is not the Paul I usually see.

"Emily, I know I don't have much time. And I know you've really meant it every time you've asked me if there's anything I need. Well, this is all I'll ever ask. I need to let David know that it was all right. I need for him to know I don't hate him for leaving me."

Now he lets me take his hand.

"Well, sure, Paul. I mean, I can try. But does David even know what you said after he left?"

"He knows. I'm sure of it. Otherwise, why would he have done such a good job of hiding himself?"

"Maybe he felt guilty and didn't know whether you'd be open to his contacting you."

"But why go to such lengths to disappear? Other people feel guilty when they leave people, but they don't completely vanish without a trace."

None of it seems to make sense, but then, what do I know?

"Would you want to call him, if I could get his number?"

"He'd hang up on me. He'd listen to you before he'd listen to another gay man. He was *so* phobic, Em. That was maybe our biggest problem. He had trouble accepting that he was gay."

Paul sighs. Our hands slowly drop apart. I can tell he's getting tired. Soon I'll have to leave him so he can rest a little before the nurse comes in with lunch.

"So, what else can you tell me about him? Did he attend the Art Institute? Where did he work?"

"No, he went to some state school, in Ohio. He worked at Field's, but he left there right after he left me."

"Do you know anything that could help me find him? Maybe his social security number, or what town in Ohio he was from? How old is he?"

He shakes his head slowly. "He's my age. He didn't tell me anything about his family. All I have are those snaphots–there's another one of him with me in there somewhere–and the drawing. You can take the pictures."

I carefully remove the snapshots from the album.

"I'm asking you, Em, because I think he'd run from anyone he knew through me. He didn't know you. With anyone else he might think something was expected of him, and nothing is."

"What will I say?"

Paul gives me a wan smile.

"Just tell him. You'll know what to say. You'll tell him that none of it mattered, what happened or didn't happen, and that I didn't understand but that I did love him. And still do."

He's closing his red-rimmed eyes now, just breathing, resting, trying to gather strength.

"If I can find him, I'll tell him. Why don't you just try to sleep now?"

I lean down and kiss his eyelids, stroke his forehead. Just like I used to do with George.

"Em?" He doesn't open his eyes.

"Hmm?"

"Don't tell him where I am. I don't want him to feel obligated to respond in any way."

"But Paul! Don't you think he should have that choice, that he should know?"

"We were always really careful. No way he could have gotten it from me–"

"That's not what I meant!" I'm almost shouting. "Dammit, Paul!" My fists are clenched now, and I know I'm angry not at Paul but at everything, all of this, the missing pieces Paul can't find, the missing answers to his life and to this disease and to Mercedes's cancer and to all of it. "I meant, don't you think it's possible he might want to say something back? Maybe he'd like to have the opportunity to explain? To do anything?!"

Paul's eyes fluttered open briefly when I first spoke so loudly, but now they've closed again.

I sit and hold his hand. I can tell it's almost too much effort for him to speak anymore. And I realize he's chosen me rather than someone else for the task because we are both recovering alcoholics. He knows I'll understand why it's important to him to do this. It's a part of his program. Step nine of the twelve-step program requires us to make amends. For everything, sooner or later. You acknowledge what you did wrong, and you change your behavior. The actual doing of it is easy, once you're ready. It's getting to a place where you're ready that's the tough part.

Paul wants to make an important amends, and he knows I'll understand two things about that: one, that it's essential to his peace of mind to do it, and two, that a true amends requires no response from the other person. It's done because the recovering person needs to do it and not for any ulterior motive such as seeking approval or forgiveness from the other person.

"All right," I tell him softly. "If I can find him, I'll say what you told me. I won't volunteer anything extra."

Unless David asks, I think, as I walk down the hallway. If he asks me, I won't be able to lie. And somehow Paul will just have to understand *that.*

If there's anything to understand.

If there is such a person as David Miller, not one of those listed in the Chicago phone directory, but one who six years ago loved an artist and five years ago left him. Who might be living in any city, anywhere. Who wouldn't welcome a call from a gay man, nor probably from a lesbian.

I'm too exhausted, not from my earlier run, but from the conversation, to run back up north. Instead, I walk along the lakefront, thinking hard, but my thoughts go nowhere. I watch the young, healthy bicyclists, joggers, and sunbathers enjoying their bodies, their freedom.

Trying to Track Down David

A few days later I'm having lunch in the basement of the State of Illinois building with Mark Berger. We each pick a spinach calzone smothered with tomato sauce.

"We'll have to bring back a sandwich for Zee, or we'll be sorry," I joke.

Mark laughs. "No 'glop with slop' for her."

Zee doesn't like messy foods, except, she says, when she's at home.

Mark and I find a table and sit down. His tie is askew, and he's rolled up his shirtsleeves. My blue skirt isn't perfectly pressed and my blouse is missing a button on one cuff. What a pair. Zee doesn't care what we wear as long as we make an effort, days we're in the building, to dress more or less as professionals. That, to me, means no blue jeans and no sweat pants. Mark has to dress this way every day, because he's in the office, working with computers. His beautiful computers. Unlike Catherine, who in her job uses them to generate corporate reports and training manuals, Mark uses his to track people and paper trails. Sometimes I can just give him a name and presto! his computers spit out where the person is. David Miller, however, hasn't proved so easy. Somehow, Mark got into the Ohio state university system and got some social security numbers and matched them with Field's employees and came up with the person he thinks is Paul's David.

"My friend at the bank says none of the creditors has any address more recent than three years. My pal over there at the Secretary of State's office"—he points beyond the eating area—"says he didn't renew his license when it came up last year. As far as we know, he hasn't applied for another license in another state, either."

We munch for a couple of minutes. Then I have to ask.

"Do you think he's still alive?"

"Well, a few Millers have died in Illinois in the last five years, but as far as I can tell, none seems to be the one you're looking for."

"What do you think it means that no one, including the post office, has an address?"

"Well, the last address he had was one of those single-room only hotels in Uptown. It's been torn down. So he might have moved in with someone and never bothered to tell the post office. The lease, the phone, the electric–none of it would be in his name. I checked with welfare. Nothing there, either. Just goes to show, Big Brother isn't quite *everywhere*. Not yet," he says wryly.

I don't know what to say. Normally, the limitations of state and federal prying would be a consolation.

"Listen, we don't have to give up just yet. I'll see what else I can find out. There's more to explore in Ohio, but maybe you could try asking around, some of the people who used to know him here."

"Paul says he never knew any of David's friends, that they always hung out with Paul's friends. No one seems to know anything."

"But he *did* live almost in your neighborhood for a while. He had to have gone to stores, bars, places." We finish up our lunches and start cleaning our table. "The people I think are his parents have an unlisted number I'm trying to get. I'll keep doing what I can through the computer, but maybe you should take those snapshots around and see if anyone has seen him."

Once a Week Is Not Enough

Inevitably, I want to see Catherine more and more. Once a week is not enough. I call one evening to suggest we meet for dinner sometime during the week.

She pauses for a minute. "Just checking my calendar," she says. "Well, I've got my appointment with Fiona Wednesday. If you like, we could meet for dinner afterward."

"That would be fine."

"We'll have to make it early, though, because I want to be home and in bed early. It's an awful week at work."

"All right. Or better yet, why don't you just bring some clothes and stay over?"

"Oh, I don't think so, Emily. I'd have to carry so much stuff with me–two days I'd be walking in and out with an extra bag."

Catherine hates the stares of her middleaged secretary and other staff when she walks in or out carrying a bag.

"Oh, come on," I say. "They'll just assume you're seeing Patrick, won't they?"

Catherine laughs. "Maybe they *would* assume that."

She has no intention of coming out at work. Ever. It's none of their business, she told me once. She finds it fascinating that I'm out to my boss, but can't imagine herself enjoying such freedom.

"I'd like to hold you, Catherine."

"Mmm," she says. "That would be nice." But she won't say for sure whether she'll stay over Wednesday.

So we agree only to meet at Leona's on Sheffield after Catherine's appointment. I tell her I won't be surprised to see her carrying a bag or not carrying one. But I want to tell her life is too short. That I need to see her more often. Need to touch her. Need to introduce her to my friends. I don't tell her these things. I sensed last Saturday, when we met for dinner, that she was tired. We went home early and cuddled, and she fell asleep early. Several times I awakened briefly to find her arms loosely wrapped around me, though we never had sex. She seemed preoccupied Saturday night and Sunday morning, yet somehow comforted to have me near.

Tonight, I crawl into bed with Mango, who stretches out long beside me and lets me stroke her luxurious beige fur. I remind myself that George and Eric weren't together every night either, even though they were very much a couple. I try to convince myself that it doesn't matter that I've said "I love you" to Catherine a few times and she's never said it to me. She's a reserved woman, not given to gushy displays of feeling. Actions speak louder than words, I tell myself. She's not one to make promises she can't keep. I think of Bonnie, who said she'd love me forever. Time to grow up, Emily, I tell myself. Still, I fall asleep hoping I'll be holding Catherine in my arms on Wednesday.

No Kissing in Public

When Catherine walks into Leona's, she's carrying no bag. She joins me, sliding gracefully onto the seat across the booth. She's wearing a taupe skirt, a cream-colored blouse, and a lightweight houndstooth jacket. The jacket complements the solid skirt beautifully. A rust-colored scarf, expertly tied, lies loosely around her collar.

"Hope I'm not late."

"No. I was here a few minutes early and went ahead and got a table. Looks like they're getting crowded now."

The place is bustling, as it always is, and I'm glad we have a booth. A handsome waiter takes our orders for large salads.

Catherine talks about two incompetent people who work in the department she directs. She's reluctant to fire them.

"I told Fiona about your inviting me to stay tonight."

"And?" I try not to appear too eager to hear about her sessions with Fiona. I want to respect Catherine's privacy, determined as I am to become a larger part of her world.

"She thought it would be fine for me to stay over during the week. Apparently, she doesn't think we're seeing too much of each other."

Our salads arrive, and I dig in, sending loose croutons skidding across the table. Too much lettuce, too many large pieces of green pepper and other vegetables packed into one bowl.

I want to ask Catherine, so why haven't you brought your bag? Don't you want to see me as much as I want to see you? But I don't ask.

"It's just me, Emily," Catherine says. "Maybe next week we can do something together, and maybe, if you'll have me, I can stay over."

"Sure," I say. "I'd like that. And what about this weekend? Maybe we could get together Friday and see a movie?"

"I'm afraid I have to go to Rockford on Saturday. Mom's been bugging me. So Friday I have to go home and get things done."

"Oh." I hope my voice doesn't sound as disappointed as I feel.

"Listen, it's just as well, Emily. I have a terrible meeting Friday that I'm dreading, and I'm not sure you'd even want to be around me."

I don't tell her that she's wrong, that I'd want to be with her anyway, just because I want to be with her. We finish, pay our bill, and leave. At the el we smile at each other, but don't kiss. No kissing in public. I've known only a few people who would kiss in public. George was one. Bonnie another. Another, my friend Rosalie, who usually does what she wants without thinking. It's as if the rest of us are wearing muzzles. Catherine climbs the stairs to the el platform. I walk myself home.

Love and Grief

Something is wrong. Catherine and I meet at the Music Box Theatre for a showing of *The Dressmaker* the following Thursday after work. She is tired, almost haggard, and on edge from a day of frustration. She is a manager who likes to manage people who manage themselves. People who can't manage themselves irritate her. Now it seems there are not two but three such people who work in her department. Tonight, I'm not sure how to gauge Catherine's mood, whether her tension extends to me.

During the film, I refrain from touching her. I sense her need to be left alone. Suddenly, after I've become absorbed in the film, for two or three sweet minutes I feel Catherine's hand on my thigh. I want her to touch me like this, on her own, more often. I want to touch her more often, hold her and sleep with her more than once or twice a week on the weekends.

Although we are both impressed with the acting, the ending of the film disappoints us. Murder seems like such a cheap solution. The British are so good at dramatizing sexual repression. The symbolic murder was clear enough. Why a "real" one?

But Catherine and I do not talk for long about this.

"I don't care where we eat, as long as it's close, and we can sit down, and we don't have to wait forever for our food," she says.

We go to the Chicago Diner. It's busy, and we are seated at an open table next to a woman eating alone. I had hoped for a booth, but all are full. As Catherine is studying the menu, I spot a couple leaving their booth. I stand, tell Catherine a booth is free, and pick up my backpack from the chair.

After we are seated, I ask, "Is this OK? I mean, if we'd sat there I would not have been as comfortable talking with you. This is more private."

"Oh." She still looks distracted, her hair slightly mussed, her eyes and mouth distinctly lined with weariness. "Well, I wouldn't have done it, but I don't mind that you did."

Ever tactful, that's Catherine. Except, she has warned me, when she gets sarcastic. She has warned that she can be cruelly sarcastic. But I haven't felt her supposed cruelty yet, and I suspect she exaggerates it.

Catherine orders vegetable fried rice, one of my favorites, and I order an Indonesian specialty I've never had before.

"Barry has invited us to a party at his house next Saturday," I say after we've both begun to relax the tension of hunger. Before Catherine, Barry was my movie buddy. I've told Barry about Catherine, and he says he can't wait to meet her. He's happy for me. He's also going to help me look for David Miller. Even though Mark thought it was a long shot, we've tried the phone books and information, and have called most of the Millers, none of which have turned out to be the right one.

"Well, don't count on my going," she says.

I don't know what to say. I eat more of my mashed squash or whatever orange-yellow material is on my plate.

"Catherine," I begin, trembling. "You were gone last weekend to see your mother. You're spending this weekend with Patrick. And now you're saying you won't see me next Saturday, either."

"I didn't say that."

"Well, it sure sounds like you did. I don't know. Maybe I was wrong. I thought you *wanted* to be with me." I cannot bring myself to say the words: once a week is not enough.

"I didn't say I didn't want to be with you. I said don't count on my going to the party. I just can't see myself standing around like a foreigner who doesn't know the language with a bunch of your friends. I don't know any of them."

"Because you haven't been willing to meet them," I spit back, surprising myself and regretting it instantly.

"Look," Catherine says after a pause during which I avert my eyes, "I never said I wasn't willing to meet them. But do I have to meet them all *right* away? Can't it wait just a bit?"

"But we've been dating three months, and I haven't even met Patrick, and he's your best friend!" I blurt out. "And he gets to hear everything from you about what you think about me, and, well, I just–"

"Could we just not continue this discussion right now, right here?"

I stop. I can't finish my food. Catherine has been distancing, and now she's treating me like some irritating employee, not a lover. I can't bear the thought of being perceived as an annoyance by her.

We leave the restaurant and walk silently down Roscoe. She has brought her bag for staying overnight. Now I am sure she regrets she did. Why is she with me? I ask silently. Why would I even want to spend this evening with her? Why did we sit through that film together? It was no better, really, than my sitting there alone, except for two or three minutes when it was unspeakably wonderful.

All the way to my apartment I do my best not to irritate her further.

"Please just make yourself at home–read or do whatever, and don't worry about me," I tell her when we get inside the door. "If you want to read the paper, there it is on the couch. I'll just read these for awhile." I pick up the latest *New Art Examiner* and sit on a chair.

Before she goes into the bathroom to clean up, she turns to me.

"Listen. I know I'm on edge. I don't know why, exactly. I'm sorry."

I nod. "Don't worry." I want to convince her that with me she can be any way she needs to be, that I can handle it. But I'm not sure I'm handling it.

Later, we crawl into bed together. I can tell she still isn't ready to talk, and I am afraid of pushing her. But I can't stand the distance between us.

We lie side by side in the darkness for a few minutes.

I turn to her, expressing physical confidence far beyond my psychological doubt. I hug her, lowering my body over hers, and kiss her on the forehead, on her ears, on her neck.

"Catherine," I whisper, "I know you're tired. You're also tense. Please, let me make love to you. I want to make love to you. And I want you just to let yourself fall asleep as I'm making love to you, and not to worry about it."

"I don't know," she murmurs, as I tenderly stroke her, trying to show her how much I care, how much in love with her I am, trying to mask the confusion I'm feeling.

"Just relax, and let yourself go, and fall asleep if you want."

Each time we've made love so far, Catherine has always been very conscientious about it—if I give her pleasure, she turns her attention to me immediately. It's as if she wants to be sure the account is kept perfectly balanced between us. But I want her, this time, to be less careful about it, to let go of the need to structure our reciprocity. I keep caressing her, and gradually her body responds.

"Well, actually, it might help," Catherine says, as if to herself.

I take my time, and her body seems to me as miraculous as if I had never seen it before. She opens to me more and more, and I am no longer conscious of being anyone but a person in love with this body, this woman, so thoroughly in love with her that its pleasure is the pinpoint of my focus, the channel of all my energy.

I do not know how long it lasts. But Catherine begins to climax with a series of orgasms more powerful than any she has had since I have known her. Her body drives her toward me and against me with a ferocity of determination. She is shaking and trembling and bouncing and contracting again and again and again. Her large hands have clamped my shoulders, pressing me down, harder than I've ever been pushed, against her body.

Eventually her body relaxes, and I continue to hold her gently. We say nothing. I am weeping silently, for love and grief. I weep inwardly because I cannot believe how much I love her and want to give her pleasure and tenderness and understanding and all the things she hasn't had enough of in this life. And I weep because she is distancing herself from me, and cannot move as fast as I want her to, as fast as I have fallen headlong into love with her. And I weep because I know that somewhere deep inside her, and beyond her body, she wants me to reach her, wants me to stay, to wait with her.

Wants my tears to reach her, to release her.

Wants me to keep chipping away at the perfect glaze.

I watch her fall asleep, and it calms me to hear her breathing change.

Such breath knows it has all the time in the world. Knows that all true things cannot be forced. Catherine is attracted to me because she sees my unguarded passion, suspects its depths may lead her to her own. And that is precisely why she is also distancing from me these days. I am always in a hurry; once I've found love, I reach for it, give it everything I've got. My intensity is raw and frightening to most people. It refuses to skate on surfaces, instead plunges deep into the heart of experience. I chip away at the ice. I cannot bear the lie of being kept apart from love. Life. It's wrong to waste it, to deny it. Yet pursuit itself can be toxic; we mortals are too fragile to accommodate a steady diet of mental and spiritual torque. I do not want to shatter anyone, not even myself.

I turn from her and lie on my side, closing my eyes. I try to match my breathing to hers. Patience is a highly overrated virtue, I think. Fine line between such virtue and ethical lassitude. To be patient is also to be calm and safe, to avoid risk. Yet to be patient with Catherine now is also to place myself at risk.

Barry's Party

I go to Barry's party alone. My friends ask me how it's going with Catherine. A woman they've never met.

"She didn't want to come," I say. I want to tell them what it is she has to do instead, but I don't know. She hasn't told me. It's OK, I want to reassure them. She still likes me. But I understand the impulse. I remind myself that it doesn't matter, that I don't need to explain.

Cass and Nora look so good together, I think. Cass with her warm, coffee-colored skin and beautiful eyes, Nora with her olive skin and smile lines giving her face a look of knowing kindness. Cass with her muscles, her reassuring solidity, Nora her trusting delicacy. Cass gives me a hug. I feel better immediately. Standing in a corner, embracing, are Judy and Pat.

So what if I'm the only person in a couple whose partner isn't here? I've had enough practice at being single that I can act as though I'm single. Everything important in life is done alone. Everything. Just because I'm "with" Catherine shouldn't make any difference–I should still do just about everything on my own. Good for me. No need to merge like putty, try to live out the fantasies of cheap love songs.

"Went to see Mercedes today," Cass says. "She's not doing too well."

"I guess the chemo can't get rid of such a huge tumor, can it?" Both of us shake our heads.

I walk out onto Barry's balcony and study the skyline. It's a lovely summer evening. I inhale through my right nostril, hold, exhale through the left. Then reverse the procedure. Over the clusters of darkened trees, over the masts of yachts in the harbor, and, farther, over the white spires of the John

Hancock and the Sears tower, I cast my question like a net: if I am patient with Catherine, and continue to see her at her pace, apart from my other friends, my other life, waiting for her to call from week to week, not knowing until Thursday or Friday whether I'll see her Friday or Saturday because she doesn't like to make plans in advance with me–if I do this, will I be sending her the message that my feelings don't count? Can I afford to be so patient?

"Great view, huh?"

Judy and Pat have come onto the balcony. They met six months ago and have just moved in together. Tall, blond, sturdy Pat sits down in one of Barry's turquoise patio chairs. Judy, a petite, pale woman with long, dark hair, sits on her lap.

"Thought we'd come out and enjoy it with you."

"Nice party, huh?" Pat says.

"Yeah."

"How are things at work, Emily?"

Judy always asks how people are, what they're doing, what they need. Habitually warm, reassuring, sweet. Unlike Catherine, who prefers to adopt such gestures by considered choice, not habit.

"The usual. More people than time to help. Small victories." Like getting the thirty-year-old man who was terrified of trains to take the CTA with me. Now he loves them, and is taking different routes just to see the city. I smile. "And how's the store doing?" Judy and her mother run a boutique in one of the suburbs.

"Oh, great, just great. We've got a lot of cute summer things now. You really should come in sometime, Em."

"There she goes again," Pat chuckles. "What she means is, if you'd come in she'd just happen to find you some real discounts." She hugs Judy even tighter.

Everything is always sweet for them, I think, even though I am suppposed to know better. Pat works from eight to four-thirty, comes home and cooks dinner. Judy opens the store at ten and leaves at six. They eat dinner, talk about their respective days, sleep together every night.

There are thousands of Judys and Pats, Jims and Bobs, even Marks and Susies all over Chicago. I wonder if Catherine and I will ever be like that. The thought of it seems to make Catherine run and hide.

"So I hear you've been dating," Judy says. Not long ago her question would have been whether I'd heard anything from Bonnie. "Yeah. I'm dating someone special."

"Anyone I know?" Pat asks, winking.

"I don't think so. She's not out to very many people."

"Well, what's she like?" Judy asks.

I hardly know what to say. "Her name's Catherine. She's different from Bonnie. She's my age. She has her own friends, a busy life."

"So she's with her friends tonight?"

"I don't know. Probably."

"You mean she didn't tell you? Did you invite her?"

"Look, I said she's not like Bonnie was. She's been very focused on her career. She's very independent."

"Oh." Judy and Pat sometimes sound like one person.

My right thumbnail is tearing away the skin on my left thumb. A nervous habit.

"I think I'll go in and get another LaCroix."

In the kitchen, Barry comes up behind me and hugs me.

"Hey, kid," he says.

I wriggle out of his grasp, turn around, hug and kiss him.

I love Barry. It would be impossible not to love him. He always hugs me when he sees me. He has endured my tales of woe from former relationships. I often wonder whether hearing about my relationships has contributed to his reluctance to get involved with eligible men. I have watched his hair turn a lovely silver-gray. He takes an instant dislike to anyone who appears incapable of appreciating me.

He, too, was hoping he'd see Catherine here tonight. But he won't torture me with the obvious. Instead, sensing without being told that I'm needy, he provides lavish affection.

"Got one for you," he says, as we both sit at his tiny kitchen table. "New guy at the office, can't tell if he is or he isn't, but nice looking. We're working on one of the computer glitches together and he says 'I was reading an article recently that said if the truth be told we're all sexual chameleons.' So I turned to him and said I've been known as a sexual comedian all my life."

Although I can't help laughing, as he knew I wouldn't be able to, I feel sorry that Barry doesn't have a wonderful life partner to appreciate him. He deserves the best. Then I wonder if I'm overrating the value of having a life partner.

"So, dahlink, when are we going out to look for your friend?" he asks.

"How about this coming weekend?"

"Great. Let's get together Saturday and pay some calls. We can do the bars on Halsted. Do you have pictures of him?"

"I'm having copies made of a snapshot Paul gave me. I don't know how helpful it will be."

"It's a start, anyway." Barry puts his arm around me. "We'll do our best, kid."

"Do your best with what?" Cass asks as she comes in and gets a bottle of LaCroix.

I tell her about Paul's request and what little I know about David.

"Was he into drugs at all?"

"I don't know. It never occurred to me."

"Didn't Paul run with a wilder crowd back then?"

It's something to think about. Cass says she'll ask around.

Later, in the living room, several of us are gathered on Barry's leather couch and in his director's chairs, cackling as he does his Lily Tomlin imitations. She is one of the few mandatory allegiances we all share. After our sides are aching from laughter, someone puts dance tapes on the stereo and we dance in pairs and threesomes and as a collection of odd individuals. Pat and Judy remain glued in their extended embrace.

Sweaty and tired, I walk home up Broadway, my hair and shirt soaked. I walk past the open doors of bars with their foul odors of old cigarette smoke and beer, and flashes of laughter and anger chase after me. A few late Cubs tourists walk by in their white T-shirts and baseball caps and mumble, "There's another one."

Another what, I wonder. I wonder what they think when they think of lesbians. And how were they so sure? Was it my short, sweat-soaked hair? My black tank-top? My cotton shorts? My muscular build? Do they assume that all women walking in this neighborhood without a man must be lesbians? Or does what and who I am write itself all over my face, in my lines, my lips, my eyes, my teeth, my bones? If so, what, if anything, does that have to do with any other human being I might or might not touch? Or is it instead not the look of a lesbian so much as the look of a romantic, of a lover, with or without a beloved, that instantly betrays itself to the eye? The lover obvious to all, except, of course, the one beloved she seeks.

Romantic to a Fault

The vulnerability of the romantic is a visible sign to those adept at locating wounds. Tenderness has marked us, and we are easy to find if you have the instinct for recognition. We wear our weakness like a faulty skin. Sparks of cruelty or half-hearted hostility or mere indifference flash at us from all directions: tangible lightning and thunder to those born without the proper shields. We are not special–simply inadequately prepared.

Catherine's apparent indifference causes me pain despite the absence of intentionality. No one controls where and how the lightning strikes. It finds us on its own, passing through others on its way, and sometimes we mistakenly attribute its source to these random, temporary points along its path.

When I walk into my apartment, my gaze immediately travels to my answering machine. The red light is not flashing. It is already midnight, and Catherine will not call tonight. She's in bed by ten o'clock on weeknights (unless a very special performance has run late), and she will not use the telephone after that hour, even on weekends. I know I must not call her. Does this mean I must not want her? I become more and more confused. I thought I understood, but now I understand nothing at all. I am becoming a person who has difficulty managing herself. Perhaps I was wrong about Catherine. Perhaps this won't work after all.

I sleep, off and on, restlessly, and dream of women who put their arms around me and tell me they love me. I know these women are myself, and in the morning I take my medicine like a cooperative invalid: looking at my face in the mirror, I pronounce audibly, "I love you, Emily." I smile, but though the words are convincing, they do not suffice. I run my errands, do my chores, answer calls from friends, but no calls come from Catherine. I call and leave a message on her machine. Lighthearted, now, Em: don't want her to suspect you're a depressive or needy type. No pressure. I tell her I've found a book she was looking for and will keep it for her.

By the time I've read the Sunday paper, it is evening. I set up the ironing board usually sandwiched behind clothes at the back of my closet. Out in the middle of the bedroom floor, I iron. I dig around and find every cotton shirt, every pair of cotton pants, and even a couple of skirts. I iron them while playing Mozart concertos on the stereo. At 9:00 I find I've only got a few pieces left to iron, and after 9:30 it's almost too late to call. I dial Catherine's number.

The line is busy.

I iron my last shirt, and dial again.

Still busy.

I iron a pair of trousers. They are baggy and have three pockets which I iron carefully. I turn the pants inside out, iron the pockets, then turn them back. I line up the seams. I smooth the wrinkles out of the fabric with the caress of the hot iron. I take my time; the heat of the iron comforts me. But when I hang the pants up and change the record, it is getting closer to 9:30, and I still can't stop thinking I must talk to Catherine.

I dial again. Again, the busy signal. Unlike me, she doesn't have call waiting. Tonight is the first time I have pondered the significance of this difference. Catherine doesn't need to save money. She chooses not to have call waiting. Not to be accessible to everyone, all the time. Does the fact that I have it mean that I am too accessible to everyone and anyone? Should I, too, set up barriers, perhaps monitor all my calls by leaving the machine on? How many times have I picked up the phone and immediately regretted it when it wasn't someone I wanted to hear from? It's true that by not having call waiting you are accessible to only one person at a time. You give your full attention. No interruptions. Keeps things simpler, maybe.

I wonder whom Catherine is talking to, and why this person and not me. She's home and has chosen not to return my call. Bad sign indeed.

By 9:40 I've bitten every one of my fingernails far past the skin. I've ironed my last pair of clean pants and turned off the iron. There's a cool breeze from the lake, but my forehead is sweating. Catherine's line is still busy.

At 9:45 and 9:50 the same.

At 10:00 I try again. It rings. She answers.

"Hello?"

"Hello. It's me. I know it's late, but the line was busy."

"Oh, that's all right," she says calmly. "I thought of calling you, but it's late and I was just on the phone an hour with Deb, and when I looked at the clock I thought, well, I could call Emily or I could just go to bed. So I just started to go on to bed."

"Oh. Well." I guess I shouldn't keep you, I almost say. But I can't.

Catherine says nothing to fill in the silence. I don't know what to say, and she isn't helping. Why haven't you called me? I want to ask. How could you possibly go for two days knowing I've been crazy worrying and not explain, not call? Are you trying to avoid me? Are you breaking up with me? What is this? What's happened to our time together, our tenderness, what we shared?

But my throat feels paralyzed.

"Well," Catherine says. I feel it's a signal: hurry up and talk or I'm saying goodnight.

"Catherine," I begin. "This isn't working, is it?" My voice shakes with terror. Please don't agree, please tell me I'm wrong, please explain, anything oh anything but running away from it all without an explanation, denying what's happened between us.

"What isn't working?"

Is that really innocence in her voice? How can she be innocent, let alone pretend innocence? How can she *not* know how much she's been hurting me by avoiding me?

"Well, uh," I try to control my voice, make it sound less shaky, but also softer. Gentle and understanding, that's what I want to be. Not angry. Not intolerant. Not demanding. Not accusing. Not any of the agonized raw pain I feel. "Uh, you know, how last week was. And then, when I didn't hear from you..."

She sighs. It sounds like angry exasperation to me. Have I become an annoyance after all? A mere pest? Someone she'd like to be rid of?

"I didn't call because I got home at eight, I cooked dinner, then I had to call Deb because she'd left two messages and she needed to have some information tonight. Your message didn't say to call back or anything. And as I told you, it was already late and I was tired by the time I finished with Deb."

"Oh." Has she missed the obvious?

"And I know I wasn't my best on Thursday, but really, Emily, what can I say? Didn't I apologize already? And I told you I didn't want to go to that party. Did you expect me to change my mind, or what? I didn't realize there was any agreement that I would call you yesterday. What have I done that's so wrong?" But her tone says she hasn't done anything wrong and I'd damned well better not imply as much.

"I know," I stumble. "I guess it's just that, well, since I didn't see you, I was kind of hoping we could at least *talk* or something, a little, this weekend."

At this moment I hate Catherine, hate her for not understanding the obvious, hate her for making me say these things, for making me overqualify, tone down, modify, practically apologize for saying them. How can she be so callous? How can she *not* want to see me or talk with me for a week, so early in our relationship? How can she *not* know I have been thinking of her? How can she not have been thinking of me?

Again she sighs in what I interpret as exasperation.

"All right, Emily." She sounds bitter. "I got up on Saturday, and I cleaned house. Then I took a box of stuff over to my mom's. She needed help with some things around the house, and by the time we finished I stayed for dinner. By the time I got back I knew you'd be at the party. Patrick called and we were both restless, so on the spur of the moment we went to a late movie."

Stop it, I want to say. Stop with the catalog of events. I don't want an accounting of what you do. "How does any of this pertain to my wanting to see you or talk with you?" I finally say.

"Well, I'm just telling you what I did this weekend. On Sunday, I slept late, and then I went to brunch. Then I went to the grocery store, came home, did my laundry, and paid bills. *When* would I have called you?"

I'm about to say, how about Saturday morning. Or tonight, before you returned Deb's calls. But if I have to tell her, isn't it pointless?

"I'm sorry I called," I say.

"What have I done *now*?"

But she is daring me to answer her, and I won't give her yet another reason to be angry with me. How can we terminate this conversation without terminating all contact?

"Look. I guess what I've been trying to say is, I just missed you. That's all, Catherine. I just missed you."

I wait.

"Oh." She doesn't sound angry.

"I know it's silly, but I just really wished I could see you." Stop apologizing, I tell myself. Stop setting yourself up as the powerless one, the victim.

"Well, that doesn't sound so silly." She pauses. "But sometimes I just have to catch up on things, you know that."

"I know."

"And besides," she says, as though she's decided something, "I was afraid of calling you yesterday."

"What?" This I hadn't expected. Catherine afraid of *me*?

"Yes. You seemed angry at me because I wouldn't go to the party with you. Actually, on Saturday, just before I went to my mother's, I thought of calling you and asking if I could come. But I decided not to, because I didn't know whether if I came, you wouldn't still be kind of angry. Why would I want to go somewhere with someone who's angry with me?"

Why would you make that person even angrier by doing more of the same–the thing that makes that person hurt and angry, I want to say, but can't find a voice for the words. Instead, I ask,"Are you saying you won't see me or talk with me if I'm angry?"

"Well, I'm afraid of what I might say. And I'm afraid of what you might say."

"But Catherine, we *have* to talk. Too much distance is not a good thing. We haven't seen each other in more than a week." Here I am, ignoring patience.

"I don't know."

"Catherine, do you want to break up with me?"

"What?!" She sounds genuinely shocked. "Not unless you want to break up with me."

Great, I think. *She's* afraid that I'll break up with *her*. What a pair. "No. I want to see you, not break up with you." I feel like you've banished me as punishment for being angry, Catherine.

"Well, I don't know. Maybe it's not–"

"Catherine, listen. If you're afraid one or both of us will get angry, we'll just agree ahead of time that either of us can leave at any time. And if it's at night, then we'll each insist that the other provide safe transportation so we don't get murdered on the train. What's the worst that can happen if we see each other? If somebody doesn't like the conversation, that person can end it, period." I am seducing her now with the same eagerness with which I first bedded her. But it's a tougher challenge. Part of her doesn't want to be convinced, would distance further, let this rift go on so long we'd give up on trying to heal it. We'd drift gradually apart and never get around to facing it.

"Well, maybe. Maybe you have a point there. Listen, it's really late and I've *got* to get some sleep. I'll think about it, Emily."

But will you call, Catherine? Or must I?

"I'll call you, or you call me, later this week, OK?"

"OK," I agree. I don't especially like it, but I agree.

Not This Time

She calls Wednesday night. She suggests we meet Friday after work. I agree. I do not tell her that I spent Tuesday night telling Barry over dinner that I'm so angry I'm ready to break up with her. Bonnie left me. I'm tired of being left. I'm tired of being understanding. If Catherine is distancing because she's restless and wants to leave me but won't take responsibility for that, I'm not going to hang around and let it drag out. Too painful.

Laura comes to town Wednesday. She calls a few minutes after I've finished talking with Catherine. Thursday morning I meet her at the Art Institute, where we look at prints from Germany and France. The smooth grays, velvet blacks, and luscious whites of the photographs calm me. I tell Laura the whole story of dating Catherine. By the time we take a break for lunch in the museum cafe, I'm pretty sure it's hopeless and tell Laura so.

"I don't know, Em. I wouldn't be so hasty if I were you." Laura has always been blunt with me.

"But don't you see how she's distancing, how insensitive she seems to be?"

"Oh, I think she might be distancing, all right. I also think you're overreacting." Laura's gray eyes watch me, her high forehead and shock of henna-treated hair coming at me like an exclamation point.

I nibble at my salad, then chew a bite of croissant.

Laura reaches over and touches my arm briefly.

"Hey, Em, I remember how much you were hurt when Bonnie left. Don't you think you're going to have your panic button ringing loud and clear anytime somebody acts in any way like they might be moving away from you?"

By the tight contraction I feel in my stomach, I know Laura's striking home. I don't want to hear it, but I listen. Laura talks the way she paints: bold colors, huge swatches, dramatic, wide, intense statements. She'll paint relentlessly layer over layer of color, so they all look like they're bleeding through, rushing like electricity in motion right in front of your eyes. Her paintings are arrested motion, motion you think you can reach out and touch, if you're willing to dare. They look like they might spark, ignite something in you if you touch them.

"OK," I manage to say. "If you're right–let's say I am sensitive to that. Let's say I don't want to be avoided for days on end. Maybe I'm just not ready for a relationship. Or at least not with Catherine."

"Is that how you see it?"

"Well, I guess so." But my heart and lungs want to scream, NO! "I mean, I thought she was wonderful. She seemed to have all the right qualities–maturity, stability, intelligence, humor, you know, all those things that made it exciting to be with her. And more. But maybe I was wrong."

"I doubt you were that wrong, Em. What you're saying is that she has all these wonderful qualities that you've been looking for, and she also thinks you're pretty neat. Now something has happened that's pissed you off, and you don't like her anymore. I thought you said you were in love with her."

"I did. I was. I, I am. I love her." But I panic as I say it.

"I don't think you do love her, Em."

I feel as though Laura has just reached across the table and slapped me. Frozen, I stare at her.

"I think that if you love someone, you love them in spite of their faults. Looks to me like this is the first time you've run up against Catherine's faults, or one of them. And you can't handle it. The question is, now that you know what her faults are, can you still accept her?"

Very slowly, I make my lips form words. It's as if time has slowed down. Truth feels like that. It slows us down, because it's thick and dense, and we can only absorb so much of it at one time.

"The question is, how can I manage not to be treated like dirt and accept her faults at the same time? How do I do that?"

"I didn't say you have to take any kind of treatment from her. And if she has a habit of distancing, that will be a problem, especially for you." She smiles because she knows me so well, knows how impatient and intense I am. I talk to Laura and can listen to her because she shares my intensity. She's had two husbands who haven't been able to accept it. "But you can talk with her about it. You can come up with some strategies both of you agree on. Would she agree to let you know when she feels she needs space for a few days, so you would know you wouldn't be hearing from her and maybe wouldn't worry about it so much?"

"Hmm."

"And another thing, pal. Has it ever occurred to you, given her history of having little or no experience with this sort of thing, just how incredible a change it is for her even to be *having* a relationship with you? Has it ever occurred to you just how terrified she might feel when she sees how intense you are?"

Laura notices I haven't touched my food since her statements began striking home.

"Hey, you know *I* think it's great. And I bet she does, too. But don't you think she may have had a kind of delayed reaction, woke up the other day and *realized* that she's in a relationship with you and what it means? She might be asking herself what she's gotten herself into, and here you are adding more pressure just when she might already have all she feels she can handle."

Outside, it's burning hot. We walk up Michigan Avenue. Then we turn east and stop at Phyllis Kind's gallery. No new sales of Laura's work. Laura nods and thanks Phyllis politely for her efforts.

After the gallery, it's time to visit Paul. We're lucky. Paul's alone and in his room, awake and glad to see us. Laura and I each give him a kiss, then we sit on either side of his bed and touch him as we talk. Today we don't talk about David. Paul's full of questions about Laura's new job as chairperson of the art department at a small college in Massachusetts.

I am glad Laura is with me this time. I sit and rest my hand lightly on Paul's arm and listen to the two of them catching up.

"Why so quiet today, Emily?" he asks suddenly. "You look like you just got a whiff of my bedpan."

"Oh," Laura volunteers, "it appears there's trouble in paradise."

"Hmm."

"I'm just thinking," I tell them. "I've got a lot to think about."

"Haven't you been telling me that you thought she was Ms. Right?" Paul gives me an expression of exaggerated surprise.

I can feel my face flush. "Well, yeah, I did. But–"

"And who knows," Laura breaks in, "maybe she still is Ms. Right. Aren't you seeing her again tomorrow?"

"Yes. But I'm scared."

Now it's Paul grabbing my arm, his plastic bracelet brushing me. "Listen, girl. You just hang in there, huh?"

Neither Laura nor I can meet his eyes. I feel silly and selfish. It's like I've been having a long nightmare, and I've been talking out of turn for hours, and finally someone in the back of the room comes up and tells me, and I shut up.

Dinner with Laura

Thursday night I join Laura and several of her friends I hardly see except when she comes to Chicago. We eat at one of Laura's favorite Thai restaurants on Western. It is good to see everyone happy; Laura looks vibrant, healthy, loved. She is surrounded by a group of fans. Michael and Susan, who live together; Ed the dancer; Tom, her former painting student, now an advertising executive; Lisa, another former student, now a commercial artist; and me. Emily, the social worker who goes to their art shows. I'm the only one who's *not* an artist, and they seem to like having me around.

What unites us all is that we all love Laura. We have each caught hell from her at various times, but as her hair has become streaked with gray, she has become gentler with us. I think we tolerated her even when she was not gentle because she always knew who she was. And who she was has always been an artist. Through temporary jobs and periods of unemployment and husbands and divorces and depressions and illnesses, Laura always kept a studio. When the rents went up or the buildings were taken over for offices, she'd move to another one, but she always went to her studio at least five or six times a week and painted, no matter what. She'd live in a two-room apartment rather than a one-bedroom so she could keep a separate studio. She'd get on the train and go and paint where there was no telephone, no refrigerator, no bed. No comfort. Just rotted out floors and peeling walls and a toilet down the hall if she was lucky. Her canvases would add up and take over the space, and then she'd find buyers for them. We'd all been to her openings over the years: at Phyllis Kind's, at MoMing, at Artemisia, and others. Laura isn't like the rest of us, who intermittently complain about not having time to work at whatever we think is most important. We learned early not to complain to Laura. We watched. She worked. When she lived in Chicago, if I wanted to see her, I'd go to her studio. On weekend nights she'd have us over to her place after dinner for espresso. But when I wanted to have Laura to myself, I'd go and watch her paint, and we'd talk. When no one stopped by to talk, she'd keep her Walkman on, playing her Rolling Stones or Dire Straits. She likes fast, hard rhythms. So much to feel, so much energy to experience. Running through her like electricity. Laura can't *not* paint. The stuff just funnels itself through her. All that color on canvas.

Tonight I am glad everyone else is talkative. They have brought beer in from the liquor store down the street. I envy my friends their ease, their freedom to heighten their own intensities.

I order the hottest vegetarian dish on the menu and gulp huge sips of water after each bite. Laura and I both like our food very hot.

Laura instructs us to go and see Paul more often. There's so much she has to tell us to do with our lives, and so little time. We are all enchanted with her. Once we would have tolerated her because of her genius. Now we enjoy those aspects we once tolerated. She's mellowed, and so have we. We appreciate her just as she is, and her harsh edges have softened beyond our expectations.

I hug Laura close when I say goodbye. She is staying with Michael and Susan. Tomorrow she'll catch her flight from O'Hare back to Boston.

I take the Ravenswood el to Belmont and walk home. I strip off my shoes and clothes and stretch out on my bed. I sleep more soundly than I have in days.

Returning

Friday I awaken feeling rested, stronger, readier. I allow myself a cup of strong coffee and a huge glass of water before I stretch and go for a run. Once I get past the urine and disinfectant smell of the Roscoe Street tunnel, it's easy breathing.

There's a good breeze off the lake. I let my chest open up, my consciousness turn to my sternum. There's room for the heart to move, for the lungs to expand. I inhale and let the air travel through my torso, let my insides work with the air. My gluteals tighten, and my hamstrings pull the energy up from the bottoms of my soles, through the groin, where it joins my torso, transfers the energy up, up and out. Ground to body to air. Anchor to flight. My legs are light as wings. My chest beats and opens like wings. And it's several miles later before I return home and shower and come out dripping to answer the phone. Only after I say "hello" and hear her voice do I realize I haven't thought of Catherine all night and all morning. Yet hearing her voice, I feel again a spark fly through me, and I'm weak in the knees again.

"I called last night, but I guess you were out."

"Oh. I guess I haven't gotten around to checking my messages." Sure enough, the light *has* been flashing. Why haven't I noticed it?

"Well, should we get together tonight, perhaps meet somewhere for dinner?"

"Do you want to?" I wonder why she's used the word "should." Maybe she isn't eager to see me at all. Maybe she thinks it's better if we don't see each other.

"Well, I guess maybe we should. I mean, what I'm trying to say is, I've thought about what you said. Maybe you're right.

Maybe we shouldn't have so much distance between us this early in our relationship."

I feel my chest nearly soaring again. Catherine considers our dating a relationship. She seems to *want* it. She's not blowing me off after all.

"I've been thinking, too," I say. "I think it would be nice if we could hug. It would be nice to spend some time where we didn't feel we have to discuss serious issues. Maybe I've been pushing too much on the issues, and maybe some of that could wait a bit."

"Hmm." She sounds surprised.

We're both surprised. Surprised at one another, surprised it's different, this time, to talk.

So we meet downtown near her office.

We don't hug. We smile. I see her blush, and I wonder how I could have doubted her feelings for me.

"I'm beat," she says. "Why don't we go to my place and just order pizza and watch television or something?"

"And if you kick me out, will you promise to take me to a semi-safe train station?"

She laughs. We ignore the fact that there is no such thing as a safe train late at night.

We sit politely on the train. She tells me about work, and I tell her about Laura. I mention visiting Paul, but I don't tell her what he said. I don't mention Mercedes. Cass has told me Mercedes no longer wants to see most of us; she's too depressed for us to see her.

Catherine and I are careful not to touch, even when we leave the train. We are respectful of the conflict between us and avoid sensitive references. We talk as though we are friends but not terribly close. As we walk to her apartment, I keep wondering whether we will ever hug tonight. I don't know what Catherine's conciliatory tone means. I don't want to frighten her into distancing again.

She unlocks her door and ushers me into her hallway. We walk to her living room, where I put down my small knapsack and she her briefcase. We stand for a moment looking at each other.

And then she draws me to her and we are hugging, bursting with the relief of being together and holding one another again. I can feel her heart pounding. I stroke her back and her neck, and then I just let her hold me. She holds me tighter than I can ever remember being held. She holds me as though she's been waiting a lifetime to do this, as though I have just returned from a long sojourn in a foreign country, a voyage from which she feared I might never return. She holds me with the wild gratitude of an instantaneous discovery. In the passion of her discovery that she does, indeed, at this moment, want very much to be with me, to hold me close, her arms clutch me as though they have no intention of letting go.

We say nothing. There is nothing else to say. We wait for the moment to subside, as eventually it does, and then we make small talk about ordering pizza. We sit and watch television until the pizza comes. I hardly notice what is on. It doesn't matter. I browse through magazines on her coffee table; she goes through her mail. When the pizza comes, she insists on paying for it. It seems important to her to do this, so I let her. We take pleasure in eating it. The spinach is folded perfectly into the cheese; the crust is thick and hearty. We eat at her table, caddy-cornered, facing each other, and it seems the most exotic activity to be sitting here eating pizza together. No stuffed pizza has ever tasted as gently and superbly blended, as fresh and as perfectly baked, as this. Afterward we sit again on her sofa, at either end, not too far apart but keeping a respectful distance. Yet ever since the hug, the distance is not a tense or fearful one.

Catherine gets ready for bed as she always has, puttering in the bathroom, carefully informing me where extra towels are, inviting me, if I wish, to stay and read if I'm not tired.

"Or, if I'm through reading?"

"Then come to bed."

I follow her. She has pulled back the white cotton spread and is lying on one side, facing the door, her long legs loosely bent. I can't help but stop for a moment and study her. She is, at this moment, the most seductive woman I have ever seen. She's not even watching me but is fiddling with her clock radio, setting the alarm or turning it off.

She has the longest, sexiest legs I have ever seen. I have never known what obsessed men so about women's legs. Now

I think I'm beginning to know. I can't believe I'm standing here. Me, impatient, ordinary, silly romantic, standing in the bedroom of the most seductive woman in the world, who has no idea how seductive she is.

Catherine looks up, no doubt wondering why I'm standing here.

"I just can't help looking at you. Do you know how beautiful you are?"

She blushes right up her high forehead to her light brown hair.

"Oh, you."

I go around to the other side of the bed, take off my clothes and drape them on the radiator. A box fan is purring quietly in the window.

I turn over on my stomach, so my better ear can be smothered into the pillow. Catherine has by now stretched out on her back. She turns off the lamp. I reach, slowly, and let my arm drop lightly across her stomach, careful not to touch her nipples beneath the fabric of her sleepshirt.

We lie quietly for a few minutes. Catherine begins stroking my arm. Then she carefully lifts it up and moves it so that it lies between us. She turns toward me, turns my face up from the pillow toward her, and kisses me on the forehead.

The nose.

The lips.

She kisses my lips and tongues them open, and then kisses me fully, circling her tongue across the roof of my mouth and behind my front teeth. And then our tongues compete for each other's mouths. I tickle the back of the roof of her mouth with my tongue until her body jerks in response. She begins to rub my nipples, and then she pulls me over on top of her.

I am still kissing her, and I push her sleepshirt up so I can kiss her nipples, too. I lean down and circle her left nipple with my tongue, teasing her and feeling her body begin to writhe in pleasure. In a few minutes she lets me slip the sleepshirt over her head, and then I slide down, licking her stomach and her navel. She is still wearing her cream-colored satiny nylon panties, and I start to pull them off. When she raises up ever so slightly to help me and then spreads her legs and bends her knees, one at a time, I nearly swoon.

She trusts me. Catherine trusts me. Wants me. Wants me to bring her pleasure. Me. No one else. I'm the only woman she's slept with in about twelve years; she could have had anyone. And in all the world, this is the only place I want to be.

I lean down to lick her, to tease her into the richest desire she's capable of feeling, but suddenly she reaches down and pulls my head up, before I can get there.

I look puzzled. I know she's always loved this before, despite her fear and misplaced shame the first time I convinced her that I wanted to do it because *I like* licking her there.

She's shaking her head.

She pulls me up toward her. I lower my body back on top of hers.

"Not tonight," she says.

I panic. Will she suddenly close the door again, just at the height of pleasure, trust, sharing? I don't think I can stand it.

But she's clutching me to her. She whispers in my ear.

"Tonight, I want you to stay with me. Close. I want to be able to hold you the whole time. I want you up here. With me." She kisses me passionately, stroking my back, and she's still pressing her groin against me. I begin to understand. Oral sex can be lonely for the recipient. Catherine's trying to tell me, to show me, we need to reestablish something tonight.

And so, while she's holding me close against her and kissing me, I find a way to raise up ever so slightly and slide my hand between her legs. She's wet and slick, and when I stroke her in circles with my fingers she writhes even more. I love her slickness, her velvet, and the way it feels to stroke up and down one side and then the other, and then to tease the expanding bud, to move my hand just an inch or two away for a second and feel her body straining upward after me.

Her body wants my hand, wants my fingers, wants me stroking her faster, faster, faster, but I refuse to let it end this quickly: I make her pause, I make her savor the delicious sensation, I take her as close to the summit as I can without letting her go completely over, and then back her down easy, and she lets me, she wants me to do this, exactly as I'm doing this.

Catherine's arms are around my neck now, and her torso is rigid with tension. I tease her by rubbing hard and then gently circling, and I whisper in her ear, "I want to suck you and stroke you and make you so hot you come, you can't help it, you're going to come faster and deeper and longer than ever before, because you're so hot, and I'm making you hotter, hotter, hotter."

She's jerking up and down now, against my hand. I push easily, gently into her, three fingers, loving the slick wet sides of her, the wonderful, tight muscles, the way they hug my fingers, the way they respond when I gently stroke them. My thumb is on her too and she's clucking in her throat now, the noise I love the most, because when Catherine makes that noise I know she's feeling pure sensation for which there are no words. She's drawing me to her, hard, again, and suddenly she kisses me harder, driving her tongue deep into my mouth, shuddering and smashing her teeth against mine when uncontrollable spasms seize her.

She begins to pull her mouth away, but I won't let her; I don't care if she smashes against me, I'm with her body, I'm feeling the spasms, she's rocking so hard on my fingers and against the palm of my hand I think they might get sprained or broken and I want them to, I want them to break with the passion, with the flood she's being swept up in and I with her, and she's flying with me now, flying into my arms and into my palm and into my teeth and into my nipples and into my heart, her heart bursting with joy, the blood beating its wings so hard and fast my ribs are bruised by it, and I don't care I don't care I don't care I don't care I'm bursting with joy too with Catherine with her flooding all over my hand and my legs and smashing me harder against her, pounding my shoulders and then suddenly not pounding any more, letting her hands, then her entire arms, flop down, her arms lightly falling back to the bed, her head back to the pillow, and she's no longer kissing me because she has no shred of energy left with which to move the slightest muscle and as my head falls alongside of hers on the edge of her pillow I brush her left temple with my cheek and feel her tears.

Sometime in the middle of the night I wake up and go around the corner to the bathroom. Catherine is sleeping soundly when I return. I slide into bed. Her bedroom set is from her mother's house in Rockford. Small nightstands on either side of the bed are covered with lace scarves, like the dresser at the front of the room. On each nightstand sits a tiny reading lamp with a crystal base and a pleated shade. On top of her dresser are a few bottles of expensive perfumes I've never heard of, lotions and cosmetics, though Catherine prefers the natural look. In the dim light from a lamp in the complex's back yard, I follow the shadows across her white walls and ceiling. The fan hums steadily, an echo to Catherine's peaceful breathing. Her mattress is too old and soft, like all mattresses taken from parents' homes. Above her bed is a beautifully framed Mary Cassatt print; small prints and photographs decorate the rest of the room. Everything is small in proportion to the large expanse of white wall, unlike my apartment where huge canvases and prints by Laura and other artists dominate every available space. The matching kneehole desk along the wall opposite Catherine's side of the bed is always tidy. Never more than a few letters or bills stick up in the clip at the edge of the green blotter. I am always amazed by this. Sometimes I can't see the top of my own desk for weeks.

Although I can't read the titles in the dim light, I already know that many of the books on her bookshelf pertain to the theater. She has textbooks on film criticism and histories of drama and biographies of actors and actresses. Along the walls in her hallway and living room are more bookshelves filled with literature; we take pleasure in finding similarities among our collections. Emily Dickinson (Catherine teases me about this), Virginia Woolf, Louise Bogan, Lillian Hellmann, Carson McCullers, Katherine Anne Porter, Alice Walker, Toni Morrison, Thomas Mann, and many others are shared favorites. She has, of course, the complete works of Jane Austen. Yet she also found a place for Kerouac. D. H. Lawrence. Henry Miller. Anais Nin. Kaye Gibbons. Jane Rule. Maureen Brady. Becky Birtha. Alice Hoffmann. Susan Sontag.

Her beautifully waxed wooden floors, her maple and walnut furniture, her books and lamps and lace all make Catherine's apartment feel like home. I let myself relax in her soft bed, turn and close my eyes, lightly rest my arm on her stomach. In Catherine's apartment the past and the present are ordered neatly into place. Everything is always neat; even the white tile of her kitchen floor is spotless. But her apartment lacks the sterility of Barry's modern, high-tech condominium. It also lacks that mixed-up, cluttered look of my own place and those of other friends, with too many books and papers, too much art, furniture of various styles thrown together from this or that thrift store. Oh, Catherine keeps things; she likes a sense of the past visibly surrounding her. She collects Wedgwood and crystal: small, unobtrusive collections. Each piece has its significance, and she has her reasons for everything she keeps.

I left home early, then lived in those crummy apartments outside D.C. before coming to Chicago and moving in with George. All the while I dated men without knowing why. George's place felt like my first home. Afterwards, I finally learned how to make a home for myself in my one-bedroom on Roscoe, the right street in the right neighborhood for me.

Catherine had always created her home for herself, but until she met me she did not allow herself a lover with whom to share it. I always had lovers, but never a true home.

Catherine understands that one can be brushed by many things, touched by many things, yet stay essentially in place, knowing always exactly where one is.

This is something I want to learn. I believe that she is teaching me. I believe that I am ready to let her teach me now.

Instead of home I had water, too many tears, nothing to shield me.

Instead of an open door her home has been constructed with the architectonic purity of ice.

I am chipping away.

I listen to Catherine's measured breathing, feel her chest gently rising and falling, and am lulled back to sleep.

I open my eyes again, this time to light and to Catherine's arms wrapped around me, to her face snuggled next to mine.

"Good morning," she says. "How did you sleep?"

I love her blue eyes, her tousled hair, her smile. I love her arms wrapped around me.

"I slept fine. How about you?"

"Great. I was dead to the world. I don't remember anything after that wonderful, well, you know–SEX!" She laughs at her own nervousness, but there's a new boldness in her laugh. Then: "I'm sorry I conked out so suddenly on you."

"Oh, don't worry about that. I fell asleep about the same time you did."

"You *did*?" she asks in mock surprise. Now she's propped herself on one elbow, looking down at me with a raised eyebrow. "But weren't you feeling *deprived*?"

I look away, at the wall. Why am I embarrassed?

"Emily, I do believe you're blushing." She strokes my forehead.

"I, I wasn't feeling anything like deprived." I can hear myself stumbling over my words. "I–I was really into it with you. It was really great–I felt like I felt everything with you."

"I know." She's smiling, and her voice sounds like a silvery flute in my head. She's staring at me, at my face, my neck, my breasts, with a look of determined lust. She's got one arm holding my arm down and she brings the other down on my other arm. Suddenly, I look at her smile, and her long arms, and her tall body arching over me, and I realize she's taking over, she's going to touch me just exactly as she wants to, and I'm melting already, limp in her arms: she can do whatever she wants with me, and she will. She's in control. She brings her face down toward mine, not smiling in the same way anymore but with a look of power, the power that my body begs her to take, and I gasp before she even kisses me. She kisses me long and hard, tonguing me the way I like it, deep into my mouth. She was shy about kissing at first, wouldn't give me enough of her tongue, but now she can feel how I crave it, and my body yearns upward for contact with hers. She slides one knee between my legs and presses her thigh up against me and rubs me, and I'm wet for her, shameless. She teases me like that awhile, rubbing against me, then pulling away.

"You're driving me wild," I whisper in her ear as she sucks my nipples and rubs against me. She makes a satisfied grunt.

She comes back up and tickles my teeth with her tongue, rims my lips and gums. She moves her leg back and begins stroking me with her fingertips. She's still holding me down with her other arm, and her left leg is holding my right leg down, and I can only move in the areas she's left free.

Butch in the streets, femme in the sheets. I love it when she holds me down like this, when I can't move except as she lets me.

I'm giving her all control, am completely at her mercy. My body's arching upward now, reaching for her hand, and she's teasing me, watching me beg for her, and smiling because she sees I'm insane with desire. I put my free arm around her and press with all the passion of my need, begging her to come closer but loving it when she refuses, when she draws me up and then pauses before she strokes me again. Her torso is above me, big enough to come down and crush me, and I hope it will, I want it to. I want her hand to stroke me harder, harder, and she sees this, and she does. She's stroking me and now she inserts fingers inside me, I can't tell how many, maybe three, maybe four, all I know is it's driving me wild, and she drives her large palm up against me, I can't get enough, I'm riding her, riding her, riding her, I can't help it, and now she's staying with me, just letting me ride as fast and as hard and as long as I want, and now she's kissing me again, this time on my neck, and lowering her beautiful chest, her strong ribs and delicate breasts down against mine, pressing me, giving me all of her, giving me the contact I'm craving, and I'm bucking like a bronco and I don't care, I let myself go, I'm soaring up, up, up, against her hand and around her fingers, hugging them tighter, tighter, tighter, so tight I can scream, and I am screaming now, high, loud, piercing screams, Catherine Catherine Catherine Catherine OH OH OH OH!!!!

She holds me afterwards, keeps her fingers in me, her palm nestled against me. She knows I come down slowly and that I need to be held like this. She kisses my forehead, my neck. When I finally open my eyes, she is smiling down at me, a pure, unguarded smile.

I touch her forearm to signal that she can pull away now. She waits another minute before gradually, gently sliding her fingers out. Her touch is as tender as if she's licking me there. She takes her time, watching my face. Her fingers move so slowly, so subtly that I think my heart will break with tenderness. When she lies down again beside me, wrapping her arms around me and kissing my cheek, I am flushed again with joy.

"Emily," she says. "I'm glad you came home with me. I'm glad you stayed."

It takes me a moment to find my own tongue, lips, voice again.

"Me too."

"I feel like I have thirty dinosaurs stomping around my mouth with their muddy feet. I hope it wasn't too terrible when I kissed you."

"Catherine! You can kiss me any time you damn well please. I'm in love," I remind her. "Besides, *I* have morning mouth, too. Maybe it was worse for you than for me."

"Oh, no, mine's always worse—"

"And besides, I'm sweating like a pig. Your poor sheets."

She laughs then. I sit up on one elbow and then get out of bed and head for the bathroom. I can still hear her giggling.

Strawberries

After I come out of the shower and put on my clothes again, I find Catherine in the kitchen, where she's sitting with a cigarette and coffee. She pours a cup for me. She's wearing her nightshirt again.

"It's half regular and half decaf," she says.

The way I always make it. She told me she'd never tried that before. Has she made it this way just for me? She's smiling at me like a kid with a secret. A nice secret, one that she'll tell you if you're patient and wait until it's time.

"And I have natural cereal, and bread for toast if you like. There's some yogurt in the refrigerator." She places a bowl of freshly washed strawberries in front of me.

Catherine is never ready for breakfast first thing in the morning, but I always am.

"Just help yourself to whatever you feel like. I think I'll get a shower now."

She crosses the dining and living room. Just before she reaches the bathroom, she turns.

"You won't leave before I come back, will you?"

I laugh instinctively, assuming she's joking. Yet while she's in the shower, I wonder. Did our fight last Sunday leave her with doubts? Does she doubt that I'm in love with her, that I'd stay with her as long as she'd allow me to? Provided, of course, that she didn't just vanish for days at a time. Aha. So there's the catch. She sees that my love is conditional after all. Even though she knows I want nothing more than to stay with her, she's not sure I wouldn't leave under certain circumstances. She's reminding me that she remembers the fight and how frustrated I was with her. She's letting me know she hasn't forgotten what happened, how I feel. She must be feeling freer.

Give her space, Emily, I tell myself, and she'll come to you. See?

"About last weekend," I begin, after her shower, when she's settled down again in the chair opposite me. Birds are chattering in the trees outside her windows, and a gentle morning breeze is pleasant on my skin. "I was unreasonable. You had told me you weren't coming to the party, and we didn't have any specific agreement about calling or doing anything on Sunday. I just couldn't get my mind off of you, but I should have gone and done something to distract myself instead of worrying about it and getting upset."

"Well," Catherine takes a deep breath, "I think it's probably natural to worry, since you really don't know me that well yet–I mean, this is still a pretty new relationship. We have different assumptions about what being in a relationship means. I just don't think of calling you sometimes, when I'm busy with other things. But I guess on the weekends where we don't get together–and those do happen, when I'm out at Mom's or have plans with Patrick or whatever–why don't I just call you, even if it's a two-minute message, to let you know what's going on?"

I'm holding a fat, ripe strawberry in my hand, and I've pulled the green top off it with the other hand, and I just sit there, holding it. I feel like my lower jaw has just dropped three inches. But I can't seem to get the strawberry to my mouth.

"What?" I feel about as stupid as someone who has just spent three hours trying to figure out how to put together a piece of furniture, only to have someone else come along who assembles it in three easy steps in five minutes. "I mean, that sounds good. Fine. Easy. I mean, if that's OK with you."

I pop the strawberry in my mouth to keep from saying anything more and revealing that I'm as dumb as I feel.

"And now, if you don't mind, I have to call my mother."

I nod. She goes to the telephone in the living room. I eat another strawberry.

"Oh, damn."

"What?"

"She's already called and left a message. Either yesterday before I got home or early this morning."

I am so glad Catherine has a large apartment, so that we don't hear the phone in the bedroom. She keeps another one there but always turns the ringer off at night.

Catherine plays the message. Her mother has a voice not unlike what I expected. A woman in her sixties. A bit nasal and whiny. Or do I just think whiny because I've heard Catherine complain about her mother's personality?

"Well, just calling to see when to expect you, honey. Aunt Josie will be here, and Uncle Ralph and Aunt Judy. I'm planning dinner on Saturday for six o'clock. Love you."

Love you? In a staccato voice. Like the voice of the traffic announcer on the radio: the Edens on the brakes from Dempster to Touhy, an overturned semi and gapers' delay.

Catherine dials her mother's number and informs her she'll be there by mid-afternoon.

She lights another cigarette while she's talking. When she hangs up, she puts that cigarette out and lights another one. She comes back to the table, sits down, and sighs.

"So, you're heading out to Rockford, huh?"

She nods, exhaling smoke. Her large, graceful, expressive hands are tensed, bent at the knuckles. Usually, they're loose and move lightly through the air, making lovely gestures while she speaks, but now they look rock hard, crippled into fists.

I get some yogurt and cereal and mix them with strawberries into a bowl. Catherine is an only child, and her father left her mother when she was 12. She's been taking care of her mother ever since. Stayed at home the first two years of college, went to a state school less than two hours away the last two, dutifully returning home most weekends. After graduation she lived at home again and commuted from Rockford to a computer consulting firm in a Chicago suburb. At 26, she finally moved out of Rockford and into Oak Park. But she still went "home" every weekend.

Her mother began drinking heavily when Catherine was a teenager, but stopped about five years later. Not long after moving to Oak Park, Catherine went with a friend she worked with to her first meeting of Adult Children of Alcoholics. She's been trying to detach from her mother, one step at a time. Now she's 32 and spends about one weekend a month with her mother.

We sit in silence while I eat and Catherine smokes.

"Well," I say when I've finished. "I guess I'll be getting the train back to the city now. I'm sure you have things to do before you drive to Rockford."

She looks up, as if coming out of a reverie.

"You're right. I should get to the bank before they close."

"Oh."

I get up and walk around to her chair. I stand behind her and lean down and put my arms around her shoulders. I kiss her neck.

"Thank you for a lovely evening."

"Mmm." I can feel her neck begin to relax. I hold her a moment longer. Then she rouses herself. "Well, let's see, why don't I walk with you a little ways, then I can run my errands."

The day is lovely: cool and sunny, just warm enough, not as humid as I'd thought it would be when I was sweating in Catherine's bedroom. A perfect day for a run along the lake, or a picnic. Or a parade.

"What are you doing tomorrow, Catherine?" I meant to ask her last weekend, but the way things went, with our fight on Sunday, I never got around to it.

"I'll probably be in Rockford until late afternoon."

It's only a couple more blocks to the train station. Now I'm getting nervous. Has Catherine never thought about the parade?

"Did you realize that tomorrow is the Pride Parade?"

She stops walking and turns to me, a bit tense.

"Well, I guess I did. Why?"

Uh-oh. Sounds almost like a challenge.

"Well, I had been planning to ask you last week if you wanted to go with me." I know better than to invite her to march with my gay and lesbian church group, because Catherine is still nervous around groups of other lesbians. "I'll be marching, but if you don't want to march you could meet me at the rally afterward."

I'm hoping this conversation doesn't turn into a battle. I hope she can hear my attempt to keep my tone light. I want to see her there, but I want her to feel that it can be on her terms.

"Emily." Her tone is not harsh, but firm. Careful. "I just don't think I'm ready for that. Not this weekend. What would happen if I saw someone from work or something?"

"Well, lots of straight people come to *watch* the parade, Catherine. It doesn't mean anything if someone sees you standing there watching. Besides, if *they're* there, they're probably cool."

"Emily, I haven't even been able to bring myself to come out to my mother in all these years. I haven't even been able to let myself have a relationship with a woman until you. You know how long it's taken me. I just can't quite see myself going to the Pride Parade this weekend. I don't know. Maybe I should. But not this year. Maybe next year."

I can see she's torn. What to me comes so easily and is just a matter of fun is for Catherine a source of conflict and tension. But I've lived away from my mother for many years, and I'm out to her and out to my colleagues. Catherine's not as free as I am to watch the parade, let alone march in it.

"It's OK," I tell her. And I mean it, or at least I hope I do.

"You know, Emily, I'd like to be able to do that, I really would." She flinches slightly. I want to touch her, to hug her, but I don't dare. Not here. Not on the street in Oak Park, near where she lives. Other women do it all the time–we've seen a couple kissing outside a restaurant–but not us. Not Catherine. We all walk around on the same streets, riding the same trains, watching the same movies, eating at the same restaurants, even working at the same jobs in the same companies, and yet some of us walk as free as if we're wearing wings, and some of us are shackled by heavy chains. Others would say we have invented our chains, that we wear them to keep ourselves where we are. I'm not so sure. I want to free Catherine from her chains, I want to free her ankles, her lovely wrists, her majestic chest, so that she can soar above her pain, above even me.

Instead of reaching out to hug her, I nod.

"I know. I know you would. And one day soon you probably will. But Catherine," I look her in the eye, "it doesn't have to be right now. You don't have to do it for me. Ever. If and when you do it, you won't be doing it for me."

"But won't you be upset with me for not being there tomorrow?"

I'm determined not to pretend this time, to play nobler than I am. "I'll be disappointed. Sure, I'd like to have you there. I'd like it a lot. But I'll survive. I'd rather have you in my life ten years from now than ask you to do something you're not ready for."

Her face relaxes; her forehead is smoother now. She smiles. Her fine cheekbones and long, elegant neck give her a look of stateliness, even when she's not completely sure of herself.

"I hope you mean that." She sounds as though she believes I do mean it, but is just checking.

"I do mean it. I'll survive. But I'll survive especially well if I know I can see you next weekend."

She laughs. "All right. I won't keep you on pins and needles, dear. We will definitely get together–when? Friday night? We could actually see each other both Friday and Saturday if you want."

"My goodness! You haven't scheduled something else?"

"No. And I won't, if you're free. Maybe you're busy. I wouldn't presume that you would be free both days." She smiles.

"Well, my dear, I just so happen to be free Friday, and I wouldn't dream of scheduling anything else."

We're at the station. I start up the steps. She stays on the sidewalk.

"Friday, then?"

"Sure."

"I'll call you."

"OK" And as I bound up the stairs, past the ticket booth, flashing my bus pass, I know she will.

Looking for David

Barry and I meet later that evening for our visit to the Halsted bars. When I see him waiting at Roscoe, he smiles indulgently. He didn't know George, doesn't know Paul, and yet he's willing to help me find David Miller.

"It's so ironic," he says, as we head for the first bar, "for all I know, I *could* have met the guy during those lost years." He shrugs. Barry drank or smoked or both nearly every night for about 20 years, or so he's told me. I've always had trouble imagining it. He's been sober for five years, as long as I've known him. We met at an A.A. meeting.

He pauses to study one of the snapshots of David I've brought along.

"Good-looking fellow, isn't he?"

I nod. "All Paul wants is to let him know that it was OK, whatever it was. Paul didn't say this, but I think he wants to know that I've found him and that the message was delivered–I think he'll be more at peace if he knows."

Barry looks from the snapshot up at me. "How was he the other day when you saw him?"

"Not good. I guess the morphine makes him fuzzy. Last week he couldn't always speak clearly even when he was awake and tried to."

"What does his doctor say?"

"He says it could be a few weeks or a few months."

"Does he have any family?"

"Not in Chicago. And apparently they haven't had anything to do with him since he told them he was gay. Laura called and talked to his sister in St. Louis. She said she'd come up to see him as soon as she could get a day off."

We pause.

"Well, let's go," Barry says.

At the door of the first bar, I turn to Barry. "Listen, if this isn't comfortable for you, just tell me. I know it's not easy for you to go in to these places."

"I'll tell you," he says. "Having you along will make it easier."

"And we won't stay long, I promise. I'll just show these to the bartenders and ask if they know of any customers from that far back who still come in."

"You don't think we look like cops or anything, do you?"

"God, I hope not. Of course, you *are* distinguished with that lovely silver hair. I, on the other hand, look too dykey to be a cop, don't you think?"

"Oh, I don't know. After Cagney and Lacey, I'm not sure."

"Well, the story is I'm the executor of an estate and there's money for David in it, and I just want him or anyone who knows him to call me. Nobody needs to give their address; I'll just give mine. Shouldn't scare anyone off."

We go in. I show the snapshots to two bartenders, but neither of them has worked there longer than a year. They also don't know any customers who've been around long. But I leave my name and number anyway.

We go up the strip and try others. At one bar, the owner tells us he *has* been there several years, and it's possible David used to come in, but he really can't remember. I leave one of the snapshots with him, hoping something might come to him. Almost everywhere we go, the bartenders raise their eyebrows at the story about an estate. They assume someone's died of AIDS and is leaving David some money. Some ask me whether I've considered the possibility that David has died of AIDS. But Mark has said the David Miller I want hasn't turned up dead yet, according to his checking.

"Remember my friend who died two years ago?" Barry asks me at one bar where everyone seems to be dancing and unapproachable. I nod. "He astonished the doctors and defied statistics, hanging on past infection after infection. His doctors experimented with treatments, since their other AIDS patients hadn't lived long enough to come down with the rare infections he had. He called himself the gay guinea pig."

"Wasn't he the one with the wild streak?"

"Used to chase his pals around the apartment with butcher knives." Barry laughs, remembering. "The thing is, I didn't really *like* the guy much. Kind of nasty. Maybe his nastiness kept him alive."

I think about this. "Paul still has his sense of humor–it was never as wild as your friend's–but he's not nasty. Hmm. Maybe I wish he were." And George. George cooperated, never complained, fretted and worried over us when we visited. But, oh, how willing I am to have him back a nastier George than he was. Where some people get through life throwing temper tantrums, cursing and raging whenever they feel like it, George went far too gently into that good night.

Barry and I drink as many glasses of pop and mineral water as we can stand. We grow tired at about the same time the crowds are increasing, around midnight. Barry walks me home. We hug.

"Hang in there, kid. You're doing your best."

I nod. Really, it shouldn't bother me if I can't find David. I'm glad for the chance to try to do something, when there's nothing else I seem to be able to do for Paul. There was nothing I could do for George. Paul, at least, will leave behind his prints and drawings. He's made a will to allow for that. George, unlike Paul, didn't let most of his friends even know he was dying. Didn't want to burden them. Never asked us to do anything for him.

When he died, that gorgeous voice, that open heart, left us. Though Barry and my other friends offer their kindness, none of them is George. No one tells me I'm a proud hawk anymore, that I should always fly high. No one invites me to sing as though my voice is actually beautiful. No one sings to me, no one caresses me with words too tender for indifferent ears. George's voice was the warm water that melted everything cold you carried inside. If I had his voice, I could sing to Catherine, and she would fly into my arms, both of us soaring, the ice dropping from our wings, happy tears falling through the sky.

Reservoir

It's the hottest day of the year, but none of us who have arrived at church care about that. This morning the service will include a talk by Fiona. In the bathroom I run into Jenny and Lucinda and Nora and Cass. Again I think how lovely Jenny and Lucinda look together, and Nora and Cass.

"Hi, Emily," Jenny says. "Haven't seen you in ages."

"Not since Fiona's party, I guess," I reply.

"Yeah. When you were after that woman." She puts her hands on her hips. "So, are you two still dating?"

"Yeah."

"Good. I've never seen you look like that before."

I blush.

"Jenny said she really is beautiful," Lucinda offers.

"Yeah. I guess so," I mumble. Why am I embarrassed? Caught in the act of love. Of being in love. Does Catherine's not being here make it any less real?

"Yo, Emily," says the ever-confident Cass. She's one of those people who is energetic and talkative from the moment she opens her eyes in the morning, while most of us are still dependent on caffeine to reinvent our enthusiasm.

"Hey, Cass, Nora." We hug.

"So where *were* you this morning? Missed you in the race," Cass tells me.

"Oh." I'd run in the Proud to Run race against AIDS when George was still alive, but somehow didn't feel like it this year. Two years ago I would have run a marathon if I'd thought it would keep him around a little longer. Day after day, week after week of watching him suffer took something out of me.

I shrug. "Guess I just didn't get around to sending the registration in this year."

Cass is about to say something else when Nora speaks up.

"So good to see you, Emily," Nora tells me, and I know she means it.

"Yeah. It was a good race, Em, but hey, maybe we'll see you next year." Cass punches my shoulder lightly. From Cass, this is a sign of approval. I return her smile.

"So tell us more about your new honey. We thought we'd get to meet her today," says Lucinda.

"She had to go to Rockford. She's not ready to do the parade just yet."

"What?" Cass asks. "What's wrong with that girl?"

"Really," Nora adds. "Doesn't she know it's the social event of the season?"

"And isn't she afraid," Cass continues, "that all the single dykes will pounce on you if she leaves you unattended?!"

We all laugh.

The five of us, white and brown and tan, later sit in a row together. We are wearing white and black and red and green, our colors of pride, our tank tops, short-sleeved shirts and shorts showing off our muscles.

While the opening music—a lovely Fauré piece played by our pianist—continues, I say a prayer for George, and for Paul: Goddess, please help him. Bring him whatever comfort you can. And I say a silent prayer for Mercedes, one of too many women with cancer. I ask the Goddess to send her strength.

The service proceeds with a welcoming statement, then a hymn, "For the Beauty of the Earth." One of the few hymns we sing in the Unitarian church that I remember singing as a child in the Episcopal church back in Virginia and in the gospel choir with Brother Johnson. This always gives me hope. Then, after the announcements, comes Fiona. Though I haven't seen her since her party, I still remember a talk she gave last year on grief. She spoke of her own grief for people she was mourning. When she mentioned the name of her father, five years after his death, her voice still cracked and she didn't hide her tears. I know she'll speak from the heart.

I watch Fiona step up to the microphone. *My Fiona. Our Fiona.* All five of us sitting in this row have either been her clients or are the friends and lovers of her clients. Tall and big-boned, she stands confidently at the microphone in a multi-colored caftan. She's hennaed her hair, and it stands nearly straight up. She's wearing lipstick but little other makeup. Fiona looks like I wouldn't mind looking in my forties. You can tell she's happy with the way she looks. If anyone can help us learn self-awareness and acceptance and courage, Fiona can.

Catherine continues to see Fiona every week.

I have hope. If my wings are stronger, taking broader sweeps than ever before, perhaps Catherine's will too.

"I think that love does last forever, but perhaps not in the way we think," Fiona is saying. "The ability to love, the capacity—that is, the space for it within us—is always there, like a reservoir.

"This capacity lies within us, not "out there" or in another person.

"Love is this capacity, and not the forms or channels our society sometimes confuses it with.

"Love isn't something we choose. Although the capacity lies within us, we don't know where the supply line is that taps into that reservoir.

"Someone or something comes along and reaches inside us and turns that faucet, and the love flows. We can't choose who does it, or when or how."

The church is filled with Fiona's voice and the silence of the congregation. We are sitting on the edge of our pews, gays and heterosexuals alike. Behind Fiona is the white unadorned wall reaching up past the rafters to the pointed roof. It makes a triangle at the top, and seeing Fiona with her rainbow-colored caftan standing there, framed by the tip of that triangle arching above her, makes me understand her woman's power, framed within that ancient symbol of our strength and unity. She, and our other helpers, healing women of all kinds, are what survives of our ancient power. Why should we need myths of any kind? I wonder. Having our Fionas today is enough.

"All that we can choose," she continues, "is whether to lie about that love or not to lie about it. Whether to deny its existence, to pretend to be something we're not.

"We are here today to celebrate our capacity to love in whatever form it takes. Our love is our truth. We celebrate today our courage in affirming that truth. If we deny love, then we deny truth. And that is the only sin there is on this planet. From that single, ultimate sin come all other failures, all other things we call evil.

"There are forces that hate us, that would deny both the love within us and the love within themselves.

"But the forces of hatred will never destroy us, because we are merely living the truth.

"We must pity those who are fighting so desperately to keep their reservoir of love from being tapped. We must pity them because such a reservoir, dammed (and perhaps damned as well) can only become stagnant, polluted for lack of oxygen.

"The supply of love is endless, but only if it has some place or places to go. Neglected, unused, it will not survive. The water turns brackish, bitter, and that sourness then infects the world.

"The world is polluted from a collective failure inside the human race. We have too often let fear stand in the way of love. Our planet is dying because the answers that would save it have been left inside, blocked up. The answers lie within us, but our refusal to go inside and find them, to let them be tapped by other human beings, will make us choke on them.

"Do not choke on the fullness within you. Let it nourish you. Let yourself become ready for those who will show you how to share that fullness, that love."

Nora and Cass are holding hands tightly. Tears streak Jenny's face. Lucinda's arm is around Jenny's shoulders.

"Remember," Fiona continues, "you can't force the reservoir out of you. You can't make it flow in any particular direction. You have to let go, and let it go in the direction where it's being tapped. "Never confuse the tappers with the source. If some particular person leaves you, you still have your love. That person brought the air, the opening, the space for that reservoir to breathe and move more freely.

"It can happen at almost any time, with a wide variety of people. These moments where the reservoir of love is touched and can flow more freely are what will save us and those who fear us. It's a process.

"For every word of gratitude and love you express to that other person, be sure to express the same to yourself. You are both participants in the process, in the ongoing life of this organism we call planet Earth. It is a good deal larger than both of you.

"Celebrate your love today. Celebrate your lover, if you have one. Celebrate yourself most of all. And when you confront the hatred that results from denial, have the courage to speak the truth. Not for your lover's sake. For your sake. And for all of us."

The rest of the service is a blur of hymns and spoken words. The air conditioning isn't able to keep this many of us cool, and my cotton shirt is sticking to my back. I mop my brow. I light a candle of mourning for George and repeat my prayers for Paul and Mercedes.

After the service, we find Fiona, and she hugs each of us in turn.

"So how are things?" she asks me.

I know Catherine has told her we're dating. But Fiona doesn't seem surprised that Catherine isn't here.

"Pretty good," I say. I blush. Fiona knows my secrets, my codependent tendencies. Time to 'fess up. "But I'm probably too head over heels with Catherine. I'm trying to learn to slow down, let her take the lead more. Patience, I guess. You know," I say nervously, glancing at my running shoes, "how hard that can be for me."

Fiona chuckles, but she is kind, and so refrains from saying "do I ever." We used to discuss—actually, argue—about what words like "love" and "codependence" and "romantic" mean. Fiona's one of the few people I truly like with whom I can let myself argue intensely: one of the benefits of a therapist-client relationship. After practicing with her, I've been working up to allowing myself the freedom to argue with friends and—the ultimate goal—lovers.

"Are you marching in the parade?" Fiona asks.

"Yes. I think I'll just stay with the church group." It's always a toss-up as to which group to march with: the women from Paris bar, the Metropolitan Sports Association, Mountain Moving Coffeehouse, Women & Children First, or half a dozen others. I ask, "Are you going to be with us?"

Fiona shakes her head. “No. I have to leave in a few minutes for Wisconsin.” Fiona and her lover of ten years often go to their summer cottage near Racine.

Fiona hugs and jokes with Jenny and Lucinda, although I know that by moving in together after dating only three months they have disappointed her. She probably gives Lucinda hell in therapy about it. Catherine and I must be relatively healthy; at least we’re not together every night or every weekend, and have not discussed moving in together. Healthy, happy kids pulling it off. Hah. Where did I get all my romantic ideas about couples? Was it from seeing too many Hollywood couples? Seeing too many straight and lesbian couples do too much too soon, always together?

All right, then, so Catherine and I will be different. Or at least we’ll try. It doesn’t feel fair that for *her* it’s no trouble not seeing me, whereas for me it’s always hard work. Or is Catherine simply more adept at masking the trouble?

The Pride Parade

The afternoon sun is hot, bright like a huge spotlight, lighting us up for all the world to see. I march on the side, next to Jenny and Lucinda, one golden-haired, one dark-haired like me. Nora and Cass complete our crooked row of marchers. Behind us are an assorted mix of church regulars. We carry our signs and banners proclaiming that we are different and beautiful and proud, singles, couples, straights, gays, young, old, children, parents, healthy, sick, all together on this one day. Gorgeous men dance in skimpy bathing trunks; tall hunks in leather pose fiercely on top of floats; women smile and throw flyers for concerts from cars. There are floats from bars and social service organizations and political groups. Ours is not the only church group, either, but the most informal, the most diverse. A straight couple marches with us. Our minister is a gay man. Two children join in.

The crowds fill the sidewalks on Broadway like popcorn overflowing a box. They clap and cheer and call out the names of friends they recognize. The gay men's chorus somewhere behind us is singing in beautiful harmony.

"Emily!" someone shouts as we inch toward Belmont.

I look around, and see Rosalie waving from a window. She's got herself invited to someone's apartment for the parade. All up and down Broadway, upstairs windows are open, with people hanging out of them, sitting on balconies and ledges. I wave up at Rosalie.

"Going to the rally?" she shouts.

"Sure." I shout back.

"Look for me–up front," she calls.

I know where she means.

It feels like several hours, but it's only been about two, when we finally reach Diversey and turn east toward the park for the rally.

"That was really something, wasn't it, Em? Mayor Daley led the parade!" Rosalie has found me, running up behind me, breathless, her dark brown ponytail swinging, the nape of her neck dripping with sweat.

"Yeah." But I miss Mayor Washington. He didn't ride in the parade, but he used to speak at the rally.

Rosalie puts her tanned, slender arm around me.

"Good to see ya, kid."

"You look great," I tell her. She does. Her olive skin is clear and smooth; her green eyes dance with happiness. Her khaki shorts and white T-shirt look great on her. She has never needed to wear a bra. She's a few years younger than me, but I suspect she never will need a bra, and I envy her that. I couldn't run or be comfortable doing almost anything without one.

"How was the party?" I ask.

She shrugs. "OK, I guess. A bunch of Marty's friends, but she didn't want to go."

"Let me guess. 'I hate crowds and I make no exceptions unless it's a crowd exclusively of lesbians.'"

"Well, that's not too far off the mark. Even these friends of hers aren't coming to the rally. They decided just to stay in the apartment and play women's music and have a ritual."

"And you'd rather be here?" Rosalie loves the outdoors. She loves summer. She spends most of it on her bicycle along the lakefront all the way to Ravinia.

"Well, I'll get tired by the time they go on and on with their political speeches," Rosalie says. "But at least there's a breeze out here. And I like seeing all the people. What about you? Any plans afterwards?"

"Not really. I think I'll just go home and read."

Rosalie makes a face like a prune. "I'm sho-ore," she says, "you're secretly going to work on pleasing that EVER so wonderful boss, Miss What's-Her-Name with the painted toenails."

"Shh," I say, smiling. Rosalie was once convinced that Zee, although she's straight, hired me because she wanted my body. "This will be good. I want to hear it."

The three different choruses—Windy City, Chicago Gay Men's, and Artemis Singers–are my favorite part of the rally. But of course the real reason we're here is spoken of at length by various dignitaries in what is referred to as "the community." I've never known what, exactly, people mean when they say "community." But I do know what they mean when they retell the story of the Stonewall riots over 20 years ago. I know what it means that lesbians and gay men stood up and fought back against being arrested for being who they were. After years, centuries of violence and oppression, one night in New York City a few courageous people said "no more." They wouldn't cooperate with being beaten and abused. They wouldn't pretend it was all right for things to go on as they were. They put their bodies on the line for truth. For love. For all of us.

Rosalie fidgets while I listen intently. I even clap for a few of the speakers. Rosalie wants to dance. She's happiest when a women's band comes onstage to play rock and roll. She starts dancing on the grass, surrounded by me and Jenny and Lucinda and Nora and Cass, all sitting down. I like watching her. I think we all like watching her. We think she is good for Marty, who can't quite forget all the oppression long enough to enjoy a sunny day. Or at least, not without Rosalie's help.

Twenty minutes later, I've noticed several large, red ants crawling up my socks and have picked them off, one by one. The speakers for ACT UP! come on stage. One man, one woman. I've heard them before. They begin shouting immediately.

Rosalie has stopped dancing and is fidgeting again.

ACT UP! was still in its infancy when George was dying. I went to see him almost every day, taking him Dove Bars–one of the few things he still enjoyed eating–and the gay newspapers, which he hid under his bed so his mother wouldn't find them. Oh, she knew he was gay all right, had known for years. But even though he was dying of AIDS and Eric joined his parents in their daily watching over him,

George was still protecting his mother from references to gay sex of any kind. Or even the gay lifestyle.

Part of me must be a little like George. I feel the anger, the determination, the righteousness of the ACT UP! people, but I can't seem to join in with them. It's not my style. Their shrill voices offended George–yet ironically, I know they offer hope for saving others like him. We aren't always comfortable with what is necessary, with tough choices about what might or might not save us.

Knowing this does not make it easier for me to sit among the ants commandeering my shoes and socks. The loud exhortations. The notion that something's wrong with us. That we're not good enough. That we have to do more. *Join us. Give. Do what we say. This is the way.*

"They're right, of course," I whisper in Rosalie's ear when I stand up. "But I just can't stay around here another minute."

"Thank heavens, Emily. I was about to leave but felt guilty."

"I'll follow you," I say.

Rosalie marches vigorously up the small hill to the street. We circle the crowd of thousands–how many? A hundred thousand? The papers will confirm my guess tomorrow, I hope. Then we head north through the park again. The quiet bathes my ears like a welcome balm. My brain begins to settle down.

Rosalie takes my hand, swinging our arms between us as we walk.

"Emily, Emily, Emily," she says, "we should see each other more often. Where have the last few months gone?"

"I don't know. We get busy, I guess."

We walk halfway up toward Belmont. The rustling of the trees is the sweetest sound I've heard all day after that cacophony of voices in the parade and at the rally. I had a crush on Rosalie a few years ago. Now, walking with her, away from the crowds, I remember that one of things I've always liked about her is how easy she is to be with. I'm glad we're friends, but I know that I see her just about as often as I like. She, on the other hand, fusses over her friends, and when you're with her she gushes so much you feel like a heel for neglecting her. It's sincere, but it's just part of Rosalie—it has nothing to do whatever with reality, and both she and her friends know it. Nonetheless, her gentle chastising endears us all to her: she knows how to make a woman feel missed.

"I'm glad we got out of there," I say. "I was beginning to turn into the guilt-ridden and therefore the irritable, evil Aunt Em."

"Oh, come on. You should see Marty when she's irritable. THAT'S enough to make you look like the good witch."

"Hah. You flatter me, child."

We laugh.

"Well, here we are. There's Belmont. Are you heading back up to Rogers Park?" I ask.

Rosalie stops walking, stops swinging my arm. She drops my hand, turns to face me.

"Why don't you invite me to your place for a glass of ice water, Em? Just for a minute. I told Marty I'd be back whenever. I don't have to rush right off. Besides, I NEVER get to see you."

"All right." I shoo away a sudden instinct that says watch out. After all, Rosalie and I have been friends for a few years, she knows I'm dating someone new, and she knows I'm always monogamous. She knows I don't share her and Marty's commitment to nonmonogamy.

In my third-floor walkup I turn the fans on, but it's still hot. Rosalie pets Mango's long fur and makes baby noises at her. She stops when I bring her the tall glass of ice water.

I drink about half my glassful and then sip it, watching Rosalie drink hers straight down. Her gestures are so uninhibited that watching her do the smallest thing, like this, is pleasing.

I excuse myself to go to the bathroom. When I come back, Rosalie has put a Teresa Trull tape on the stereo. She's wiggling her torso, not really dancing, but tapping her feet and swaying just a little.

"You're only playing Teresa because she wrote that song about you," I call out.

"Hah." She wriggles and smiles. Then she turns her back.

She's standing right in front of the picture of George, with his blue eyes and his mustache and his reddish brown hair, smiling at me as I snapped the shutter. I took it ten years ago. He's the only person I could imagine being roommates with.

Pictures are all I saved from the other apartment. It was always his apartment; I guess I liked it so much because it was easier to share his home than to learn how to create my own. He made it so easy for me. So easy I didn't quite know what to do without him.

I stand next to Rosalie and look at the picture with her. She didn't get a chance to know George well, but she'd met him once, before he got sick.

"I remember how he made you smile," Rosalie says.

One of Teresa's heartbreaking love ballads has come on, after a rock tune.

I turn away from the picture, away from Rosalie. Don't, I'm about to say, don't.

Her hand is on my shoulder. Since I won't turn around, she comes around, following her hand with her arm, her body. She stands in front of me.

"Kiss me, Em. I need you to kiss me. Now."

Never a hungrier mouth, I think, watching her curving, seductive lips. Rosalie's lips are beautiful, and so is her olive skin, her green eyes, her fine brown hair. A few years ago I would have traded away my job, my cat, anything for this.

Sensing my hesitation, Rosalie doesn't wait. She leans into me, grabbing me on both arms now, and kisses me. Her lips are soft, full, wet, and warm. But I don't open my lips. I concentrate very hard on not moving my arms. My arms want to lift up and wrap themselves around her, but I won't let them. I am keeping them down at my sides, as stiff as I can hold them.

I hate this. I hate doing this to Rosalie. But why doesn't she just respect my hesitation? Why is she making me do this to her? I don't want to reject her, but I'm forced to hold myself stiff. I'm forced to be mean. I don't want to be mean. I don't want to say no. I love the way she smells, the way she feels against me right now. But I don't want to do anything about it. I don't want to kiss her back. Right now it seems like the hardest thing to do is *not* to kiss her back. She's kissing me because she feels safe with me now, whereas she didn't a few years ago. Now she thinks she could kiss me, maybe even sleep with me, and not cause me pain by leaving me. Ah,

Rosalie. Romantics like me can't afford these indulgences, sweet as they are.

Finally, after an excruciatingly long moment where she tries to tongue my mouth and my lips refuse her, she backs away, drops her arms.

"Em, I just wanted—"

"I know. You just wanted to kiss me. But you *know* I can't do that." I'm afraid my voice sounds mean. I don't want to be mean. Not to Rosalie. Not to anyone. And not to me either.

"I thought you loved me, Em." She's pouting. She looks like a wounded bird. I feel like I've run over a defenseless animal on the road and left it there to die.

"I do. At least, I mean, I care about you. You know that. I just don't want to kiss you. Like that. Can't I love you and not want to kiss you like that?"

Now she draws herself up, defensive.

"It was *just* a kiss, Em. I don't see what the big deal is."

"Just a kiss? I don't know, Rosalie. Maybe for you it would just be an innocent little kiss. I don't know whether for me it could ever be just a kiss—with you."

She's fighting back a smile now, I can tell. That's what she really needed, I tell myself—the reassurance that I'm still attracted to her.

We both stand there frustrated a minute. The Teresa Trull tape has finished one side. Finally, she starts giggling. So do I. We can't help it; whenever one giggles, the other one can't keep quiet.

"Hey," she says. "I just hope you aren't mad at me."

I look at her, asking myself whether I am. I was, just a moment ago. But seeing her smile again, her pony tail bouncing happily down her back as she jerks her head to one side to get the loose strands of hair out of her face, I can't be angry with her. She's Rosalie. Rosalie likes to kiss. It's hard to stay angry with her for long.

I shake my head. "No, I'm not mad at you. But just don't try that stuff on me, OK?"

"OK." She looks truly contrite.

"Come here, kid." I hug her, making sure to put my head side to side with hers so there's no chance she'll slip up and try to kiss me on the mouth again. She pecks my cheek. No funny stuff.

At the door, she still looks a bit sheepish, but grateful.

"Tell Marty I send regards," I say.

"Sure. Maybe we'll even get her to the parade next year."

"Hah. Not a chance," I say.

"Well, tell you what. If you get this woman—what's her name—Cathy?"

"Catherine."

"Oh. CATHerine. ExKOOZE me."

I can't help but smile.

"You're blushing."

"So what. So what about Catherine?"

"Well, you get her to come next year, and I'll get Marty to come. Deal?"

I shake my head. "No deals. Ask Catherine. Ask Marty."

After a minute, Rosalie says, "You're right, dammit. Why are you always right?"

Me? I want to say. Me? Of all people, me always right? No wonder I find it so hard to resist Rosalie.

"Guess we got ourselves a couple of headstrong girls, huh, Em?"

"Knowing us, how could we have it any other way?" Then, "Goodbye, Rosalie. Goodbye." I pretend to shoo her out the door.

She grins. I close the door and hear her skipping down the stairs.

"If AH could only WIN your LOVE, Emily," she shouts, loud enough for the neighbors to hear, in a voice just as deep and twangy as Meg Christian's or Teresa Trull's.

I walk back over to the shelf and look at George's smiling face. Is it my imagination, or do I see approval in his smile?

Calling Home

I play back the messages on the answering machine while I'm reheating leftover tofu and veggies in a skillet. A few hangups punctuate the messages.

"Emily, this is Mark Berger. Got what I think is the phone number of Miller's parents in Ohio. Call me, or I'll see you at work. You won't *believe* what Zee did."

Then I hear my mother's gentle Virginia drawl.

"EM-i-ly? Are you there? This is Mom. Just wanted to see how you were. We're fine. We've had a heat wave. Talk to you soon. 'Bye."

It's already after six, so I've missed the cheapest rates, but I dial Mom's number anyway. The same number she and Dad had for the "new" house they lived in twenty years. A red brick two-story with a small cement stoop, front and back. Like most of the others on their quiet street. Though the town grew from about 20,000 to about 50,000 people before Dad died, their street remained quiet.

"Hello?" my mother says. But her television nearly drowns her out.

"Mom? It's me, Emily." The cord is long enough for me to drag the phone into the kitchen while I stir the vegetables.

"Well, hi, honey. I didn't know if you were away for the weekend, or maybe just out running or something."

"Actually," I take a deep breath, although I wonder why I should need to, "I was at the parade and rally. Today's the Pride Parade. And the rally lasted most of the afternoon. It was bigger than ever this year."

"That's nice. Your father used to like parades."

He wouldn't have liked this one.

"Mom, it's the *Gay* Pride Parade. The mayor was in it, and it drew a hundred thousand people."

"Oh, Emily. I *hope* you didn't march in it with those people. I just worry–"

"Don't worry about it, Mom," I break in. "It's no big deal. Parents of Lesbians and Gays marched in it, and so did a lot of churches."

"Well, anyway, it's been really hot here, and I saw Eddie and Marianne and little Eddie and Cindy last night."

"That's nice, Mom."

"And you should *see* how that little devil reaches out and grabs whatever you put in front of him and runs around on the balls of his feet."

"Uh-huh. So how's Marianne doing? And did she get the books I sent?"

"Oh, sure, sure. But she won't let Cindy have them until her birthday next week. You know. I'm sure they'll be much appreciated."

I send my niece books with feminist heroines. Once or twice a year. It's not much, but I do what I can to suggest alternative realities to the Eddie-and-Marianne version.

"How are *you* doing, Mom? Did you go see about getting your ear looked at?" She builds up fluid in her ears; for a while Marianne was convinced it was Menier's syndrome, but Mom's doctors think it's allergies.

"Oh, I had it cleaned out again, but you know, it's only better for a few weeks, and then. But, oh, well. I'm just lucky I can use my hands and see to do my work. I made Cindy the cutest outfit last week. You should have seen it."

I turn off the heat and remove the pan of vegetables. "She's lucky to have a grandma like you, Mom." It's as close as I usually come to telling my mother I'm glad she's my mother.

"Well, I don't know about that. Listen, this is on your bill, so we shouldn't talk long–"

"Forget the bill. What if I *want* to talk to you, Mom? Aren't you going to let me?"

"Well, I don't know. I guess you can decide. Just tell me when. But that little Eddie, he sure is something. Walks around on his tippie-toes everywhere–"

"Mom, I've been dating someone new." I take the phone to the table and sit down. Mango jumps into my lap almost immediately and starts purring.

"And he just won't listen when we tell him to put his feet flat on the floor."

"Her name is Catherine. She's just about my age."

"When Marianne gets after him, he'll take a few steps across the kitchen floor, but the minute he sees something that gets him excited, he just runs, and it's tippie-toes again."

I give up. "Won't he hurt his legs that way? What about his tendons and ligaments?"

"Oh, the doctor says if it keeps up next year it could be a problem. But he did all the tests for reflexes and things and said little Eddie is just fine. He's a pistol."

"Yeah. I'll bet." Just like big Eddie. Used to wrestle me to the floor anytime he felt like it. But once we hit our twenties we both seemed to decide that we might as well be friends. Eddie thinks that to live in a world that includes gays and lesbians is about as unfortunate as it is to live in one that also includes people of color (Marianne still calls them "niggers"), the possibility of the ERA, female politicians, gun control, and a host of other unpleasant obstacles to nirvana. When I finally came out to Eddie (a few months after I'd come out to Mom and noticed her health had not significantly deteriorated and therefore could not be used against me), he shook his head and said, "if that don't beat all." Then, a day or two later, when he was ready to ask some questions, he told me he'd thought about it. He was so glad that he'd chickened out, one night when he was fifteen: four of his buddies found a note from another boy to one of them, and they went to the McDonald's where everybody hung out, found him, invited them into their car, drove off with him, and pounded him half to death.

"So when are you coming home, Emily? Maybe sometime this summer you could take a few days? Why don't I send you money for a ticket?"

"Uh, don't do that just yet, Mom. I may not be able to get away. I'll let you know." Go home and see Mom and Eddie and Marianne and the kids. Why not? Get my mind off

Catherine for awhile. Why am I remembering what Eddie said instead of concentrating on what Mom is saying?

Eddie had a date that night he could have canceled, but didn't. Didn't like the girl much, but he didn't feel like hurting her feelings by calling her up to break the date. "But the real reason," he confided to me, "was I was scared. I just didn't want to go beat the shit out of that guy." He went on to add that of course, if the guy had written the note to *Eddie*, it might have been a different story. Face it, Eddie, I told him. Your baby sister is one. "But it's not the same. I mean, what those guys do...it's just gross. Makes me vomit to think about it." So I let him off easy. I didn't tell him what women do, and he hasn't asked. Marianne hasn't either.

"Well, all right," my mother is saying. "But if you need anything, you just let me know."

"Thanks, Mom. I really appreciate it. But I'm all right." Finally, after those years of squeaking by on temporary jobs, I found Zee. I get by all right, even though my job's been reduced to part time. I always hated to take money from my mother, even then, when I needed it. She'd sometimes slip a check, or even cash, into a letter, and I'd open it and immediately burst into tears. It's like she's trying to make up for everything she thinks we didn't have as kids. While Dad was alive there was never enough. She could barely keep us in clothes. Let alone buy any for herself. That's why she sews. She's not particularly good at it. But she does it. She likes to make things for people. She likes to give things to people. Seems like my mother has always put herself last. Dad drank it all away, and she put up with it, and with him. Cleaned up after him. Thought that was her job. Her duty. To take care of him. And now me. And Eddie. And the grandkids.

"Hey, Mom. Why don't you come to Chicago this summer? I'd love to have you visit."

"Oh, I don't know, Emily. I've got to see the ear doctor this week, and then next week I'm sewing another outfit for Cindy, and I told Marianne I'd help her with her shower, and—"

"OK, OK. But think about it. Maybe when things aren't so busy for you. Huh?"

"Well, I just don't know. I'll think about it, but I just don't know. Well, I don't want to run your bill up, Emily, so I'll talk to you later."

"OK. 'Bye, Mom."

We've talked longer than I realized. A few minutes later, Mango has assumed her sphinx position on the table, watching me eat my cold veggies with cold rice in the dark.

A Letter from Rafik

Later, I go through the mail I've let pile up on my desk. I sort through and toss out most of it, then find a note in very careful handwriting.

Dear Miss Emily,

Thank you for helping me with job applications and with my English. I am now working full time at the Jewel Supermarket as assistant manager. I am reading more books. I will never forget you or Zee.

Your friend,

Rafik

I sit back on my sofa and smile. Rafik is a tall, handsome man from Baku, Azerbaijan. He studied English for years before finally emigrating. Like so many of my foreign clients, he vastly underrates his own performance in English, and I am always touched by this. Mark, who used to teach high school, said his American students had enormous confidence in their abilities. They would often boast of their expected *A*'s and then perform dismally when asked to write anything. Mark said it was too bad more Americans didn't have Rafik's humility. And I wish Rafik had some of the poorly prepared Americans' confidence. I wonder if I will see him again.

I put Rafik's letter in the file where I save such things—mementos from special clients who touched my heart in some way. And then I think: if Rafik can find his way around the world, from the Soviet Union to America, from his most complicated language to another highly complicated language, English, then surely I ought to be able to find David Miller. And surely David Miller has saved some shred of paper, some memento, some memory, from his time with Paul. You don't forget such things. Ever. No matter who you are. Or do some people? Perhaps some people can close the door with a clean, crisp sound. Hear the click of the handle, the perfect fit of wood against wood. And never open it again. At first I feared Catherine might be like that. I still fear it. It's still possible she'll panic, distance, decide I'm not for her, and vanish from my life. And if she does, can I accept it, let it go? Or will I torment myself with my thoughts of her, my imagination a lingering poison, a punishment far greater than the enduring silence of her absence?

A Feeling about David

"Laura? It's me, Emily." Thank Goddess, she's still at her office studio. After getting no answer at Mark's, it's good to reach someone.

"Well, hi, Em. This is a surprise. What's up? How's Paul? And how did things *go*, anyway, with Catherine?"

"Oh, well, that's going much better." I take a breath. "And thanks for talking with me about it. It helped." Before she can say it's nothing, I move ahead. "I'm still not having much luck tracking down David, but it looks like my pal might have located David's parents in Ohio. Do you know anything about them?"

"Hmm. I don't remember him talking about them."

"Paul told me that David never brought up his parents except to say if they ever knew he was gay they'd die."

Laura makes no reply. I wonder if the line is dead.

"Laura?"

"Just thinking, Em. I wonder, if I *did* know anything, do you really think it's good for Paul to drag all that stuff up?"

"Well, I guess what *I* think doesn't matter. Paul asked me, and I felt it's the least I can do to try to find out about him."

"Well, I don't know. Paul's always been like that. Doesn't always know what's good for him."

"What do you think he might find out that's not good for him? Did you know something Paul didn't?"

Again, a pause. I'm clenching my teeth again, and my fingers are curled around the telephone cord.

"Listen, Em, this goes no further, you understand? But I just think you ought to know, before you go hunting up people, what you might find. You know?"

"What is it, Laura?"

"Well, maybe it isn't that awful. But you know, I always had this feeling about David—and one time we were looking at each other, and I could just tell."

"Tell what?"

"He was hiding something, Em. And it had something to do with his sexuality. I think he just wasn't gay."

"What do you mean, wasn't gay?" If I hear one more straight person, even a straight person I love, say such a thing, I think I'll scream. "He and Paul were lovers, remember?"

"Yeah. But I think David must have been bi. I think he just couldn't handle it. Maybe I just used the wrong words, Emily, but what I meant was, if somebody's gay but just can't handle it, well, sometimes they just pretend they're not. You know. Wasn't David married once?"

"I didn't know that." But then, I never knew David.

"I think he was. I think he said it had ended some time before that. But I had the feeling that David hadn't dealt with that stuff at all. He was always nervous about living with Paul. That's when he left, I think—not long after they started living together."

"So you're saying that maybe he went back to pretending to be straight, and that it wouldn't be good for Paul to know?"

"Well, not only that."

"What, then?"

"Just not knowing. Just that there could be a lot of things about David—you don't know what effect it would actually have on Paul to hear from him again or to see him."

"Paul doesn't want that. He only wants to send David a message. Something like forgiveness or a blessing, you know. And he doesn't even want David to know he's dying. Sounds pretty harmless to me."

Laura pauses. I'm counting on her to understand.

"Well, maybe it is. I don't know. Do what you think is right. You're smart, Emily. You'll figure something out. And if you don't find him, Paul will understand that you tried."

"I don't think he has much longer, Laura."

"Well, take it one day at a time, kid. Call me if there's anything I can do. Anything."

Anything I Should Know

Monday morning I stop off at the hospital to see Paul. He's drawn, weak, but clear. His eyes brighten when I walk into the room.

"Well, what have we here? Emily in drag?"

I sashay deliberately to the chair by his bed.

"*Sometimes* even *I* wear skirts, dearie. Keeps 'em guessing."

"Well, at least it's a conservative color."

We both laugh. My skirt is fire engine red. My lemon yellow short sleeve cotton shirt hardly tones it down.

"For you, of course. Had to get your attention."

"And what about your girlfriend?"

"You mean how's her attention? Not bad. I'll see her this weekend, I hope. But I have other news for you."

I tell him I've run some personal ads in the gay papers. And I tell him about Mark Berger.

"He's going to give me the Millers' unlisted phone number today. Anything I should know before I call them?"

I can barely see Paul shrugging under the loose-fitting pajama top.

"Nothing more to tell you, I'm afraid. They didn't get along. He never stayed in touch with them. What's your scam?"

"Oh, I'll think of something. A friend from college who's lost touch."

"Girlfriend, maybe?"

I consider this a few seconds.

"No. Just a friend."

"Nervous?"

"Yes."

"Want me to call them? I could say I was a friend."

"Want to?"

"No. But after all, I'm the one who wants to find him. You've already done enough. It's not fair to expect you to do it all."

Enough? All? What if they're not even the right people?

"I'll call them. Must be this skirt. Makes me feel adventurous."

Paul's chest and shoulders seem to relax slightly on the sheets. I kiss him goodbye and go on to work.

What Zee Did

All day at the office I carry the yellow square with the number written on it in my shirt pocket. Mark's friend who works in a bank's credit section can dig up all kinds of things in books that supposedly don't exist. You name the city, he can find the street, then the name, the phone number. Or if you give him any one of those things he can find the others. Anyone who has an address. David Miller doesn't have any address in Chicago newer than the Uptown SRO he lived in three years ago. But his parents still live outside Columbus, Ohio, and even their unlisted number wasn't too hard to get. Scary.

When I ask Mark to tell me about Zee, he describes a reception the governor's office gave. Zee apparently went to it, ate hors d'oeuvres, and charmed the governor practically out of his pants. She left with his promise to take a closer look at our budget and her request for more staff.

About three o'clock Zee, her hair looking like someone just plugged her in to an electric socket, stops at my desk. She leans over and touches my shoulder. No doubt about it. She's got charm enough to make emperors relinquish their lands.

"Hey, Emily, what's new? You look sad."

I try to look down, but she leans down and stares into my face. She give me a long, sad look, like a clown. I have to smile. I can't imagine Catherine acting like this with one of her staffers. I imagine her always professional, frowning upon employees who discuss their personal lives. With Zee as your boss, you're practially *required* to discuss your personal life. She likes to play mom and therapist.

"Sorry, Zee. I guess I looked preoccuppied."

"So that's obvious already. So, spill." She leans back and puts one hand on her hip. Her smart blue suit looks like silk. Very fine.

I tell her simply that I have to call some parents I've heard aren't any too friendly.

"So big deal. What are you afraid of? You've handled tough cases before."

"Yeah. I don't know why I'm worried." Maybe I don't want to know why David left Paul or why he's wanted to avoid everyone.

I go home, change, run along the lake. Later, after a dinner of beans and rice, I pace the living room for about five minutes. I think of Catherine, want to call her. I want to hear her voice. I want to invite her over. Tonight. Even though it's a work night. She'd probably say it's too much trouble. She'd have to drive in from Oak Park and search for the one or two parking places within a square mile. I decide it's not a good idea. Mostly I'm dreading calling Ohio. I talk to the cat. "Mango," I say, "this is it. Time to have courage. Got to talk to those people. Whoever they are. Why should I be afraid of them?"

Finally I pick up the phone and punch the number in.

After a few rings, an elderly woman's voice answers.

"Mrs. Miller?"

"Yes. Who is this?"

Take a deep breath. Say it quick, kid. No dawdling, no time to be nervous.

"My name is Emily Hawk. You don't know me, but I used to know David in college, and we've lost touch. I've got some good news and I'd love to get in touch with him again–"

"*Who* did you say you are? Well, whoever you are, miss, you can just kindly refrain from calling this number. We don't know anything about him. Haven't heard a thing since the divorce."

Then I hear a short series of muffled sounds, and a gruff man's voice comes on the line.

"Listen, whoever you are, you better not bother us anymore. That boy is just the same as dead to us. Haven't heard from him in years, and don't plan to. So have some respect, huh?!"

Then there's a click, and the receiver protests with its annoying dial tone. I set it down.

Their words are swirling in my head, blanketed in gray wool, muffled and merged with Zee's voice from earlier today. None of it makes sense. I don't know what I've heard, what it means.

A Potential Feminist

Friday afternoon is cool and clear; we're having an atypical Chicago summer. I love my runs along the lake in this weather. Last summer the ozone and the heat made it harder to breathe, but now I can go up to Hollywood Beach and back and hardly feel winded afterward. Six miles this summer feels like running three miles felt most days last summer. I hope this weather holds.

I check the gay papers for the personal ads asking anyone knowing David's whereabouts to contact me. They're accurate, all right. It's hard to just sit back and wait, but sometimes that's what I have to do.

This weekend I'm seeing Catherine. We're going to a double feature; foreign films. Catherine sees a lot of films and plays. I used to think I saw a lot, before I met her. She's a member of the Film Center at the Art Institute and goes to silents and classics a lot. Before Catherine, I'd mostly go to films in the "drama" category or films that dealt with social or political issues. I saw all the Spike Lee films when they first opened. But I tended to overlook light comedies. Tonight, one film is a serious drama about an English family during World War II. One is an Italian comedy. I wear light cotton slacks and a shirt, both having been ironed a few weeks ago when I was trying not to call Catherine. Couldn't get her off my mind then. Now I walk along Addison with a spring in my step. She's called me twice this week; once on Wednesday night, and again today.

I see her standing underneath the marquee as I approach. She's wearing a tan suit that complements her light brown hair nicely. It's been done in a chic dutchboy this week; with her long neck, the style is just right for her. She's smoking a cigarette. When she sees me, she smiles.

"It's amazing," Catherine says as we leave the double feature. "I mean, even *I* was upset by the way they acted as though the women were incapable of anything but trying to get their men to marry them."

"So that Italian director got your feminist hackles up?" I tease. But I'm only partially joking. "I see your point." I'm more amazed by Catherine. Is this Catherine speaking? The same Catherine who has been too nervous to attend lesbian events? Who gets nervous when I tell her about articles I've read in *Sojourner*?

We then discuss the women in both movies. And as I walk beside Catherine, I think she has more surprises in store for me. She may be more feminist than she has appeared. I like that.

We discuss recent plays and films and whether or not they will bring changes in the way people think about each other: people of different sexes, races, cultures. Where I had assumed Catherine didn't think about such differences, I find I was wrong. She and I both come from very conservative families. Both of us reacted against much of their thinking, even as we were influenced by some of it.

"If there's one thing I learned from my grandmother," Catherine tells me, "it's that women are hard workers and strong people. She was really the backbone of that small insurance office in Rockford. Without her, they would have gone out of business several times."

"And without you, I'll bet your company wouldn't get half as much done." She doesn't like to brag, but I know she's won awards on her department's designs and publications.

"Well, it's not just me—I can name three other women there who direct departments and do the work of ten people." I know the three she means already. They also take turns, with Catherine, serving as volunteer tutors one evening a week in the Cabrini-Green tutoring program sponsored by Montgomery Ward. They get a lot done, and yet they do more. I think how surprising all of us can be sometimes.

The English film explored not only family tensions, but also racial tensions; one woman fell in love with a black American soldier. He was from Chicago. Working for Zee, I've grown more and more aware of the new all-volunteer army and how young African-Americans growing up in Chicago join up. I think of how sexism and racism still permeate our lives, of the overwhelming challenges we still face. I think of Jenny, who volunteers time with Bethel New Life and their affordable housing program. Cass's mother and sister still in the projects. A client I worked with last year who turned up dead of an overdose. Another client who barely survived a fire that killed her family. Fiona helped me get her into the shelter, and she went back to school. She has her own home and hair salon now in Logan Square. There's one success, anyway. That's what Zee would say. Take every client one at a time. This one might make it. You never know. But when I see the pain in this city, I wish I could change it all.

Suddenly, as we turn off Broadway and onto my street, Catherine slips her arm around my waist. We walk like that, with her arm around me, for an entire block, and I don't say a word. I just let myself feel it. In her dressy corporate clothes, carrying her briefcase and a small overnight bag in the other hand, she keeps her arm around me.

We get to my complex. I reach for my keys. She drops her arm, steps slightly apart from me. I can see she's ready to come in, has brought her overnight bag to stay the night, though she had not promised she would. Just before I reach to turn the key in the lock, I look up and meet her eyes. She's smiling calmly, watching me steadily, like a woman who's sure of her choice. I unlock the door.

Breakfast

By Sunday I don't know where the weekend has gone, and I don't care. Catherine has scheduled breakfast with Patrick, and I am to meet him for the first time. We each take showers in the morning. Catherine always washes her hair and dries it with the blow-dryer, but this morning she seems to take longer than usual. She smokes a cigarette before we leave, and lights up another on the way to the Melrose.

"You seem nervous," I say.

"I am nervous."

This surprises me. Catherine, nervous?

"Why are you nervous? You've already told me it's OK if I don't like him."

"Yes, but what if both of you really don't like each other? I'll be sitting there uncomfortably, not knowing what to say and wishing I hadn't introduced you."

I take her hand briefly, then let it drop.

"Don't worry. I'll do my best not to say anything that will make you uncomfortable. You've already warned me that he's sometimes sarcastic, so I don't think there'll be any major shocks. Of course, I *am* worried that he won't like me."

"Well, I think you both know that even if you don't like each other, it won't affect how I deal with either one of you."

She means it, I think.

"Patrick and I have never agreed on everything. He loves Michael Feinstein and I can't stand him. I love Barbra Streisand, and he can't stand her. So," she says, leaning down to nuzzle her face close to mine, "you shouldn't worry, Emily."

"And neither should you. Try not to worry about whether or not Patrick and I are having a wonderful time."

But Catherine still walks briskly, her hands a bit more active than usual.

"There he is—out front." She waves to him. He's even taller than she is. A large, handsome dark-haired man many of her coworkers and friends assume is her boyfriend.

"Glad to meet you," he says in a deep baritone, and takes my hand warmly.

"And I'm glad to meet you, too." We both grin awkwardly, the way people do when they know the other person has already heard a great deal.

Patrick tells stories of Catherine's wild younger days, their pranks in high school. She blushes but smiles. He's surprised she's already told me about some of them.

The two of them used to dance in the nude on the balcony of his parents' home. They'd go to movies, plays, musicals together, talking about the men they dated until Catherine figured out why she never really liked any of the men.

"You should have seen her, dancing on that balcony, just praying that her 'best friend' would walk by."

We laugh. Catherine blushes.

"No doubt you've noticed her obsessive-compulsive disorder. Back when she had her first apartment, I'd come over and find her down on her hands and knees scrubbing her kitchen floor. She did that *every week*. She used to clean for hours every day. Now she's gotten better."

"Definitely. She even sleeps and goes to work," I offer.

"Yeah. Now I think she lets the floor dry by itself at least. But I remember once her telling me what a mess her place was and it turned out that one perfume bottle was a half-inch out of alignment on the dresser top."

"Don't be cruel," she teases. But breakfast is going very well. Suddenly I notice Rosalie and Marty walking in with Jenny and Lucinda. I wave. Rosalie waves back, then points me out to the others. They take a table at a far end of the room. Rosalie pauses to stare at Catherine and to smile a knowing smile at me, as if now she knows my secret.

"Don't worry about Cath," Patrick says. "She's a headstrong girl. Tough as nails. I've been trying to get her to move into the neighborhood for ten years. You see how she listens to me."

I watch Catherine.

"Oh. Have you considered moving to the neighborhood, or at least somewhere on the north side?"

She fires Patrick a look. It says: watch out. Leave well enough alone. Then she turns to me.

"Well, yes. I have."

Patrick, reading her face, puts down his coffee cup. "Yeah. She's considered it, but it takes Cath ten years to think about something and then another ten to act on it once she's made up her mind. Look how long it took her to go after that job she got this year. On the other hand," he casts a friendly glance across the table at me, "maybe now that you're in the picture, Emily, she'll be more motivated."

I'm delighted that he says this, but nervous at the same time. Catherine is lighting another cigarette. She's no longer smiling. I look at Rosalie's table, but everyone seems busy, and none of them is looking at us.

"So," I volunteer, trying to think fast, "I hear you've done some acting, Patrick. Catherine says you're quite good."

As I concentrate on Patrick and his stories of college productions and his self-deprecations about his bit parts in non-equity productions since, I don't dare sneak a glance at Catherine. I don't know if she appreciated my changing the subject or not, but I hope I've done the right thing.

"Emily, I think someone's trying to get your attention," Catherine says as we stand to go. I look over at Rosalie's table. She's giving me the quizzical look. "Is that a friend of yours?" Catherine asks.

"Yeah," I say, wondering why I feel like my stomach has decided to reject breakfast. "That's Rosalie. I think I told you about her. She's with some other friends."

"Well, if you want to go over to talk to them, I'll just wait outside with Patrick and smoke." She heads for the door. We've paid our bill, and Patrick joins her.

"Hi, everybody," I say when I reach Rosalie's table.

"So, Emily, is that the new girlfriend? And who's the guy?"

"Yes, that's Catherine. Jenny remembers her—we met at Fiona's party."

"So she says." Even Marty, usually somber, suppresses a giggle.

"The guy is her best friend, Patrick. Don't worry girls, he's a member of the family too."

They laugh.

Rosalie pretends to breathe a huge sigh of relief.

"For a minute there, we didn't know WHAT to think, Em. We thought maybe you had us all fooled and were really into three-ways."

While I'm feeling my face grow hotter, Lucinda says, "So, aren't we good enough to meet her, or what? Are you trying to keep her under wraps, Em?"

"Oh, I don't know. I guess she's a little shy–you know, just to be introduced on the spur of the moment like this. It took this long for me to meet Patrick, and she was nervous enough about that." I'm wondering, though, why Catherine seems afraid of meeting other lesbians.

"Don't you just love it—Em and her skittish girlfriend. I'll bet she's not at all shy in other ways." Rosalie smiles a knowing smile.

"Oh, leave her alone, Rosalie. Go on, Emily. Don't keep her waiting too long," Jenny says. "She seems like a nice woman."

"Yeah," Lucinda adds, joking. "Emily's probably ashamed to introduce her to us, the way we're acting."

I try to protest, but they wave me away. I join Catherine outside. Patrick has already left.

"I hope you don't mind," she said, touching my shoulder briefly, an unusual gesture for her. "I just wasn't up to meeting them today."

"That's OK."

Why I Haven't Met Her Mother

"Beach deprivation," Catherine says. "That's what I've got. It strikes those of us who work downtown from eight to four-thirty. When summer comes, we watch the weekend weather reports. When it's nice, watch out."

I'm not as enthusiastic about the sun, so she goes by herself. Later, I meet her there, lying on her blanket between Fullerton and North Avenue, and we take the train to Oak Park. We listen to a Barbra Streisand CD, read, and go to bed.

On Monday the weather isn't bad, but it's not the perfect beach day. A bit hazy. We laze around all morning. Catherine has both Monday and Tuesday off for the Fourth of July holiday. This is the first time in years, she says, that her mother has not insisted that she come home.

"I'm really surprised," she tells me as she irons clothes in her living room. I'm lying on the sofa, supposedly reading. "I guess she and Ronald didn't make any plans that absolutely required my presence."

Catherine's mother has been in the habit of calling her, sometimes as late as mid-week, and expecting Catherine to appear on Saturday. But Catherine went home last Saturday only after determining that there would be no need to go back for the Fourth.

"I've been trying to wean her gradually. I used to go home nearly every weekend, especially when my grandmother was sick, and after she died, for about a year. But I haven't been doing that for a year or so now." She hangs a freshly ironed white blouse on a hanger and begins ironing a skirt. "It's one of the things I've been working on with Fiona."

"Hmm."

"I just find her dependence on me harder and harder to take. Even those last two years when I went away to college, I didn't really get away. I went home far too often, and of course was there all summer."

Headstrong girl, boss lady to her department at work, lover who calls the shots and won't let me push her around: that's one side of Catherine. Another side is the wild one who loves to shock Patrick, match his sarcastic wit. Yet another side is the Catherine who finds it almost unbearably difficult to resist her mother's demands.

"Catherine," I say. "I couldn't help but notice, on that message your mother left for you on your machine, how she ended it with that 'love you' thing."

Catherine stops ironing and looks at me.

"You heard that?"

"Sure. I mean, it made me wonder. Does she always do that?"

"Oh, sure. Every time she calls."

No wonder, I think. No wonder Catherine hasn't ever said, "I love you, Emily." No wonder she refuses to commit to things–dates, plans, declarations of feelings–when all her life the one person who has consistently and insistently professed "love" has continually tried to hold Catherine back, keep her tied to Rockford.

We watch the video about the making of *The Search for Signs of Intelligent Life in the Universe*. I saw the show with Barry when it was in town. Catherine saw it with Patrick. The jokes are still funny. I laugh out loud, as I always do: boisterous, raw laughter. Playwrights and actors love it when I'm in the audience. They tell me my hoots and screams are infectious. I find them embarrassing sometimes. Won't controlled, dignified types like Catherine find me too vulgar? But Catherine looks over at me from behind her ironing board and smiles.

When it's over, Catherine has finished her ironing. She brings us tall glasses of mineral water and fresh strawberries to nibble on.

"I wish I could take you to Rockford sometime with me, Emily," she says, sitting next to me on the sofa, "but I'm afraid. Even though I'm not 'out' to Mom, I could bring you home as a friend. But I guess I don't want to do that. I'm afraid you wouldn't like her, and you wouldn't enjoy it. She just complains so much, all the time, it might really get on your nerves. I've learned to tune it out. When she gets really whiny, I go outside and wash her car for her, or wash mine."

"So *that's* why it's always so clean!"

She laughs and reaches over to pat my thigh. She doesn't know it, but I'm wet for her again. I stretch my legs in front of me, fold my arms behind my head.

"And, I guess I'm afraid," she says, slowly, watching me, "that you might not be nice to her."

I turn to her. "Now, that's a surprise. Whatever do you mean?" I'm hurt, thinking Catherine underestimates my ability to be polite to mothers and other straight people.

"I mean, that you'd see how she is—you'd argue with her, I think."

"Why on earth would I argue with your mother? For God's sake, Catherine, I know how to behave myself, and certainly could put up with just about anything for a day or two, especially when it's your mother." I assume my most indignant pose, straightening up on the sofa.

Catherine reaches over again and takes my hand.

"I've noticed you, Emily. You're protective of your friends in general, but I think you're also protective of me."

That one stops me. I don't know what to say. It doesn't sound as though Catherine's pointing out a flaw. I relax back into a semi-slouch.

"Well, hey. If your mother is really so hard to be around, why would I care whether you take me home to meet her or not?" I meet Catherine's eyes. "I don't have to meet her. Certainly not anytime soon." I move over and sit next to Catherine, stroke her hair. She puts her arms around me as I kiss her on the lips. The strawberries sit untouched in their bowl on the coffee table.

Fireworks

"I can hardly believe I'm finally here," Catherine says, as we spread her blanket on the grass across Lake Shore Drive from the Monroe Street Harbor. "For years I've wanted to see the fireworks in Chicago, and I've never been able to." Always the dutiful daughter, going home to mother's, I think. I have to remember this. Won't the anger from years of such duty and consequent resentment eventually be displaced onto me? But maybe not. Catherine's smart. Too smart for that.

She unpacks our picnic sandwiches and fruit and sets them between us.

"And *I* can't believe I'm here. A million and a half people at Taste of Chicago, and every year I thank the Goddess I don't have to go anywhere near the place. I've seen fireworks in Virginia. But I never thought I'd bother to come down here with all these crowds. True codependency, I'm sure. I'd better call Fiona and make an appointment this week."

We laugh. Catherine is surprised I've agreed to come along, surprised I didn't panic as we walked through the crowds, surprised I've relaxed and actually appear quite calm and content to be here. I'm surprised, too.

Loud, drunken young white men are raising a ruckus behind us, drowning out the music from the bandshell being played on a radio near us. Catherine and I eat our sandwiches, watch the crowds gather in front of us, watch the street lights slowly come on farther down the Drive. When unauthorized firecrackers go off behind us, we jerk our heads around, disconcerted. But when the Tchaikovsky comes on the radio, the young men seem to have moved away. I lie flat on my back and watch the leaves in the tree above us and the night sky between the leaves. Pretty soon we're all watching the sky.

The fireworks are extravagant, excessive: too many are fired all at once, and no pauses are given between to let the experience sink in. I find it hard to savor each one as I would like to. Huge glittering bursts of green confetti, five at once, are followed by red and gold exploding circles, then a series of fire-engine red circles, like serpents chasing their tails, and then the brightest white slivers of light burst like giant illuminated icicles pushing out from the center of light. Again and again and again our eyes are overtaken by color and brightness and shapes. Gold confetti, gold pinpricks of light, blue, red, green, all the rainbow is there breaking out above the harbor. Catherine has slid over on the blanket, closer to me than I would have expected. After we both murmur our small additions to the chorus of delight all around us, she slides even closer to me, so that our forearms and shoulders and hips are touching, though we're both looking straight ahead. We sit like that, drinking in the feast of colors with our eyes, and suddenly it's over.

We gather our things and head back toward Michigan Avenue, along with the million and a half other people.

"It was so intense," I say as we walk. "I remember seeing fireworks shows in Virginia where they'd shoot off just *one* of those big ones, then wait a minute, then shoot off another one. Nothing like this shooting three, four, five at one time, and then another set of five, without any pauses in between. It was just too fast to be able to appreciate each one as it happened, I think. They were so beautiful–I needed more time for each one."

"Hmm," Catherine nods. "It was beautiful, wasn't it? I hope you're not sorry you came."

"Oh, no, not at all. Just please keep me from getting separated from you in this crowd!"

Catherine, taller than me by a head, knows what I mean. I'd be hard to spot: she, easy. She takes me in hand and leads me quietly through the throngs until we head north on Michigan Avenue. We decide the el will be hopeless, as will the buses along Michigan for the first half hour or so. We see a few go by, crammed with people long before they reach the Chicago

River. No room for us. So we walk north. We walk up Michigan Avenue, see the Wrigley Building lit up like a giant ice castle, see more pedestrians crammed at one time on the bridge than we've ever seen, more than we think the deteriorating structure can hold, but we file along in the crowd anyway. The pavement vibrates under our feet.

Finally, we leave the crowds on Michigan and head over to State Street. I'm ready to walk all the way home rather than risk more crowds, but Catherine insists we try the Grand Avenue subway stop.

We wait in line to get past the agent, then wait on the crowded platform. Every ten or fifteen minutes, a packed train zooms by—people jammed in up against the doors, no room for new passengers. Finally, when the third train comes, Catherine tells me, "This is it. Just get on however you can. I'll push from behind and get in after you."

Of course, several other people decide they can elbow in ahead of us, but Catherine times it right, placing us on the platform just in front of one of the doors. When it opens, she shoves me in. I go right up against a woman and her boyfriend, pressing hard into her.

"Whaa—"

"I'm sorry," I mumble. "They're pushing me." I want to tell her how much I like her dredlocks. But I'm too nervous about being mashed up so close, already invading her privacy.

Somehow, Catherine gets herself smashed up behind me, just clear of the doors. I'm hunched over the woman's shoulder and can smell her boyfriend's bad breath. The woman rolls her eyes. Then she giggles. I giggle. The boyfriend grins. It's one of those rare occasions when Chicago citizens decide to laugh over the absurdity of their predicament rather than to scream at each other.

Catherine is pressed up against my back. I can't even see her, but I can hear her voice.

"You all right?"

"Yeah. I guess we made it. Sort of."

At Fullerton, many people exit, and I can stand up straight until we get off at Belmont. When we're on the platform, I look at Catherine and shake my head.

"You did it. I'm impressed. I really didn't think we'd get on that train."

"Well, I guess I was tired enough and had enough of a headache. I was determined not to wait for another one or have you force us to walk."

"Just what I like. A headstrong girl."

At my apartment, the headstrong girl conks out soon after taking aspirin and drinking a tall glass of water. Mango moves over and makes room for us in bed. I fall asleep against Catherine's shoulder, and dream of the rainbow hues of fireworks. I sail through them in my dream, through all the space in the world, calling out, "Where are you, David Miller, and are you a blue speck or a green speck or a gold one or a red one?" How would I find him in all that space, those colors, with light almost too bright to look at?

A few hours later, it's still dark outside. I've come back from the bathroom, and now Catherine, who probably heard me and woke up, is there. She comes back to bed and slides her arm over my stomach. I move closer to her, reaching half under her to touch her nipple. I kiss her hair, her temple, and slide one leg over hers. Then I move her arm, and she turns up to face me.

"Mmm."

I want to stroke her more, but before I know what's happening, Catherine reaches and grabs my arms and turns me back and crawls over me. She holds my arms down and slides one leg between mine and starts kissing me passionately. I've been wanting her since the fireworks, since she sat so close to me, and my groin arches toward her already. She strokes me there and kisses my breasts. She does this for a very long time. She rubs her leg up against me, just behind her fingers as she continues stroking me. She takes her leg away. Then she brings it back again. My body arches up, toward her leg. When she takes her fingers away, I writhe like an animal. I let myself become an animal. I close my eyes, and in the silence I am hearing the fireworks again, seeing their colors. Red circles with gold sparks chasing them round and round. Green confetti, blue stars floating down, tickling me, teasing me. Then brighter and brighter bursts, shafts of white light, radiating out from the red center. She's rubbing me harder and harder, and suddenly her tongue is licking me, soft and insistent, it's everywhere, and she's tonguing me up, down, around, and the wetness is everywhere. A wide blue-black sky rushes towards me, and then big booming noises sound in my head, and I'm seeing red explosions blotting out the sky, and then gentle cascades of fine, fluid gold falling down the sky, spiraling toward earth.

Missing Persons

Hot, hot, hot. The July sun has come out today in force. There's an accident on the Drive. From the bus stop I watch the traffic crawling along. Three days later, I'm still thinking of fireworks, of Catherine, tasting passion in the steamy air off the lake. I watch an elderly woman, her back bent slightly, walking toward the highrise behind me. When she gets there, she looks confused. She continues walking past me to the next building. Then again, she looks at the front door and appears puzzled. She's petite, compact; her hair lies neatly against her head despite the wind. Her green dress and matching jacket look well cared for. She looks up and down the street, seeming more and more bewildered. The 145 express pulls up to my stop. Passengers begin boarding. I decide not to.

"Are you looking for someone?" I ask in my best social worker voice. "Can I be of any help?"

She turns toward me, looks me up and down. Then she looks at the cars and buses moving past us. Then she turns back to me.

"Well, I, I guess I was looking for my house, but then I realized there are no houses here."

"Do you know the address?"

"It's a little tan brick bungalow. We live on West Foster Avenue, let's see, I think the number is–" she stops, and for a moment, a look like terror distorts her cameo features. "Oh, no. That's not right. Foster Avenue is where I used to live." Then, looking at her empty hands, "I wonder where I left my purse."

"Can you tell me where you live now?"

"I live on Sheridan Road." She tells me the number; I recognize it, a senior residence.

"That's not far from here. Why don't I get you a cab?" She doesn't show much perspiration, but not knowing how long she may have been wandering around in this heat, I decide it's best to get her back as soon as possible. I'll be late, and Zee won't be happy. As a part-time employee, I sometimes put in full days, sometimes half days, depending on Zee's instructions. Today she wants a full day. We're in a phase where Zee expects us to do 24 hours of work in an eight-hour day.

"I don't want you to go to any trouble," the woman tells me as a cab pulls over and I reach for the door.

"It's no trouble, Ma'am." I usher her in. Then, instead of just handing the driver some cash, I get in too. I want to be sure the address she gave me is her home.

The driver reminds me of Nora. She has a wooden back massager draped over her seat. We arrive at the senior residence in under ten minutes. I pay the driver and escort the woman into the building.

"Mrs. Hardwick!" the doorman says. He's tall and friendly looking; he could be a talk show host. He also looks relieved. "The pharmacy called half an hour ago to say you left your purse there."

Mrs. Hardwick explains to the doorman that she must have forgotten her purse and then forgotten where she was and where she lived.

"Then this nice young lady, uh–"

"Emily," I say, "Emily Hawk."

"This nice Emily asked me where I was going, and suddenly, I remembered." She turns to me. "It's been several years since I lived on Foster Avenue. Once in a while, that happens. If I'm upset, or if I wait too long to get my prescriptions."

"Does your doctor know about this?"

"Oh, yes. I have an apppointment, let's see, on Monday. Yes, that's it."

Reassured that Mrs. Hardwick has regained her clarity, at least for now, I nod and mumble "no trouble" in response to her thanks, then head back out to the street to catch a bus.

Zee is not exactly pleased, but she shrugs and says, "At least that woman had a home to go to." Zee has worked with Fiona and with other agencies to keep people temporarily housed, but we all know the number of homeless people has risen dramatically, year after year. Tomorrow Zee's going to see a state representative from Chicago about a bill he's sponsoring in Springfield. She's had most of us involved in some way in preparing her report for him. Her hair is full of bounce today, and in her yellow suit and white blouse she looks like a woman who's confident she'll win, eventually. A similar piece of legislation, designed specifically to protect the differently abled, was sponsored by the same representative last year. The current bill would apply, depending on circumstances, to the homeless and to other groups.

I'm busily summarizing recent client data when I notice Mark looking over my shoulder.

"When did you get here?"

"Just now," he says. "Wanted to see how long it would take you to notice." He pulls a chair up and sits next to me. "And I bet you didn't know where I was this morning."

"I was late, too." I don't bother to mention details.

"Well, *I*, your devoted public servant, was out there working on Miss Emily Hawk's case while you were dillydallying around."

"Oh?"

"I see that raw, greedy curiosity. Pipe down, pipe down. All I did was have lunch with a pal who works on missing persons. A friend of my friend in the bank."

"A cop?"

"You could say that, yes. I won't tell you where. When my efforts via the world of computing and your efforts via the telephone led to naught, I asked him to see if he could help. You can't declare your friend officially missing, of course. You'd meet none of the police requirements. But my pal was willing to do some checking for me."

"And?"

"And. Nothing much. As far as jails and hospitals, he's clean. If he's in the area, he doesn't have a current mailing address. The last address anyone has is the same hotel in

Uptown I had before." He looks at me evenly. "By the way, did you know he was married once?"

"What?"

"Married. Apparently not for long. But one of the charge cards he had was in both names. An Amy Miller. That was older than the other accounts."

"Amy? When were they married?"

"Nearly ten years ago, apparently." He pauses. "It wasn't too hard to find her; she's still got credit cards and a telephone and a mailing address. You can even find her in the directory. Her maiden name is Rejikowski. She lives in Evanston. I called her, pretended I was doing a credit check. She said she hadn't heard from him in three years or more. Last address she had was the same one in Uptown."

"You called her?"

"I figured you'd had such a rough time with the parents that I might as well. She was nice enough. But I believed her when she said she hadn't heard from him. I even did some checking with the shelters. Nothing, but you never know. It's likely he's not even in the area. Maybe not even in the state."

Dead ends. I take a deep breath and exhale long and slow. Mark waits. He's seen me do this before. Finally, I say, "Well, thanks for trying. And thank your friends for me. Seems like if he were findable, you or your friends would have found him."

"'*Nobody is ever missing.*'"

"What?"

"It's John Berryman. Or rather, Henry. Anyway, it's from *The Dream Songs*. You know–Berryman, the poet who threw himself off a bridge in Minneapolis?"

I nodded. His was exactly the kind of despair Paul had managed to overcome.

"Any luck with the bars or with the ads?"

I shake my head. "Not yet. Maybe there's something else I can do. Any ideas?"

"You could try showing the photos to people at the shelters, but you know that even if they recognize him, most of the guys won't tell you."

"And the workers, however well meaning, may or may not remember a face from the hundreds they see."

"It's all a long shot. I mean, if she hasn't heard, and the parents haven't heard from him and/or won't help us, I don't know. I'll keep trying. Meanwhile, though, I think you need to realize you might not find him."

"You're right. I probably won't find him. I'm not even sure Paul really expects me to. Maybe David *really* doesn't want to be found."

Zee comes breezing through, her yellow skirt rustling pleasantly.

"Find whom? Who's Paul?"

Mark and I exchange looks. I start to tell Zee about Paul.

A couple of sentences later, she interrupts me.

"Look. So you do, so you don't find the guy. Maybe he's not lost. Or maybe he's lost the same way thousands or millions of others are lost. Friends, lovers, homes, health, jobs. But I know we're all gonna be lost if we don't get this report finished. You'll be putting your own names on that missing persons list."

Mark scurries over to his desk and I go back to my summaries. I make a mistake, entering "Mrs. Hardwick" instead of the name I intend. Mrs. Hardwick was lost, or was she? I didn't find her; she found herself. Maybe it's true that nobody is ever missing.

Or maybe we're all missing persons, longing for someone to find us.

Dance of Death

In my dream I am with George again. We are dancing in large, spinning circles on a marble floor, black and white squares. We are dancing a dance of death.

Maybe it doesn't matter, now that George is gone. Missing. Lost not to himself but to us. But George had hundreds and hundreds of students who never knew he was gay. Students and colleagues were always calling him at home or inviting him to dinner, needing him to listen to them. So he listened. He listened to all of us, whenever we needed his kind, sympathetic ear. His heart was open. He shared all he had, and sang for everyone who asked. Yet when he was dying he hid from them all. He didn't ask the world to listen to him, to pay attention to who and what he was.

Eric, knowing he's HIV positive, waits. We got together a few times for lunch not long after George died. Then, for awhile we didn't. It was too painful for him. When he saw me, he saw George in me. He saw another person who was there at the end. And it brought the end back. Holding George in bed, trying to keep everything away from his sensitive feet, repeating back to him the words we thought he was trying to say. When he could still understand and enjoy books, I'd read aloud to him.

I think how ironic, yet how fitting, it is that Eric and I are in touch again, this time because of Paul. How it won't be long before we're saying another goodbye. How I wish I could do the one thing Paul has asked me to do.

I go to the bedroom, strip off my clothes and shoes, pull back the top sheet, and lie down. Mango jumps up on the foot of the bed and walks up toward me. She climbs on my chest, purring and kneading my breasts. When my breasts are sensitive, I won't let her do this. It hurts a little, even when they're not. She finally seems satisfied and settles down, her eyes staring into my face, her body resting on mine. I stroke her from head to tail, and she purrs loudly. She closes her eyes. As I stroke her, the sense of being lost without George diminishes. I'm awake an hour longer, lying in bed, petting her, because I need to.

Moving Day

Nora and Cass are moving in together. They've bought a house in Ravenswood. "Needs fixing, but it was too good a deal to pass up," Nora tells me. The lesbian attorney who drew up my will not only handled their closing but also drew up a partnership contract for them. Who will get what, if. What happens to the house, if. Fiona has coached them well. They're trying to be level-headed and not to follow impulses blindly. They waited longer than Jenny and Lucinda, for one thing. Dated for nearly two years.

Jenny, Lucinda, Judy, Pat and I all meet at Nora's apartment in Rogers Park at eight-thirty on Saturday. Nora has rented a 14-foot truck she says will be big enough to hold both hers and Cass's stuff. The six of us form a brigade and pass the boxes down: I'm at the head of the two flights of stairs. Nora hands boxes to me, I carry them down one flight, Pat carries them down to Judy, Judy passes them to Jenny, and Lucinda loads them on the truck. We're done in less than an hour. Then we go after the furniture and the loose stuff in twos and threes and load it on. Nora doesn't have much. Pretty easy, so far. When we're finished loading the front half of the truck, we take a break and drink ice water. I like the sweat rolling down my face, neck, and arms. We all take turns in the bathroom before we leave and head for Cass's place in Edgewater.

Marty and Rosalie are already there, helping Cass finish her packing. Rosalie has put all of Cass's plants in their car. "It'll be too hot in that van." Cass has the biggest sofa I've ever seen. She and Marty take the ends, and two more of us support the sides. Cass's building has an elevator. We carry the sofa to the elevator, then Cass and Marty and I push it so it's nearly vertical. But it's too heavy. Nora acts fast to keep it from falling. She leans into it, and we manage to get it into the elevator.

The rest of the stuff is easier. When we're just about finished, Cass gets her cat from the bathroom where she's kept him all morning and carries him in his plastic kennel to Marty's and Rosalie's car. I ride with Nora in the truck. Jenny and Lucinda ride with Judy and Pat.

At the new place, we form a brigade again, and Nora directs us where to put things. It's a nice little house, a two-story crackerbox. Great light from the upstairs windows. It needs new siding and a paint job, and there's only one bathroom, but it's livable. Wooden floors. They'll need work, too, but at least it has wooden floors.

Cass takes me down to the basement while Nora is unpacking the kitchen things.

"Here's where the leg machine will go. And the bench press will go over there along that wall, just under that window." It's damp but cool down here. "Nora's buying me a set of free weights and a curl bar for my birthday next week." I can see there's plenty of room here for all these things.

"I'm jealous, Cass."

She punches my bicep affectionately. "Well, hang in there, kiddo, maybe your woman will buy you one in a year or so. Took Nora a while to decide it wasn't all just my foolish vanity."

We laugh.

"I miss the gym," I say. We stand awkwardly a moment.

"Me, too."

The gym is where we met. Cass and I were regulars. Both of us had worked out in other gyms before Strongwomen opened. Mercedes and Paula bought a run-down building, gutted it, put in fat new pipes all the way to the street for the hot showers, new flooring, new walls, new electrical circuits for the air conditioning, the sauna, the whirlpool. They used pastel tiles imported from Italy, the best cedar in the sauna, the best fixtures. They built a suspended floor for aerobics and hung art on the walls. They painted everything in semi-gloss white, mauve and gray. Three years later, everything still sparkled. An entire karate dojo, housed upstairs, sent two dozen women out in two years to place in nationwide competitions. Feminist zen. There were aerobics for every woman, self-defense courses for women of all ages, yoga, body awareness, you name it. And the weight room, where Cass and I hung out on weekday afternoons when I wasn't working for Zee and she wasn't welding. Cass usually welds at night, but her shifts change every few weeks.

"Have you heard from Paula and Mercedes?" she asks.

I shake my head. "Nothing much new. She's really sick with the chemo, but she's hanging in." Mercedes left two weeks ago to participate in an experimental, hyped-up chemotherapy program in California.

"Where's the justice?" Cass asks, her chin jutting out, her head tilted slightly down. "That's all I want to know, Em, all I ask. Explain it to me. Where's the goddamned justice?!!"

I purse my lips, inhale a deep breath through my nostrils. Cass knows I have nothing to say, doesn't really expect an answer. But we need to be here like this, away from the unpacking upstairs, just a moment longer.

"I mean, goddammit, the two of them worked their butts off, built the place for us, knocked themselves out day and night to keep it open, set the best damned example I've ever seen of lesbians creating a good, healthy business serving real needs of the women's community. They brought this community the best damned place we ever had, and what did they get in exchange? Half my fucking friends telling me they don't have the money to join! Women who refuse to support them! They drop thirty fucking bucks every weekend at the bars, they don't deny themselves a fucking thing, and then they tell me they don't have the money for a membership at Strongwomen! Hypocrites!"

"I know, Cass. I know what you mean. And what really bugs me are the ones who left to go to other gyms. Cheaper. Whatever."

"It was worth every penny!" Cass makes a fist and smashes it against a fat wooden support post. "You ask me, I'll *always* wonder whether, if maybe Paula and Mercedes hadn't had to worry about making ends meet, live under all that stress all that time, whether they might neither of them have developed cancer!"

The words hang heavy in the damp basement. The concrete floor is an ugly, mottled gray, sloping unevenly toward the drain in the center. I want all the toxins, all the malice, all the mistakes and fear and suffering, all the cancer cells and HIV and herpes viruses to flood through, flow down here, down into that drain. If I look at it long enough, if I just stand here, real still, maybe all of it will.

"There you two are! I should have known." Nora calls to us from the stairs. "Come on up; the kitchen's all set. Let's party!"

We sit in the living room on Cass's couch and chair and on boxes. Nora plugs in the telephone and informs us it's working. Jenny takes pizza preferences, says she knows just the place in the neighborhood, and calls in a big order. Somebody has found Nora's stereo (a bargain model from Sears) and unpacked it. Judy and Pat bring in tapes from their car: Tracy Chapman, k.d. lang, Deidre McCalla. Pat puts Tracy Chapman on first. Nora sits on Cass's lap with an open beer.

"We're here, hon!"

Cass smiles. Like me, she doesn't drink. She raises her can of diet cola and toasts Nora. We all do the same with our various beers, colas, sparkling waters.

"Happy housewarming!"

We're sweaty and tired, and it feels good. Marty sits in the corner on a box across from me.

"Where's Rosalie?" I ask.

"Upstairs with the cat. Said she'd help it get settled."

"It! Can you believe she calls him 'it'! This woman has ice in her veins!" Cass teases.

"And if she'd only give poor Leonard a chance, I'm sure he'd win his way right into her heart, wouldn't he?" Jenny adds. Lucinda touches her elbow.

"Listen, girl, we're lucky she even visits us, with a male in the house. Even if he is just like his namesake—nonsexist, sensitive, nurturing, and all that." Cass winks at Jenny.

Marty rolls her eyes. But she doesn't seem angry.

"Now don't you all be giving Marty a hard time," Nora says. "She really helped us out, cat or no cat."

"Are you big, bad dykes ganging up on Marty *again*?" Rosalie has come into the room. We laugh.

"What I'd like to know is, what did the *men* do to help you move, Cass? Did any of them offer to come over and help you pack or clean or move?"

"What men, Marty?" Judy, sitting on Pat's lap in the chair, seems completely surprised.

Nora gets off of Cass's lap as Cass lets out a long sigh. Nobody's laughing or even smiling anymore. Nora stands up near the sofa, looking like she's ready to play traffic cop if necessary.

"She means," Cass says to Judy, as if hoping she wouldn't have to do this, "the men in ACT UP! Or maybe the men I run with in Frontrunners. Or maybe the guys I volunteer with over at Howard Brown Clinic."

"Oh." Judy still looks confused, but like a student who's afraid to admit she doesn't understand because she thinks everyone else does.

Jenny, however, doesn't hesitate. Maybe she didn't notice Lucinda's gentle warning.

"But wait a minute. Why should it bother you, Marty, if Cass hangs out with men sometimes?"

Before Marty has a chance to respond, Nora butts in.

"Now, wait just a minute," she says, as if to all of us. Rosalie is standing nervously in the doorway, looking down at her feet, twirling a loose strand of hair. Nora looks directly at Marty. "Marty, you don't have to answer that if you don't want to. Listen, gang, do we really have to go into this again?"

Marty sips her beer and sets it down on a box.

"No, really, Nora, it's OK. I'm getting used to it. It never ceases to amaze me that I get asked such a question. What happened to the seventies, anyway? Didn't we used to have a women's community? Back then, it wouldn't be *me* having to defend or explain myself. Am I the only lesbian separatist left?"

Dead silence. I wonder how it's possible that most of us in this room feel sympathetic toward Marty, don't want to challenge her, don't want to make her feel isolated, yet we have no way to show that because we don't call ourselves separatists.

Marty looks around the room. The Tracy Chapman tape has stopped playing, but no one goes to the stereo to change it.

"Marty, you know I'm not a separatist, but–"

"Hah. That's the understatement of the year."

I ignore what she's just said and go on, "I think it's a term some of us have trouble with these days. Maybe it's just not a term some of us are comfortable with."

"Bullshit! Don't you dare, Emily Hawk, don't you *dare* try to turn this into a semantic argument. That's what you bureaucrats are good at, I know." She begins to imitate a high-pitched, nasal, phony voice. "If we just fill this out according to the state's instructions, in the proper bureaucratic language, then I'm sure we'll find we're all really in agreement."

Eyes turn toward me. My face is burning. I'm holding a bottle of mineral water in my hands. It's sweating onto my fingers, and I concentrate on the cool drops of condensation.

"By the way, Marty," Cass says, "I *did* get offers to help from two of the guys in Frontrunners. You'll excuse the men on their deathbeds, I hope, for not jumping right up to help us."

Marty glares at Cass. Cass glares at Marty.

"And did you tell them no, thanks?" Rosalie raises her head and watches Cass. She hasn't looked at Marty since the glance she gave her when she first came in the room.

Cass takes her time before answering. She turns from Marty to Rosalie, briefly, as if thinking about her answer. Then she takes a sip of her diet cola and sets it back down as she turns back to Marty.

"I told them thanks, but that I had plenty of friends helping me already."

"Yeah." Nora tries again. She spreads her arms gently open as if to include the entire room. "And our friends did help. It's really wonderful that all of you came."

"I think it's just great that Cass is involved with all these AIDS things. Maybe we should all go over to Howard Brown. I mean, don't we all need to pull together?"

Sweet, naive Jenny. Yet her goodwill goes beyond naive. She donates her carpentry expertise to families who help build houses they can call their own.

"You sponsored me in the race, Jenny," Cass says gently. "I think if everyone would do at least one thing like that every year, we'd make some real progress. If more women–"

"If more women devoted their energies to solving the men's problems and constantly putting our own issues on hold, postponing, delaying, then later, someday, women would get to devote attention to these lesser issues!! Oh! I am sick and tired of that line; I can't believe we've fallen for it for centuries and now even my *lesbian* friends are falling for it!"

Marty sounds angry and tired, as if her voice is about to crack. Why doesn't Rosalie at least go and sit by her? I wonder.

"You mean, like violence against women?" Jenny asks innocently.

"Yes! That's what she means!" Pat is apparently tired of leaving everything to Marty. "One in four women is sexually molested at some point in her life! Look at the battered wives! Look at the fact that none of the women in this room can walk alone after ten o'clock at night in this or any neighborhood!"

"And now those assholes are going to take abortion rights away again!" Lucinda chimes in.

Marty doesn't meet anyone's eyes. I can't help but think she's relieved not to be the only one raising these points.

"Yeah!" Judy says, perking up. "That's something we've absolutely got to get involved in, *right now*. If we lose abortion–"

"If *you* lose abortion, maybe," Marty interrupts. "I'm also sick and tired of our giving all our energy to fighting straight women's battles, only to have them turn their backs on us because of their homophobia."

Marty got burned, I remember, by the NOW people ten years ago, when they were paranoid about lesbians. Even though they've got lesbian rights agendas now, NOW is still too phobic, according to her.

No one says anything for a moment.

"Marty," Pat says. "I think I know what you mean. But Judy's not straight. Please."

"All right. I know that."

"It's okay, Marty," Judy says. "I'm a member of NARAL, and I don't care who knows. When I was straight, I had to have abortions. Twice. And I'll always care about it."

"And if they get outlawed again, there will be another JANE collective to help women get them illegally," Marty said. "And you know who took the greatest risks in JANE?"

We listen respectfully. We know that Marty is a close friend of one of the women who kept JANE going.

"The women who took the greatest risks were lesbians. And they did all of it for those straight women. I'm not saying that's a bad thing. It was good. But what I'm saying is, will I ever, once in my lifetime, see lesbians working on lesbian issues *first*?"

"Like what?" Judy asks, truly interested.

"Like joining the coffeehouse collective. They always need more members. Like showing up every now and then for a *Hot Wire* mailing party. Like helping your lesbian sisters who are unemployed, on welfare, in prison. Like demanding to know why it is that gay men have all this money and all these bars and all these clothes and all these cars and all these condos and most of us have no money. Things like that."

"Hmm."

"Or supporting Strongwomen gym while it was here," says Cass. Marty looks up, surprised.

"Well, Cass and I were able to get this place," Nora says, smiling, waving her hand to indicate the nebulous benefits of owning such a structure. I know she mentions the obvious not because she wants to disagree with Marty but because she feels guilty about actually having anything. Like other lesbians I know–mostly white–from middle-class backgrounds, Nora has trouble allowing herself to own things. Marty is even worse, according to Cass. A guilt-ridden white woman determined to stay downwardly mobile. Cass, who grew up in the projects, has no guilt about acquiring anything. It was Cass who convinced Nora, finally, that they should buy the house.

"But you're the exceptions," Marty says. "Very few of us will own property. Or retire with a pension. Or any of that."

"You're right," Cass says. She and Marty seem calmer now, but tension still swirls around the room. My quadriceps and calves are flexed involuntarily, and my gut is tight.

And then Rosalie does a strange thing. She's still standing in the doorway, not looking at Marty. Now, when we're all silent but slightly relieved that the storm seems to be ebbing, she raises her head and looks across the room at Cass again.

"But, Cass," she says out of nowhere, "I was just wondering if you were telling the exact truth a while ago. About your two men friends."

"Huh?" Cass looks puzzled. Then she apparently remembers, and nods. "What about them?"

"Well, you said you told them you already had lots of help, but I was just wondering. Wasn't the real reason you didn't let them help because you thought they'd be uncomfortable?"

I can never tell if Cass is blushing. She seems cool. She looks over at Nora as if to ask what to say.

"Well, not exactly," Cass begins.

"Because Marty would be here?" Rosalie asks.

For a few excruciating seconds the room is absolutely quiet. Marty looks stricken. She's sitting with her right arm bent, her palm covering her mouth. She doesn't move.

The doorbell rings.

Cass doesn't answer Rosalie.

Nora, already standing, strides across the room. Just before she passes Rosalie in the doorway, she says, "Hey, gang, you know what? I think we're all tired and hungry, that's what. And thank the Goddess–the pizzas are here!!"

The next few minutes are frenzied. We all jump up, digging in our pockets. Nora and Cass want to buy the pizzas, but Jenny insists that the two of them shouldn't have to pay anything. Finally we all stuff bills into Jenny's hands and she lets Nora give her a few for the tip. Then we're opening the cartons and eating fat slices we hold in our hands. Tomato sauce drips down my chin, and I don't care. Somebody puts a new tape on, then thinks better of it, takes it out and flips on a rock radio station. We huddle in groups of two and three, scattered around the room, carefully leaving Marty in her corner and Rosalie wherever she scurried off to.

More people are beginning to arrive before we've finished eating the pizza, and the music gets turned up. Two or three couples I don't know and a couple of apparently single women. Not sure whether I want to leave yet, but needing a break, I go upstairs to check out the rest of the house.

Rosalie's petting Leonard, who has curled up on a futon in one of the bedrooms. He's tortoise, mostly gray with some white and a few streaks of burnished orange. Short but thick fur and a massive head.

"Hey," I say.

Rosalie's pouting like a child who knows others might be angry with her.

I watch her stroking Leonard's chin and the side of his face. I take a few steps closer. I squat down next to Rosalie and let my right hand dangle in front of Leonard's face, so he can sniff it. He wrinkles his nose and pokes his head forward, then circles it. Rosalie's stroking his back, following the curve he's positioned himself in. I slowly reach one finger to the side of his face and gently, slowly stroke it.

"I guess everybody thinks I'm awful, huh?" Rosalie says, without turning toward me and without interrupting her strokes.

"I don't know. I doubt it. What do you think?"

She doesn't say anything for a minute. I glance around for the windows. She's already opened them, but it's still too hot up here.

"I don't know, Em." She sighs.

"I used to just tune it out, thinking that Marty had her beliefs and other people had theirs. It doesn't bother me not to bring men by the apartment or to talk about them. It's not like I know many. It was just seeing how–how sharp, how mean, how goddamned sure she's right and other people are wrong–I've seen it before but today it bothered me like crazy. And then I saw how everybody has to take Marty into consideration before they say or do anything, just because she's like the President of the Lesbians or some damned thing."

I suppress a smile. Leonard stretches out his full length, lets Rosalie stroke his side. I've stopped petting him, and just watch the two of them.

"You know, Em? It's been getting to me, I guess."

"Hmm."

"And you! Why didn't *you* let her have it after what she said to you?"

"What?" I had to think for a second. "Oh, you mean whatever she was implying about my being the opposite of a separatist?"

"*Understatement of the year,* she said. What the hell was that about, Em? She just assumes that you're, like, consorting with the enemy, just because you have some male friends."

"Yeah. I guess so. Well, I do work with men—I have some male colleagues. And George was an important person in my life. And I guess I'm kind of involved with Paul. And then there's Barry. So maybe I'm giving some energy to certain specific men. I guess that might be what she meant."

"Yeah. To Marty it doesn't seem to matter whether you do it in an organized way like Cass or just by having friends, like you. But you know what, Em? I see you and Cass both giving women your energy, too. Maybe it's not like a little container of energy, the way she'd have us think. Maybe it doesn't work like that at all. Maybe if you didn't have your male friends and Cass wasn't doing her AIDS work and stuff, then maybe neither of you would be the same people or have the same energy to share with women."

Leonard turns to lie on his back, lets Rosalie stroke his belly. His rear legs spread, his paws hang limp in the air.

"I don't know what to think about any of it, Rosalie." I take a deep breath. "But none of that is the issue, is it?"

She's silent for what seems a very long time. She stops stroking Leonard. He doesn't change his position.

"Maybe if she hadn't said that about you, Em—"

"Cut it out, Rosalie. Hey," I soften my voice, but think better of touching her arm or shoulder. Instead, I get out of the squatting position and sit on the floor. "I'm flattered, sure. But what you did down there had nothing to do with me. If you're angry with Marty—"

Rosalie waves me away. "I know, I know. If I'm angry with her, I should confront her when we're alone and not embarrass her in public. Spare me the lecture, Ms. Emily. Maybe I wanted to embarrass her."

I say nothing. I'm thinking I've meddled enough; I shouldn't have come up here. Let Marty, hurt as she is, go after Rosalie. Or not. It's their stuff to work out, not mine.

"Maybe I wanted to hurt her. I don't know what I wanted. Or want."

Rosalie moves to the futon, lies down alongside the cat. She strokes Leonard's belly again, long, slow strokes from his chin nearly to his penis.

The door opens behind us. I hear laughter, then quiet.

"Oh, excuse me." I turn my head to look, but hardly need to.

It's Bonnie, standing over us, looking down at Rosalie's tanned arm sensuously stroking the cat, at me sitting next to them. She stays only a few seconds, then turns and goes out again, closing the door behind her.

"My God," Rosalie says, propping herself up on one elbow. "Em, I had no idea she'd be here."

I don't answer. I'm already up and halfway to the door. Even Leonard has picked up on the changed energy. He's sitting up now on the futon, staring as if to ask us to explain.

It's been a year, more than a year, I keep repeating to myself as I go downstairs and find the kitchen. Bonnie must have been looking for the bathroom when she found us, so probably I've got a couple of minutes to collect myself before she appears again. If I'd been within earshot of Nora, she would have warned me the minute she saw Bonnie come through the door.

When I walk into the kitchen, I'm relieved to see four or five women standing around, no Bonnie.

"Em! There you are," Judy says. "Pat went to look for you."

"Too late," I say wryly. "I already saw Bonnie. Or Bonnie already saw me. Whatever." I grab a bottle of LaCroix out of the huge cooler Judy and Pat brought.

When Pat comes back, she looks at me with a quizzical expression, and I shrug.

"Well, sometimes such disasters can't be averted," I say.

"She betrayed me," I hear Marty say loudly behind me. She's followed by Cass into the kitchen. The two women I don't know leave the room.

"All right, so I'm not saying she didn't. If that's what you say it was, then it was. Some kinda betrayal. OK. But does that mean—"

"It means—excuse me, Em, just wanna reach in here and get a beer—it means, dammit, Cass, I'm through with the little bitch. I've been deluding myself, thinking her lack of political backbone didn't have to get in the way, but—"

"Talk about lack of backbone, Marty," Pat maneuvers her way in as she slides along the counter, makes room for Marty to lean against it. "Did you see who came in a few minutes ago?" Pat nods her head in my direction.

"Uh, uh, who?"

"Must be Bonnie she's talking about," Cass says. She's standing next to me, punches me lightly on the shoulder. Extra lightly, for Cass. "Didja see her, Em?"

"Yeah. For about half a second."

"Didn't talk, huh?"

"Uh, no. Not yet."

"Think ya might?"

"I don't know."

Marty and Pat and Judy are silent, watching me.

"Hey, pals, I mean, come on, it's been over a year." I wonder if they think I've convinced myself.

"Besides, you've got yourself a new girlfriend now, Emily," Judy offers. "I hear she was spotted with you in a public place having breakfast not long ago. One of these days, we'll all get to meet her, right?"

"Right.

"Maybe we'll see you at Michigan?"

"Yeah," Cass says. "What is it, Pat, three weeks and counting?"

"Think so."

"Well, then, it's a deal. We'll all get out our cameras when Emily introduces us to this new girlfriend she's gaga over. What's her name again—Catherine?"

"That's what I need," Marty says.

"What?" we ask in unison.

"A new girlfriend."

Cass rolls her eyes.

"I give up," she says. "You're completely insane, girl. Let me outta here."

I follow Cass out of the kitchen and into the living room. There's Bonnie again, this time nuzzled up next to her new honey. The one she settled in with not long after we broke up. I meant to walk briskly through the living room and out the front door, but I can't help myself. I stop and stare. This time Bonnie's with another blond like herself. Is that woman obviously more attractive than me, or do I automatically think so because of low self-esteem? The woman's name is Rhoda or Rita or something like that. She's taller than I am (which is also true of the vast majority of human beings on the planet), has a slender body, but it's sharper, tougher: not delicate like Bonnie's.

It still hurts. After a year, it still hurts. The smell of her. Vanilla. Lemons. The taste of her lips, her tongue, and more. Everything about Bonnie is sweet and loving. Used to lose myself in her long hair. It used to fall in cascades all over my face when she kissed me. Which she did. Often. Passionately. At night, after dinner, sometimes she'd get out her guitar and play and sing softly, just for me. Love ballads she'd written just for me. She'd never play in public or even at small parties. Just for me. And now she's right here, in this room, but a long ways from me. Touching this other woman the way she used to touch me. Singing for her at night. Telling her her dreams.

Ah, Bonnie. Always available when I needed her. Any party to go to, sure, she'd come along. Friends to meet? She was eager. Wanted to meet all my friends, wanted their approval of her. Of us. Together. Sing me to sleep. Pamper me. Did things Catherine will probably never do.

But there she is, with that other woman now. Doesn't know quite who she is apart from her lovers. Is that why she just can't stay with any of us as long as we'd like? Trying us on, thinking we're the perfect fit. Easy to fit when you don't have too many edges yet. And isn't that the loveliness of her? Those with edges, nerves stripped by time and grief, should all be so lucky as to have the love of a woman like Bonnie, at least once in our lives.

Bonnie's watching me watch her. Other women are standing, talking between us. I show Bonnie my smile. She studies me a minute, hesitant, then smiles back. I let my smile say what I don't need to put into words. And I give her a little wave as I walk out of the room.

Wanna Dance?

It's not far to the train. I'm home within an hour. Catherine has left a message on my machine saying she'll see me tonight, reconfirming the time. But I'm disappointed there are no other messages. Nothing from David Miller or anyone knowing of his whereabouts in response to my ad. At least Mark's computers turned up *some* information. I'm getting zilch.

I shower off the sweat and dirt and start getting ready for Catherine. Tonight, she's promised we'll go out for dinner and then dancing. This is a big step for her. We haven't been out dancing yet. The normally poised Catherine panics at the thought of going into a lesbian bar. She's gone around to men's bars and mixed bars over the years with Patrick. She's even danced with him, but always after a few drinks. Tonight, she's ready to go out with me, to be with me around other lesbians. She's been to Paris only once before, at Fiona's party.

I put on my nicest dress slacks, a crisp black-and-white print shirt, and black western boots with fancy tooling and three-inch heels. I put on elaborately carved silver rings, a dangling ear cuff, and a matching necklace. Even a splash of cologne.

Catherine rings my buzzer right on time. We mumble hello, then hug. She seems genuinely delighted to see me again. We walk down Broadway for a leisurely dinner. I order marinated vegetables over rotini with lemon sauce, and she orders broiled chicken. We watch each other over our food, smiling often. She's wearing a peach blouse with white slacks. How good we'll look on the dance floor, I think. Her whites with my blacks. Her pastels with my deep shades. Dark and light. Maybe no one will notice the height difference after the first few seconds. Catherine is wearing muted makeup and her conservative jewelry: a diamond ring, a watch of white gold with a yellow gold filigreed edge, a delicate gold chain around her proud neck.

We walk to her car. As she reaches to start it, I reach out and touch her hair, stroke her forehead.

She smiles and then turns to me before pulling out from the curb.

"Emily," she says, "there's something I have to tell you."

For a few seconds my heart jumps. Oh my Goddess. Have I been so wrong in thinking she looked delighted to see me? Is she really angry underneath? Maybe interested in someone else? About to break up? Slow down, Emily, I tell myself.

"I know it's weird, but I have this thing. I just can't stand to be touched in any way while I'm driving. You'll just have to remember that if you're going to ride with me."

I'm laughing inwardly at myself.

"Oh." I smile. "Well, that will be hard. I guess I can just sit on my hands. But sometimes they might forget, and they might just impulsively touch you before I've had a chance to stop them."

Catherine smiles, looking ahead at traffic.

"Right," she says, not falling for it a bit.

"So what happens if I forget and touch you?"

"You don't want to find out," she says in a mock ominous tone.

"Oh, no! Not the MEAT CLEAVER, I hope!"

She laughs wickedly. So do I. I want to reach over and put my hand on her breasts, touch her crotch. I want to take her home right now and make love. But I promise her I'll behave. Don't give her any reason to avoid weekend trips. As in: Michigan. She hasn't said for sure she'll go, but she's been leaning in that direction lately. Going out to dance with me tonight is a good sign, too. If she survives dancing with me in a room crowded with lesbians, surely she'll feel less intimidated by the idea of the Michigan festival.

Paris is busy. We get the last parking place in the lot.

Inside, we make our way toward the tables in the back room, but none are free. Catherine's about to ask me something when a cute redhead I haven't seen since Michigan last year comes up.

Kerry's impressed that I remember to ask about her job as a physician's assistant at a clinic in Uptown. She has a new lover. We all exchange pleasantries, but soon there isn't much to say. After a minute or two, I excuse us politely, and we walk into the front room, finding a small clear space in front of the wall with its narrow shelf for drinks and ashtrays. From here, we can watch the dance floor, and Catherine can use the ashtray. She's smoking her second or third cigarette since we came in; I can tell she's nervous.

A few dancers are on the floor, and some lively rock music, with lyrics and melody is playing. Then the fast song ends and the DJ plays a slow song. I can't believe it. Seems like the few times I've been at Paris, I've hardly *ever* heard a slow song. Once every hour and a half if you're lucky.

"Catherine, I can't believe it. They're playing a slow song. They *never* play slow songs."

"Emily, we just got in the door. This is way too soon for me. I told you I can't dance at first."

"But this may be *the* only slow dance."

"Sorry. Not yet. I'm just too nervous."

So we watch the couples dance. None of them looks so exquisitely talented as to make anyone else feel inhibited. That's good. I hope Catherine will find it reassuring. She's told me she's afraid she looks like a bad puppet when she tries to dance. I find this hard to imagine, because she's so graceful in the movements I've seen her make. And I love to dance. I love to let music charge through my body like electricity, get in there and drive my spine and my arms and my legs, flowing out my hands like someone's playing me.

Now the music is fast rock and roll again.

"The music will get worse later. We should dance to songs like this while we have the chance."

"It's so soon, Emily. Give me a few minutes. I'm just not ready yet." I'm puzzled. She's told me she's afraid to dance, but she moves beautifully. She even manages to smoke gracefully. I know I am the only person who will say this. That's the romantic's way. My beloved this, my beloved that. She's the most beautiful woman in the room, and I'm with her. I imagine everyone envying me. By now my internal bullshit alarm has gone off several times and warned me that Emily Hawk is hovering dangerously near the abyss.

Catherine, needing something to do, volunteers to go and buy drinks. I watch the dancers. I see two or three women I recognize. That's Paris. You can stay away for months or a year and come back and see a few familiar faces. Is Paris *all* these nameless faces and I have in common?

Catherine returns with a diet cola for herself and a LaCroix with lime for me. She stands against the wall shelf, nearly rigid, like a mannequin. She watches the dancers.

"See that couple over there?" I ask. "They're good."

"The one with the beige shirt and black pants?"

"Yeah. Sexy."

"I prefer her partner."

The partner is curvy, hot. They're both hot. Hot for each other. Long, dark, curly hair on the partner; lighter hair, an interesting face with bold lines and the look of a thinker, above the beige shirt.

Other dancers are lusterless, barely moving, as though their bodies can't feel the music, can't feel anything. And a group of three young women are throwing themselves up in the air and back down again in clumsy but energetic jumps. I like them. I wouldn't want to dance with them, but I like their irrepressible spirits.

"And have you noticed this woman dancing near us? She and her partner have some very subtle moves."

"Yes." We watch them, admiring the close-fitting skirt, the large breasts, the fluid elegance of the coffee-colored woman nearest us. Her partner, white and thin, follows her and backs away as if drawn by a string from the center of those heavy breasts, from the heart.

A woman I have met once comes up, shoving a can in front of my face with the sensitivity of a robot. She then enthusiastically solicits for an AIDS group. She's never acted pleased to see me before. I throw in a dollar and wave her on.

She passes Catherine by. Catherine hasn't even noticed. She's watching the dancers. She's not had any friends diagnosed with AIDS. A flash of anger crosses my mind like a torch, then disappears. She still has Patrick, but in my selfish judgmental mind I know he's no George, that he lacks George's generosity of spirit. Immediately I strike the thought from my mind. It's thinking like that that makes people crazy. It's easy to feel cheated. But it's better to live in the world as it is, even as I try to change it. It's better to dance.

I'm itching to dance. I've been moving to the music without lifting my boots from the floor. Catherine doesn't move at all.

"Now here's a good one, Catherine." They're playing Aretha Franklin's "Freeway." Catherine is clutching the shelf.

"I'm sorry, Emily. I don't know what's wrong with me. I just can't go out there. Why don't you ask someone else?"

"But I only want to dance with *you*." Damn. Pretty soon the music will be getting undanceable.

When the DJ plays the Pointer Sisters' "Jump," I try again. "Please, Catherine. Remember how I told you there are some songs that, if they play them, I can't NOT go out and dance? This is one of them."

Again she's sorry, but no, she can't.

"I thought you said you've danced before, in other bars."

"I've always had a couple of drinks first."

"Catherine, if you want to have a drink, please have one. Just because I don't drink, that doesn't mean it bothers me if you do." If it'll make her dance, I'm willing to encourage just about anything.

"But I don't really want to have a drink."

Can't argue with that. She's too nervous to dance; I can see her still shaking slightly, standing too stiffly, holding onto her glass too tightly.

"Hey, it's the Hawk! Long time no see! Where ya been, Em?!"

It's Susie, cute as a button. She used to work out with me at Strongwomen when it first opened, but she left after a year. Felt she needed a more high-tech professional bodybuilder's gym. Like Cass, I felt less impressed with Susie after that. She's always at Paris on the weekends but couldn't keep up a membership in a feminist business important to us all. Let go, Emily, I remind myself.

"Around," I say. Susie's apparently here alone tonight. Last time I was here, a few months back, she seemed smitten with a soft, pale, dark-haired femme. Susie's all of about 105 pounds but loves to play butch.

"This is Catherine. Catherine, Susie." They murmur hello, and Susie smiles knowingly, as if to tell me I'm a sly old fox, before she heads on toward wherever it was she was going.

I remind myself that the important thing is to be with Catherine. If she can't dance, she can't. Why should I care?

The music gradually gets worse and worse. Catherine's body never seems to relax. I put down my LaCroix bottle and lean into her. I give her a bold kiss on her neck, then on the top of her chest at the open neck of her blouse. I smell her light perfume. Catherine leans back into me, presses one leg against me. I'm ready to close my eyes and fall into her arms. She's so tense she's trembling. She smells so sweet, feels so warm, needs so much to relax, needs me to lean into her, needs me to kiss her gently.

We stay like that a few minutes. Then I stand on tiptoe in my high-heeled boots to whisper in her ear.

"Know what?" I say. "I don't care whether we dance or not. So long as I get to go home with you. That's what's important. It's a treat just standing here with you. Just being here. With you."

"Mmm," she says, as if she's inhaling the scent of a fragrant rose. I hold her until she's not trembling anymore.

On the way to her car, she's apologetic. "I'm so sorry, Emily. I really had no intention of taking you there and not dancing with you. I really thought I could—that if we stayed for awhile, eventually I'd be ready to dance. But I just couldn't." She unlocks the door for me and I slide in.

"Don't worry about it. But I do hope we can come back sometime and try again."

"I'm sure we will. I just have to get over being nervous around so many women."

She starts the car. I decide it's not a good time to mention the Festival.

I reach for her, then stop my hand in mid-air, draw it back in front of me, and slap it with my other hand. Catherine bursts out laughing.

"Whew!" I say in mock relief. "Almost lost it that time."

She drives to Roscoe Street. We're there in what seems like a minute or two, and luckily, she finds a place to park only a block away.

We reach my building.

I pretend to slap one hand with the other again. "Bad hand. Tried to touch the driver." Then I reach up and hold her face in my hands.

She laughs, grabs my hands, pulls them away from her face. But she doesn't let go of them.

"Hey," she says, after we step into my apartment. "I guess I'll have to make an exception, just for you." She takes me in her arms and bends to kiss me on the lips. My heart coos like a dove.

Meddling

I sleep a long time. I'm awakened out of vague, gray dreams of being somewhere underground, digging or crawling through a tunnel. But the images are fading fast. It's the telephone, ringing in the other room. I reach for the silent one near my bed.

"Hello?"

"It's Eric, Emily. I'm at the hospital. Just thought you should know Paul's taken a turn for the worse."

"What's happened?"

"Well, he's got a new infection they can't pin down yet, and they had to take him off the AZT because of his white blood cells dropping. The T-cells are down to like, nine or something. Bad."

"Should I come down?"

"I don't think so. I don't think he'll know you, Em. He doesn't seem to recognize me anymore. His sister from St. Louis is here, and he doesn't recognize her."

Paul apparently hasn't told Eric about wanting to find David Miller, and Eric doesn't ask about it.

"Is there anything I can do?" I ask.

"Not at this point. I just thought you'd want to know. I'm not sure he'll last another month. Maybe not another week."

I draw in a breath.

"Well, thanks for calling me, Eric. I'll call Laura."

"Sure. See you."

Catherine comes in the bedroom, bringing me a cup of coffee.

"I wanted you to sleep longer, but I hesitated to answer the phone."

I take the coffee and sip it. "That's fine. How long have you been up?"

"A while. I was just reading your Sunday *Trib.*"

"That was Eric calling from the hospital. Says Paul doesn't recognize anyone. Probably won't be long."

"Oh."

I'm handling this much better, I want to tell her, than I handled it when George was sick. I don't know whether I'm glad Catherine didn't know me then. I don't know how she would have reacted to my pain.

"I have to face it. He may die without ever knowing whether his message reached David. I wonder if David is still alive."

"Hmm. No responses to the ad, huh?"

"Not yet. His parents acted like they don't care if they never hear from him. And nobody at the bars seemed to remember him. Well, one guy thought he might have. Sort of." I'm sitting up in bed, frowning into my coffee. Catherine is sitting at the foot.

"Well, Emily, do you think it's so important that you find this guy?"

I watch her, wondering what she means. Ever since listening to Cass and Marty yesterday, I've been wondering myself. Maybe I am directing too much energy in inappropriate places. But when someone you care about asks you to help, how can you refuse?

"Maybe it's not so important whether I find him. I'm not sure what I think anymore." Then I tell her about what went on yesterday at the moving party.

"My God," Catherine says when I finish, "I'm glad I wasn't there. Sounds like a miserable afternoon."

I nod. "It was, in a way. My tendency is to freeze and run from any conflict like that. But maybe it was good for me to be there, to realize it wasn't the end of the world that a group of friends couldn't agree on things. By the end of it, Cass and Marty were more accepting of each other. I think the rest of us didn't quite know what to do with ourselves." I don't tell her about what Rosalie said.

"I can't stand disc–arguments like that. People get so childish and hostile."

"How do you avoid them at work? Surely you've got at least one or two temperamental types in your department? Even computer people aren't calm *all* of the time."

"Well, I do my best to see that they don't come to that sort of thing."

"But what about when they lose it?"

"I don't respond in kind. I remain calm. And if I'm right, I stay firm on my position. After a certain point, I won't enter into arguments with them."

Minimalist management, I guess.

"Well, you must be stronger than some of us."

She shrugs those beautiful, broad shoulders of hers. "I don't know. I just try to keep things on an even keel."

"Hmm. Maybe I'm too invested in helping my male friends. Maybe Cass is right–maybe only organized efforts really count."

Catherine smiles. "I'm the last person you should ask about those things, Emily, and you know it. I'm just beginning to find out what it's like to be a lesbian actually having a relationship. I'm ignorant of half of the political groups you've mentioned as it is."

"All right, then," I say. "But could you have said no to Paul if you were in my shoes?"

She looks down at her cup. With her other hand she strokes my calf. She looks up and watches me.

"Well, Emily, since you ask. I guess I have to tell you I don't think I would do what you're doing. I think it's very sweet, what Paul told you. The idea is nice. But don't you think, if Paul really meant it, he would have managed, sometime during all those years, to find the guy himself? And don't you think that if the guy wanted to hear anything from Paul, he would have been in touch by now?"

"Hmm." I've thought those things.

"I think if I were this guy David I'd resent someone chasing me down like that. If I had managed not to communicate in all those years, then probably there was a reason. Probably he doesn't want to be bothered. I think it's wrong to invade people's privacy like that, Emily."

"Wrong?"

"Yes. You asked me. Now I've told you."

"Wrong how, exactly?"

"Like I said. It's meddling. It's thinking you have the right to decide what other people should know, or what's good for them. Boy, have I seen enough of that. My mother's a prime example. Screwing things up for other people because she just can't respect anyone's wishes to be left alone."

"Oh."

I don't know what to say. It's hot already, and a small trickle of sweat is running between my breasts. A light breeze comes through the window. At any second, Catherine might get up from the bed, gather her things, and leave. Does she think I'm a meddler like her mother? I fear she's angry with me. Then I remind myself that these are classic feelings. Fear of the other person's anger, of the other person's disappearance. Natural.

"Emily."

"Huh?"

"I'm sorry about last night. I really don't know what got into me. I had every intention of going there and dancing with you. I thought for sure I could settle down enough after a half hour or so."

"Oh, that's all right." Last night seems far away. I excuse myself, go into the bathroom, and come back.

Now Catherine's sitting in the middle of the bed. She's put her empty coffee cup on the floor. Mango is lying belly up, legs spread, in the doorway.

"Elaine called me yesterday."

Elaine. The straight woman Catherine was in love with for ten years. Spent lots of weekends together, went on trips, even slept in the same bed. But Elaine kept saying she was sorry, she just didn't love Catherine in that way. *That way. That way.*

I watch her face. "How was it?"

"Not too bad. She was polite. She's moving into a new townhouse and realized she still had some of my records." The two had parted abruptly one weekend after a fight, and neither had contacted the other since. Catherine had been working with Fiona in therapy on getting herself out of the relationship, and Elaine made it easier by blowing up at her one day and telling Catherine she had never been much of a friend.

"So, are you going to get them?"

Catherine laughs. "No, Emily. Don't worry. I have no intention of seeing her. She offered to send them to me, but I told her that whatever they were, I'd managed to survive without them this long and probably had replaced the ones I like with CD's by now anyway."

"So that was all? Sounds like it went well."

"Well, that wasn't quite all. She also said she wanted to tell me she hoped I understood and hoped that I didn't hate her."

I need for him to know I don't hate him.

I wait for Catherine to go on. When she doesn't, I ask.

"And what did you say? Or what do you feel?"

She looks off, away from me, toward the window. Perhaps she's following the dappled light on the oak leaves.

"Oh, it doesn't matter. I mean, it makes no real difference that she said it. I guess I don't feel much one way or another."

Ten years, and you don't feel much one way or another? But I don't say it. Catherine's body belies her words. I can see the tension in the way she holds herself, the quickened breathing. Control. Her priority is maintaining self-control. She's very good at it. Too good at it, she told me once. Lay down your shields, I want to say. Lay them down. Stop blinding the beasts with the harsh light of your shield, and they'll stop howling. But I say nothing. Instead, I reach out and stroke her ankle. I keep stroking it. In a few seconds, she turns back to me.

"And what about you, Emily? I wondered if you were worried we might run into Bonnie at Paris last night?"

I blush. I can feel it. Time to tell her about the rest of yesterday. About Rosalie. About Bonnie. I take a deep breath and tell her about seeing them both.

When I finish, Catherine is smiling, delighted at the absurdity.

"So Bonnie's convinced you and Rosalie are having an affair?!! Oh, that's rich! I'd love to have been a mouse in that room!"

"Except for Leonard," I manage to say between giggles.

"Oh. The cat, right?"

"I wonder what poor Leonard thought."

"Oh, you and cats, Emily." She points toward Mango, who has raised her head because when I said "poor Leonard" I used my baby-talk voice reserved for cats. "More coffee?" Catherine takes our cups, refills them, brings them back.

"It's almost getting too hot for another cup of this stuff. I should get in the shower and hose myself down." But we both sit on the bed, sipping. Then Catherine sets down her cup and reaches over and strokes my face.

"Catherine," I say. "Do you think I'm a meddler?"

She doesn't answer me at first. She takes my coffee cup out of my hands, pulls me down on the bed so that my face is just above hers. She's holding me tightly by the wrists.

"Right now, I think I'd like you to meddle with me. I'd like to meddle with your body." She kisses me on the lips, drives her tongue back up against the roof of my mouth, stroking it. We kiss like that for several minutes. Then she lets go of my wrists and pulls my flimsy undershirt off, over my shoulders. She pulls off her own sleepshirt and throws them both on the floor. Slowly, deliberately, she licks the sweat between my breasts. She starts sucking on my right breast, and uses her right hand to play with my left nipple. I'm on my knees and falling backward; she's pushing me backward with her tongue sucking me, her hand pushing my breast. She pushes me down and climbs on me and I reach up and put my knee in her crotch. She flinches with pleasure, already horny. I'm bucking against her thigh, wet and sticky and I don't care. We ride each other, taking our time, rubbing ourselves into a sweet, sweet desire. Then I pull back. I reach up and push her leg back a bit, take her hand from my breast, push her torso upwards.

"Come up here," I whisper. I urge her body up over me, pushing her up, perpendicular to me. I urge her legs to come forward, on either side of me, so she's straddling my chest instead of my crotch. "I want to taste you," I whisper. I can see the apprehension in her eyes, but I know she'll trust me. "I want to suck you, just like this." And I pull her waist down so her crotch is right above me, and I start licking her. She's slick and swollen already, and I circle the bud with my tongue. I love the feel of her velvet-soft folds, the coarse, curly hair. I love the rank smell of her love juice, flowing for me. I love the little gasps she's making up above me. I love the way her hands are holding on to the side of my head. I'm writhing beneath her, my own desire intensifying unbearably, as I feel her muscles hugging my chin. Then I move my tongue down, slowly drive it in and around, then flick it back up. I draw my tongue back for just a second, and her body lunges forward, hungry, desperate, needing me to lick it again and again. And I do. I'm moaning with pleasure at the wet, raw taste of her, the feel of her, the swelling, the milky juice, the bucking and sucking and thrusting and now she won't let go of me, she's gripping my head, my ears so hard it hurts, and I don't care, I want her to hold on with all she's got, to hold me and ride me and ride my tongue, my tongue inside her, stroking her, pulling outside her, licking her up, down, up, down, and now I'm sucking hard and she's riding my chin and screaming don't stop don't stop Oh yes Oh yes Oh yes OH OH EMILY OH!!!

This Michigan Thing

"It's a pleasure to meet you," Barry tells Catherine as they shake hands and sit down. "I've heard so much about you."

"And I about you." She gives him a warm smile.

"I'm surprised we got a table without waiting. Our lucky day," I say. Trio is usually crowded until Sunday afternoon.

After we order, Barry asks Catherine about work, and they talk about computers. They show no awkwardness. I drink the glass of water in front of me while they discuss their favorite actresses, films, and shows. They both love Katharine Hepburn, Kathleen Turner, Meryl Streep, and, of course, Lily Tomlin. They've both seen Ellen Burstyn on stage.

When Barry snorts like Ernestine and then impersonates Trudy, the bag lady, I know Catherine's won his heart. I watch Catherine's beautiful hands. She's only smoked two cigarettes so far. Her hands, now free, are describing small circles in the air, punctuating her animated conversation. She *likes* Barry.

I sit and watch them, these two people who are so special to me, and a wave of deep satisfaction gently washes over me. I love the frail, fresh periwinkles on our table, the splash of sunlight from the window as it strikes my glass, the delicate, young crow's feet wrinkling at the edges of Catherine's eyes when she laughs at one of Barry's jokes. And I wish George were here. If she likes Barry, how she would have loved George. How he would have enjoyed meeting her. He would have been happy for me and for her, and she would have seen how much there was to love in him.

When our omelettes arrive, we mumble how nice they look, and start eating.

"So, Emily," Barry says after a couple of bites, "you've been quiet over there."

"Have I? Well, I guess I was just enjoying hearing the two of you."

"Didn't realize how talkative I can get when I find another person who's powerless over celluloid, huh?"

"Oh, you." I pretend to throw my napkin at him.

We've all three seen a dozen or so films we can discuss, and each of them has seen a dozen more I haven't. They discuss their favorites, ancient and modern, and then the conversation moves to books, and then to films made from books we've all read.

"And what about *The Rainbow*?" Barry asks. Catherine and I saw it together.

"Well, it sure wasn't as good as *Women in Love*," Catherine says. "But I was glad I saw it."

"I was glad I saw it too," I say, "but it was disappointing. As I recall–it's been ten years or more since I read the book–even Lawrence, who had some pretty strange attitudes toward lesbians anyway, did show a kind of intellectual and emotional relationship between Ursula and her teacher Winifred. Seems to me they already knew each other and had grown to love each other before the sex scene in the lake."

"That's how I remember the book, too," Catherine says.

"But Russell changed all that–makes Winifred out to be a really butch swimming coach who takes one look at Ursula, and Bang! Instant lust for the body. Pounce. It really cheapened it, for me. Russell gives an unfortunate impression of lesbian attraction–like the worst stereotypes."

"But they do have much more than a sexual relationship later, even in the film," Barry points out.

"Yeah. It gets better. I just didn't like the way he handled the first part. Not to mention that sex scene."

Barry's raising an eyebrow, smiling, encouraging me to explain. Catherine's watching me intently too, though she's already heard my opinion.

"Well, there's this incredible buildup to the rainstorm and the dip in the lake. They finally strip their clothes off, and you see them running naked into the lake. Then there's that wonderful plunge into the water where the camera goes underwater with them–and just when it's getting good, that's it. Kaput. Cut. No actual touching, stroking, or sex—that scene ended exactly where it should have just begun."

Barry laughs. "You know, you're right."

Catherine's smiling at both of us. "Wouldn't you just love to see what was left on the cutting room floor?" I like the wicked gleam in her eye.

Our checks arrive, but we're in no hurry, and the waiter refills our coffee cups. We put our money on the table and just sit, sipping. I feel warm and happy inside. The three of us agreeing. Enjoying each other. About as perfect as life gets, I think.

"Well, I should be going," Barry says. "Got to do some laundry today. I'm so glad I got the chance to meet you, Catherine."

"I've really enjoyed meeting you."

"Now you can finally see that Catherine exists, that she's not a figment of my imagination."

Barry slides his chair out, stands up.

"And a very nice-looking figment, too!"

Catherine blushes.

"Listen," Barry announces suddenly. "I just remembered. I have to go out of town for the company—it's just to Kansas City, dahlink—in a couple of weeks, and I've got a couple of extra theater tickets I'd love to give you. They're for a new show by a Chicago playwright at that new CityLife theatre."

Catherine looks over at me, waiting for me to say something.

"Well, sure—if you can't use them. What night is it for?"

"They're for the second Friday in August. I won't be back until Sunday. I bought a charter subscriber thing, and so they'll just go to waste if someone doesn't use them."

"Sounds good, huh, Emily?" Catherine looks excited.

"But that date—that's, that's—yes, I'm sure it's the weekend of the music festival. Michigan."

"The one where everybody got sick one year?"

"No. Yeah. Well, I didn't get sick. A lot of women did, but I didn't. Most of my friends didn't, either. Anyhow, it's that same weekend."

"Oh." Barry shrugs. "Well, too bad. I'll ask around and find someone else." He gives us a little goodbye wave. "I'll see you later."

"Thanks for offering the tickets, Barry," I say.

"Yes," Catherine says. "Thanks a lot. Nice meeting you. 'Bye."

Then, she's silent.

"You seemed to like Barry," I say.

"He's wonderful," she says. But somehow her voice is different.

We leave the restaurant and walk up Broadway.

I put my arm around her waist. She shrugs away.

"Too bad about the tickets," I say as we enter my apartment. Catherine doesn't say a word. We gather our things for the beach.

I stand across the table from her as she stuffs her suit and things into her bag.

"Catherine."

Nothing.

"Catherine, what's wrong?"

She keeps looking down, her hand reaching for things to put in her bag. She adds another book, even though she already put one in there. She picks up the newspaper from the table and begins to throw it in, then takes it back out.

"You've already read that."

She looks up then, glaring at me. My stomach feels queasy all of a sudden.

"Emily," she begins. I can see she's shaking. Her voice is cold with a hostility she's never directed at me before. She pauses for a minute, apparently to control her anger. Then she steps back from her bag and the chair it's resting on, letting her hands fly back toward her shoulders, her palms facing me, her fingers spread. Her hands go limp and fall to her sides. She shakes her head as if to clear her vision.

"What is it, Catherine? Whatever it is, just tell me."

She sighs. "I don't know. I don't know, Emily. Maybe I just made a mistake."

"About what?"

"About this Michigan thing. I mean, you seem to have assumed that we're going."

"Well, you've known about it for months—and I told you we don't have to make plans, we can just go at the last minute."

"So did you just figure you could talk me into it at the last minute? If it hasn't worked so far, why did you think it would then?"

"Well, you told me your big concern was camping. But remember when I told you about my tent and my sleeping bags? You said we'd need a thermos of coffee and plenty of bug repellent. I thought you sounded more like you might want to go."

"Emily, I said *if. IF* we go camping. Sometime. Not meaning, necessarily, Michigan. I *told* you I just couldn't see myself out there with all those women running naked."

She lights a cigarette and blows smoke defiantly up at her bangs. I don't like the way she's looking at me. And she sounds very, very sure of her position.

"So you'd rather have tickets to that play?"

"I wish it were that simple. Yes, I'd rather have tickets. And I didn't like the way you just decided for us that we couldn't take them."

"Well, if you wanted to go so bad, why didn't you speak up? Barry would have given them to you."

"Right. And have you going hysterical on me because I contradicted you? In public? No way. You told Barry we wouldn't use them. Barry's your friend, and it wasn't my place to speak up then."

This is it. Catherine is really angry. And she's decided I'm just an hysterical woman. Someone who might really do something stupid in public. Someone she'd rather not be seen with, in that case. Someone who can't manage herself, can't maintain control.

Well, maybe she's right. Maybe I'm all those things she fears I am. I'm standing here watching the woman I love stare at me with a cold dislike that makes me feel it in my chest. My whole chest cavity is shrinking, recoiling, from the stomach up through the lungs and the sternum. The heart. A wing spreads across the sun. A chill ripple blows across my heart.

"So what you're saying is, number one, you're completely firm about not going to Michigan?"

"Right." She closes her lips over the word, as if biting it.

"And number two, you're pissed off at me for assuming you'd go and for turning down the theater tickets?"

"I wouldn't say pissed off."

"Well, mad."

"Not mad. Disappointed." She sighs, exhales smoke. "I don't know, Emily. I know it's important for you to go to Michigan. That's why I said you could go ahead and plan to go with any of your friends if they asked you."

"I thought you were teasing. You knew I didn't want to go with anyone but you."

"That's just it, Emily. Look at us. We're different. You really wanted me to go to Barry's party a few weeks ago. I felt bad about it, but I just didn't want to go. You love to go dancing at Paris. You've seen how nervous I am at Paris. If I'm that nervous there, how could I possibly be comfortable at Michigan?"

"I know."

"It's a lot of things. Emily, you have a lot of friends I'll probably *never* want to meet. You want to go to all these things and to have a lover go with you. But to me, the thought of walking into the coffeehouse or the bar and becoming known as Emily's lover, or as the woman Emily brought into the community, just makes me panic. I just don't want to be in a couple like that. Maybe you want a woman who will do all those things with you."

She looks down now. Her chest is rising and falling visibly.

But that's not what I want, Catherine, I want to tell her. I want *you*. But I can't speak the words. I'm afraid she won't believe me. I'm afraid she'll think I just can't admit that she's right. And maybe she's right. So I stand here, confused, not saying anything, hoping she doesn't notice my silent tears.

"It's not you, Emily," she says at last, gently. "It's me. You know how long it's been for me. I waited all those years before I was ready to try having a relationship, and maybe I just wasn't ready. Or maybe I'm just too set in my ways for any woman to put up with me." She puts her cigarette out. "I have no desire to be part of a couple that requires that I blend with all of my lover's friends, or that I spend every weekend with my lover. Maybe I'm just too unreasonable. But this is how I am, Emily. And I think right now I just can't do these things with you."

We stand there breathing for a few minutes, not looking at each other. Time has slowed down again, and every pore of my skin feels the sweat beading up from the physical heat.

"Well," I say at last. "What do we do now? Somehow I don't think going to the beach together is a good idea."

"No, not right now. I can go home early."

She stands there. I look up now, watch her. Just like a bad moment in a Ken Russell film, I think: we're ending this scene just when we ought to begin something.

"No, Catherine. You take your things and go to the beach. I'll stay here. I was only going to the beach to be with you. I don't love it the way you do."

"Emily, I–"

"Just go!" I say, more passionately than I intend. "Just go, would you, please?!"

"Emily, I'm only saying I need time to think. I need to be alone for awhile. I mean, we'll talk another time, all right?"

Catherine's shaking as she holds the door open.

Right, I think. She needs space. Needs to be alone. It would always be the same thing with her, wouldn't it? I'm standing here perfectly passive and quiet while inside my guts are screaming NO! Don't leave! Please don't leave!!

"No," I make myself say, as though I'm acting a role. "We won't talk. You'll be happy at a distance from me, where you can keep me safely out of your life except on your terms, and as long as I keep waiting eagerly for you to invite me into some small corner of your life, maybe every third Tuesday or so. Well, don't. Don't call me, Catherine. Maybe you're right. Maybe I really would like to have a lover who wouldn't mind going to lesbian events, who would be happy and eager to dance with me in public, who would also assume that we'd go to Michigan together, who wouldn't be afraid of being known both as herself and as Emily's lover–what's so terrible about that–and who wouldn't think I was a meddler for trying to help my friends!"

I bite back that last statement, but it's too late. It's out. I've said it. I feel the chill of severance. Great, Hawk, now you've done it but good. You'll probably never see this woman again.

You'd better hope you don't. She'll ignore you if you run into her, and you'll be ashamed even before she does.

She hovers for a minute longer in the doorway, her bag slung over her shoulder. I know she's seen my tears now, and I know my voice has not been steady. But before I finished speaking, I saw tears begin streaming down her face too. And she's not making any effort to wipe them away. She just stares at me as if in disbelief. Then she walks out the door, pulling it gently shut behind her.

Grief

After she's gone, I stand just inside the door, shaking. Eventually I find myself moving toward the dining area, sinking into one of the chairs at the table. I'm soaked through with sweat from the heat. My chest feels as though someone's strapped metal strips around it and pulled them much too tight. Mango jumps down from her perch in the windowsill and comes walking over to the chair. In reply to her "meow," I reach down halfheartedly and stroke her. And then I'm sobbing, great spasms. They come from deep within me. I'm crying for Catherine, and for all of it: all my grief for George comes back, grief I thought I'd finished but know now I'll never come to the end of; and Bonnie, and the gym, and my dad, and everyone and everything I've loved and lost. Rough, jerking thrusts of pain come from the center of my body, my heart chakra breaking from the pressure, the constriction, fracturing into shards of sorrow.

Lifting

"What a bummer, Emily," Cass says, as she takes me down the basement steps. "I never even laid eyes on the woman, but I think you're bound to be better off without her."

We start working out. Cass uses the bench while I do curls. "I guess so. Guess it just wasn't meant to be. Sure is a crummy week." It's been exactly eight days since Catherine left. She hasn't called. I've been fighting off urges to call her every day and every night. "Still no responses to my ad about Paul's ex. Saw Paul yesterday and he didn't recognize me. He's out of it now. They say he'll be gone in three weeks."

"Listen, Em, you still might hear something. Don't give up yet. I'll keep asking around, too."

For awhile we just work and rest, work and rest. Our breathing gets louder, then settles down, then gets louder again. I do four sets of curls, then add another five pounds and do four more sets. While I'm resting between sets, I spot Cass on the bench. Her big shoulders and biceps seem to expand right in front of my eyes. She grunts softly, heaves up, then slowly lowers. Over and over. Cass is the strongest woman I know.

"Maybe I really was awful, Cass–assuming she'd go to Michigan with me. Maybe I just got too unreasonable."

Cass finishes her set, and I help her set the bar back in place. She wipes her brow with a towel. Our sweatbands are already soggy. I pick up the 10-pound dumbbells and work my triceps while Cass sits on the bench, resting.

"I don't know, Emily. I'd have trouble with a woman who wouldn't go to Michigan with me. I mean, hell, you know Nora and I are about as different as they come, but I tell you,

I draw the line when it comes to anything remotely smacking of a straight woman."

"Straight?!" I set the dumbbells down. "Catherine's not straight! She was a lesbian before she met me!"

"Maybe. I know you said she was. She said she was. But what was it, one affair? All those years of calling herself a lesbian privately–to no one but herself and her one friend–and not doing anything about it?"

"That's not how it was, Cass. She was in love with Elaine and stayed with it even though Elaine never did come around. That's why she didn't get involved with anyone else all those years."

"OK. If you say so. And didn't want to meet any of us? Didn't want to go to the parade? Doesn't go to anything, doesn't support any organizations? Come on, Em. What kind of a woman is that? Let her figure things out first, get herself clear of her homophobia, then you can date her. Meanwhile, you're better off dating someone who doesn't have those hangups." She moves to the leg press, climbs on, begins working her quads.

I begin my dumbbell flies, to work the chest. Spread the arms out on either side, keep the back straight against the slanted chair. You can do this exercise using only the arms, not involving the chest at all. But I like to do them with my arms light as feathers, the real work taking place deep inside me, in the muscles surrounding the heart. Today I have to concentrate. Lift from the center. My torso opens. Energy flows in the expanding space, through the thoracic region of the back, along the upper spine, and forward through the sternum. I lift and breathe, lift and breathe. I'm lifting hard to open myself up, struggling against the other feeling, the one that wants me to close up.

"Come on, Em, you don't have the energy for that shit. Listen, why don't you go to Michigan anyway? You can come with Nor and me. And Rosalie."

I put the weights down. "Rosalie?"

"Yeah." Cass stops lifting and watches me. She's finished with her quads. "Didn't you know? They broke up."

"When?!"

"A few days after the party. Come on, Em, you saw how it was. Rosalie told me they'd been having problems anyway. I guess Marty just decided she couldn't handle it, so they split."

"Rosalie moved out?"

"Yeah. Friday after work."

"Where'd she go? Did she get her own apartment?"

"No. Not yet. She's here, Em. She's staying in the extra bedroom for a while."

"Wow."

"Yeah. It's gonna work out fine, for now. She and Nor can take the train together in the morning, and she'll be company for Nor while I'm working nights."

"Some 'company,' Cass."

"Hey, don't worry," Cass laughs. "I think old Nor is one of the few women in this city who doesn't lust after Rosalie. To her, Rosalie's just a kid. If anything, Nor will mother her too much."

I laugh. I can see it. Rosalie will get lots of attention and sympathy. And if George were alive and my roommate, I'd be getting lots, too. But he isn't. And I'm alone. Laura's moved to Massachusetts, Paul's about to die, David Miller will remain a mystery. What good is any of it? Strongwomen is closed. Gone. Mercedes is off in the California hills, fighting for her life.

"Cass?"

"What?"

"Let's send some flowers to Mercedes."

"Now that's a good idea. We'll go fifty-fifty, get something nice. You know the address?"

"I've got it written down somewhere at home."

We work faster now, and don't talk again for twenty minutes. We work out well together. We can talk and then be comfortable not talking. It's almost like it was at Strongwomen. Maybe that's why I'm here. Maybe Cass and I are both trying to keep something alive from those days.

Our T-shirts and shorts are soaked. My hair drips sweat down my face. Cass hands me her towel. I rub my hair and face with it.

"I'm going to bring the fan down here from upstairs next time."

"I don't mind, Cass. It's cooler down here than at my place."

"Yeah. Listen, feel free to come use it anytime. We'll get keys made for you."

I stop and stare at Cass. I feel a cool, soothing balm of acceptance wash over my sweaty body.

"Thanks," I mumble.

Later, I order pink roses for Mercedes. I hardly expect they'll cheer her up. But I like the color. I like hearing myself tell the florist to write "Love, from Cass and Emily" on the card.

That Was Different

I hear the sudden intake of breath when Laura hears my voice. She knows that any time now one of these calls will bring the inevitably bad news.

"Still no improvement. I sat and held his hand for about an hour today, and he never did recognize me." His hand was limp, like an inanimate object attached to his body.

"Do you think I should come, Emily?"

"Only if it would help you. He doesn't seem to know anyone anymore. Might be kind of hard for you—come all that way and he'd never know you were here."

"I'm supposed to give a workshop at this conference in Boston next week. Maybe I should get out of it."

"You know Paul wouldn't want you to do that. He knows how hard it was to get this job."

We both pause.

"Well, what can we do, then, Em?"

Laura's asking *me?*

"His sister's here. I think she's going to stay."

"What's she like?"

"Not too bad. It finally sunk in on her, I think. And she has all this stuff she wants to talk about with Paul, and he just isn't there anymore. So she cries a lot. She talks to Eric and me. Asks questions. Wanted to know about you. Wants to see his drawings now. It's like she wants to catch up and get to know him. Only it's—"

"Too late." Laura sighs. "Why do people never figure stuff out in time?" She pauses. "Did you get in touch with David's parents?"

"They haven't seen him in years. Sounds like they just wrote him off completely. Wouldn't talk to me."

"That's too bad."

"And guess what? I did find out he'd been married, just like you said. Only she hasn't heard from him in three years, either. I took out personal ads, went to the bars with his picture. My coworker has found out everything a bank's credit bureau can find out. It's like he just disappeared."

"He asked you to look. Not to conduct an all-out federal case about it. You've done your best, Em. You know what I think matters? What matters is that Paul got to a place where he really let go of David, of what had bothered him. That's what counts."

"But it *does* matter. He wants the message to do some good—for David, not just for him—if it can. That's why I think he needs to know I found the guy. But he won't know. Not now. Even if a miracle happened tomorrow, it would be too late. Paul can't understand me if I tell him."

"Then you're going to need to let go of it, Em."

"Yeah. You're probably right about that."

"So, any news from Catherine?"

"No. I don't think she'll call. I guess I really blew it. I was probably too intense. I moved too fast for her. Guess I put her off."

"That's too bad, Em. It sounds like you still care about her."

"Yeah, I guess I do. Can't stop thinking about her. I mean, so many things *did* seem right—you know, it's always hard when you've gotten your hopes up, and then you find out the person's not the person you thought she was."

"Now, wait a minute. I think you found out a few weeks ago that she wasn't the person you thought she was, and you hung in there, didn't you?"

"OK. Yeah. I remember that. But that was different. This time it's not just a matter of a day or two of distance. This is finding out she really panics at the thought of being considered part of a couple. With me. Going places like the Michigan festival together. You know. Pretty basic stuff."

"Hmm. I don't know, Em. After all, I've never met her. But it sounds like she's not rejecting you, exactly. Sounds like she's coming up against that same thing from a few weeks ago. And maybe you're right. Maybe she's just not ready for a relationship—for all the things that being in a relationship means." She lightens her tone. "Apparently, being in a relationship with you means going to Michigan and doing all those other things."

"No!" But what does it mean? I don't know. "I think it doesn't mean going to all those things, but maybe not always being *afraid* of them, either. You know? I don't know. Cass says I don't ask for enough of what I want. But maybe I expect too much. Maybe Catherine got a whole lot more than she bargained for when she found out what I'm like in a relationship."

"Maybe so, Emily. But remember–if you were more than she bargained for, then maybe you need to be with someone who can appreciate how much of a bargain she's getting. Someone who'll love it that you have so much to offer."

"Hmm. I'm beginning to wonder if that will ever happen."

"Well, I'd say your chances are excellent. After all, look at me. I think I've found a man like that–he's not threatened, he's not afraid to commit, he thinks my art is great and likes it when I stand up for myself."

"Laura! That's great! How come you haven't told me before?"

"Well, it started a couple of months ago, and I was real cautious at first. I just took my time. Watched him. Watched myself, how I felt when I was around him. I liked what I saw. I like the way we are together. It's good. You'll find something good, too, Em."

"Yeah. Maybe. Sometime. Right now I just wish I could find David Miller."

"I still think I should cancel that workshop and come see Paul. I think I will. Maybe he'd perk up. I could pick up those two prints for the group show next month."

I suck in a deep breath. "I hate to say this, but you'll be turning right around and coming back for the funeral."

"I'll talk to the people at the conference. You call me anytime. The slightest change."

No More Ex-Lovers

The air is cooler in August. On my lunch hour or my days off I visit Paul's room, where it hardly feels like I'm visiting Paul. I listen to his sister talk and ask questions and answer the best I can. I go to work and don't laugh much when Mark or Zee make jokes. Sometimes I walk past the building on Michigan Avenue where Catherine works. Every night I wonder whether she's home, whether she'd talk to me if I called her. Then I decide it's best to leave her alone. The summer's gone and I've goofed up the two most important things. I'm just no good at hunting up people I don't even know. And I'm no good at keeping the woman I love from running away.

At night I walk along Broadway, feeling an autumn edge to the wind. Too cool for August nights. I walk right past The Closet nearly every night. I can still attract the eyes of a woman or two in there, I think. There's nothing wrong with me. I walk by and stare at the people sitting at the windows, looking out at me. And I wait for my legs to move me up to the door. But they don't. I feel no desire to go in. I think of Bonnie, her gorgeous long hair. This was where we met. Where *she* came up to *me*. A gorgeous woman picked me out, wanted me. I didn't have to do the pursuing. Happened here once. Might happen again.

But always, I turn and walk away. Always, I wind up on the tree-lined sidewalks of Roscoe Street, picking up my mail and heading up my stairs. I pet Mango, who spreads herself out before me and purrs contentedly. I stir-fry vegetables and eat them with slices of whole wheat bread.

I decide I don't need more ex-lovers. What would I do with them? My photo albums and drawers are full already, full of the photographs, the old letters with promises they couldn't keep. I think of Paul and David. Bonnie and me. The men I slept with and the women I loved before Bonnie. Then I think of Marty and Rosalie. Too much suffering. Not worth it. And then, sometime during the night, I wake up and remember what it was like to wake up with Catherine. I wince with pain. It's cool enough this week to pull the covers up again. Cool enough to drape our arms over each other again, to snuggle up close. If she were here.

Back to Fiona

"I didn't want to call you. Didn't want to see you." I'm staring down at my dirty shoelaces, gray from running on the cinder path along the lake.

"Oh. Do you want to tell me why?"

Finally, I look up and meet Fiona's eyes. Her voice just now had that tone it always has when she's trying to be very "adult" with me but is suppressing some gentle humor. Damn it. She knows me too well. On the phone I told her some of what had happened the last time I saw Catherine.

"Because I'm sick and tired of always being brokenhearted over somebody or other who couldn't keep their commitment to me, and of having to run to you to fix me. That's why."

Fiona puts her hands up, palms toward me. "Whoa. Just hold on there a minute. Where's this *always* come from? You aren't exactly into and out of flings every month or so. You've had two recent ones, and both of them seem to have ended, and you're feeling the pain of that."

"Yeah, so, why can't I just feel the pain and deal with it? Haven't I learned anything in all these years of supposed growth?"

Fiona is wagging her head as though she's bored.

"Yeah, right. We should all be declared perfect, crisis-free, for the rest of our lives. Permanently wise and strong. Right."

I sulk for a minute. Fiona waits for me. I realize that sulking in Fiona's office is expensive: about a dollar a minute.

"A couple of my friends think I should go to Michigan. I've got to tell them tonight if I'm going, because they leave tomorrow."

"What do you think? Do you want to go? And what would it be like to go with these friends?"

I sit and think. "I'm not sure. It would probably be good for me. But right now I just don't feel like it. Having to socialize. Watching all the lovebirds. Running into people from the past."

"Like?"

"Like Bonnie. She'll be there with her new lover, I'm sure." Last year Bonnie said she wouldn't go, because she thought I'd want to. She tried to be kind.

"Would that be so bad? You've survived seeing her around town a few times already."

"No, I guess it wouldn't be so bad. I could go to those workshops for women who've just broken up with their lovers. That was pretty good last year." But I don't feel like I've broken up. Maybe I'm just holding on to the idea of Catherine long after the real Catherine has disappeared. Like the idea of David Miller, maybe. I just don't want to give her up.

Fiona waits for me to go on. She can see I'm hesitating. I don't want to say the embarrassing truth.

"So?"

"So. Remember that old crush I used to have on Rosalie?" She nods, encouraging me to go on. "Well, we spent some time together at the Pride Rally, and afterwards she, uh, tried to kiss me. You know, not like just a friend. And I didn't let her. But she's the other person going with my friends to Michigan. It's sort of understood that she and I would share a tent."

"Oh. And what do you think would happen if you did?"

"Well, I don't know. But I know I'm not feeling like the tough dyke I was then. I guess I kind of hope she would try again. I guess I kind of think that would be nice."

I'm thinking about it now. Rosalie's lips.

"And?"

"I guess I'm afraid I might do something stupid. Like sleep with her."

"Why would that be stupid?"

"*Because I'd feel terrible!*"

I'm breathing harder than usual.

"Why?"

"Because I love Catherine. I don't want to sleep with Rosalie, really. I don't love her like I love Catherine. I don't want to be just another of many lovers of Rosalie. I want to be the only lover. Monogamous. Committed. To Catherine."

I feel like a boring person, a dull conservative. This disappoints me, of course. We romantics like to think we are unusual. But commitment is back in, I hear. An overreaction to the sexual revolution and venereal diseases and AIDS. Maybe it's gutless. Maybe if I were truly liberated, I'd let myself kiss Rosalie any way she wanted me to. Why not?

"Have you talked with Rosalie about Michigan—about what the expectations would be? You could talk to her about it, you know. Make some agreements."

"Right. She told me we might as well share a tent. Bonnie thinks we're having an affair anyway."

But Fiona won't let me off so easily.

"So who cares what Bonnie thinks?"

"It's not that. And it's not Rosalie. I guess it's that I don't trust myself to go. I'll get needy, and Rosalie will be there, and I just don't want to put myself in that situation, because I think I'd regret it later."

"Why would you regret it later?"

"Because, like I said, I love Catherine. I know that's insane."

"Who says it's insane?"

"Well, she doesn't love me back. She's gone. We aren't seeing each other."

"How do you know she doesn't love you?"

"She never said she did."

"So big deal. Some people don't say the words."

"She hasn't called."

"Didn't you tell me *you* basically encouraged her to leave and not to call you again?"

"Well, yes. But she wanted to leave. It wasn't just what I said. She was really disgusted with me, I think." It's all I can do not to ask Fiona if she's seen Catherine. I know Catherine was still seeing her when we were dating. I'm sure Catherine's been in to see Fiona since. I don't dare ask. Fiona would lecture me on client-therapist relationships and refuse to reveal a thing.

"Regardless of disgust or no disgust—the point is, you told her not to call, and she hasn't called, and you're taking that as confirmation of rejection."

"Well. Isn't it?"

"Can you think–I know you have a mind, Emily, so just try applying it here. Think. What do you know, in general, about Catherine? Is there anything about *her*, that has nothing to do with you, that might lead her to call or not to call? How is she with the telephone, anyhow? Does she call up women and ask them for the first date?"

I laugh. "She'd be terrified. She's super-smooth boss lady when it comes to work, but in romance–well, I definitely had to make the first moves. But hey, she knows me now. It's not like a first date."

"But it is, isn't it? It would be taking a risk, wouldn't it, to call a woman who didn't try to stop her when she decided to leave? And who, when she offered the chance of getting together to talk in the future, said no?"

When Fiona puts it like that, it seems so clear. But was that really Catherine and me? Was that what happened? How come I feel like she's the one who left? Even though I know I'm the one who made one fight into the end.

After I leave Fiona's, I'm still thinking. Am I just a romantic wimp who orchestrates relationships so that they can fail, so that I don't have to do the unglamorous work of thrashing out the issues between us? Or are there too many issues between Catherine and me? A light rain is falling as I walk home. Already I anticipate a rainy fall and a premature winter. Yes, I can feel it now, like a rain hood I'm pulling over my head. The deepening descent of a romantic's gloom.

Tents

At home, I get my tent and rainfly, and head for the train again.

At Cass and Nora's place, Rosalie comes to the door.

"Emily!" Her eyes flash enthusiasm.

"Here," I say, handing her the things while I prop the screen door open with my leg.

"Well, what's all this? Come on in, now."

She takes the tent and sets it on the floor in the hall.

"Nora? It's Emily."

"I'm on the phone. Be there in a minute," Nora calls from upstairs.

"Is Cass working tonight?"

"Yeah. Wanted to get in one last shift before we leave. You know Cass."

"Well, I just wanted to bring the things by. Rosalie, I'm not going. You can use the tent."

"But I thought we'd have such a good time. I mean, it would be so much more fun if you'd come."

"Thanks. But I don't think I'd be much fun. Listen, it's getting late, and I'm sure you and Nora have packing to do tonight, so I'll just get the train."

She follows me out the front door.

"I'll walk you to the train."

We walk. She's quiet. A solicitous quiet. I like it.

"I really wish you would come. I'm not just saying it. And I'd promise, no funny stuff, OK? If that's what's bothering you. We could just be like Girl Scouts, you know?"

I stop walking and watch her animated face. She puts one hand on my arm.

"Don't you see, Emily? It would be good for both of us. I, I, well, I'll be *lonely,* dammit, if you don't come."

"Lonely? You'll have Cass and Nora to talk to, and all kinds of women to meet." Judy, Pat, Jenny, and Lucinda will be there, and Marty too, no doubt. "Not to mention everybody's ex-lovers from their entire lives."

She smiles back at me.

"Come on, Emily, you know what I mean."

An openness I haven't felt all week floods through me. I take Rosalie in my arms and hold her.

"I know what you mean."

Not Like a Festival

By Thursday afternoon the rain has moved on, and the sun is out. The temperatures zoom back up into the nineties, and I try to convince myself there's still plenty of summer left. I roam around my apartment, going through drawers and stacks of papers, throwing things out. Bonnie's old letters. Several times during the day I find George's framed picture in my hands. I can't decide whether to put it away. Mango rubs between my legs, meowing. She picks up on my restlessness.

Finally, I talk myself into going out. I run along the lakefront, down past Fullerton and North and then past the high-priced condos and mansions of the Gold Coast. At the hospital, I spot Paul's sister Betty sitting in the hallway outside his door. She's petite, like Paul, and sits like someone who through habit doesn't take up much space.

"No change?"

She shakes her head. She looks worn, ten years older than she is. She's a year or so younger than I am. "He doesn't even know I'm here."

I peek in the doorway. Paul is sleeping. His skin looks grayish-yellow. I close the door softly and sit down on the bench next to his sister. After a few minutes, I mumble something about coming back tomorrow. Restless again, I leave.

Should have gone to Michigan, I tell myself. But I don't feel like a festival. I jog slowly back home, taking my time. Still restless, I talk to Eric. He's been going to a group for people who have lost loved ones to AIDS and other diseases. He invites me to go with him to the meeting tonight. I go, but somehow I can't concentrate much on what anyone is saying. I look around the room at the faces—mostly men—and remind myself that more than half of these people have lost not one or two but five or ten friends to AIDS. Buck up, Emily. Chuck the self-pity.

On Friday it's worse. I go to the office in the morning, and work on another set of domestic violence statistics for Zee. Mark is busy solving a computer virus. Zee flits in and out. There's no one I feel especially like talking to. Everyone seems to be preoccupied. I go home and think about going to the hospital, but just can't seem to make myself leave the apartment. I don't feel like running. I have a key to Cass and Nora's, but I don't feel like working out. I feel like calling Laura, but I've already called her twice this week. Too much. I'd give anything to be able to sit down and pour my heart out to George. I know I'm depressed when I feel an urge to call Bonnie. She's in Michigan, so I can't. Judy and Pat are in Michigan too. So is Marty, and Jenny and Lucinda, and just about every lesbian I know.

Except Catherine.

She won't be there. I know she isn't in Michigan. Where is she? I could call her office. I could call her at home and leave a message. Tell her I miss her and I'm sorry and I wish we could talk. Tell her I love her and I didn't mean half of what I said. Tell her she's right about everything, and I'll do anything. Just to talk to her. Just to see her again. My fingers hover above the telephone. I lift the receiver, put it back. Again. And again. Now I know I'm in trouble.

I dial Barry's number at work.

"Hey, kid. What's up?"

"Sorry to call you at work, sweetie, but I'm not having such a good time. I need help." So far I've only told him she left me. He was surprised to hear it but hasn't pressed for details. "I guess it's kind of silly, but I'm having real trouble not calling Catherine. I keep picking up the phone and nearly dialing her number."

"And do you think that's a good idea? What effect would it have on you to call her? That's all I care about, kid. How will you feel afterward if you call her?"

"Probably like shit. She might hang up on me. Or worse, she'd be exceedingly polite. But distant. And I'd feel like a real nuisance. I'd feel like I was proving her worst fears about me true."

"What are her worst fears about you?"

"That I'm a needy, clinging person who won't let her have her independence. That I want too much."

"What do you think?"

"Maybe she's right. Maybe I am too needy." I can hear my voice almost cracking. "But I want her, Barry. I really love her. What's so wrong with loving someone?"

"I doubt there's anything wrong with loving someone, so long as you don't hurt yourself. Listen, Em, I've got some stuff I've got to get worked out on the computers right now, but would you like to get together tonight? The seven o'clock meeting, then dinner?"

"OK."

"Good. See you there. And, Emily. Thanks for calling. I mean that. You've done the right thing."

And I know I'll go tonight. I'll go to a meeting and see Barry. But I keep remembering the party line, the groupthink doctrine of my time: at all costs, do not ever give the impression that you are too much in love, that you are possibly suffering over another person you care about. Codependence is the new taboo. After alcohol, marijuana, cocaine, sugar, caffeine, and all the rest, that's the weakness against which we are ordered to maintain constant vigilance. Right now, I'm a romantic in rebellion.

At dinner, after the meeting, I ramble while Barry listens. He knows I'm not reasonable; I'm full of ideas like toxins that need to take their course through me.

"I'm tired of being good," I tell him. "I'm just in one of those pissy phases where I'm tired of it all. I'm tired of being told I'm not supposed to need anybody. I'm tired of being made to feel guilty because I'd like to share my life with someone. I'm tired of always having to hold back my feelings, always having to be careful not to let the people I love see how much I really love them, how much I want to settle down and make a commitment."

I know I sound outrageous, whiny, self-indulgent, and adolescent. But my romantic's dander is up now. Barry has learned to wait while I wear myself out.

"I'm tired of listening to everybody call love a disease. I'm tired of feeling apologetic for who I am: someone who loves. I love Catherine. I don't know what's so wrong with that." I take a bite of my salad, shifting my eyes from Barry back to the table. "Except that she didn't love me back. Doesn't." Or did she love me? She did, I think. She didn't. I don't know.

Barry waits to see if I've really shut up. We chew our food for a few minutes, sip our decaffeinated coffee.

"You and your romantic fantasies, Emily," he begins, with a gentle, liquid voice. "One of the things I find so charming and lovable about you. You always think it will last forever."

"Yeah, maybe you're right. I guess I always take it seriously."

"And that's not bad, Emily. Just try to lighten up a little, huh? And try to look at what you *do* have. And realize you *did* have Catherine, too, for awhile. Would you rather you'd never gotten involved with her?"

"No. You're right. At least I had the experience. Brief as it was."

We chuckle. I'm chuckling to cover the pain, but it helps.

Later, he walks me home, gives me a hug and a kiss when we get to Roscoe and part ways.

Inside my apartment, I notice the red light is flashing on my answering machine.

"Hi. I'm calling in response to your ad. I used to know a David Miller. I don't know if it's the one you're looking for. But maybe I can help." It's a man's voice, probably about my age or a little older. Hmm. You lousy pessimist, Hawk. Feeling so down on human nature, and look how wrong you are. People *do* try to help people. Sometimes. They don't all judge and point fingers. Thank the Goddess.

Calls

Saturday morning I go for an early run before the cinder path is crowded with Lincoln Park couples and the running and walking clubs. The morning is bright and cool, although by afternoon the temperature will hit 90. I wait until after I shower and finish my cereal and yogurt to return the call. It was too late last night. Maybe the guy won't be home. I never did get to the hospital yesterday. It would be great if this person can put me in touch with David Miller. I could go to the hospital today and tell Paul. Or try to tell him. Just stand there and think it real hard and squeeze his hand and maybe he'd know. Maybe his heart would pick up the white light of healing.

The guy didn't leave his name, just his number.

"Hello?" The same voice from the message last night.

"Hi, my name is Emily Hawk. I'm the person who ran the ad about David Miller. I hope it's not a bad time to call?"

"Oh, no, not at all. My name's Brad. I'm not sure the David Miller I once knew is the one you're looking for. But your description sounded like a guy by the same name I knew in high school. Blond, about six feet tall, brown eyes. He'd be about 35 now, give or take a year. Like me."

"First, if you wouldn't mind, could you tell me which ad you saw? I mean, what newspaper?"

"Oh, it was in the *Trib*. I was stuck on the el with nothing but a classified section someone had left on the seat. The ad said Ohio. My folks used to live about 30 miles outside Columbus. They moved to Florida about ten years ago. David's parents might still be there, though. They were kind of weird. Real conservative."

Yeah, I know. "When was the last time you saw him?"

"High school graduation. He went off to college. I never saw him, but I heard once that he was in Chicago."

"Uh-huh." Probably never knew David was gay. "Listen, Brad, I really appreciate your responding to the ad. It's important. Can you think of anyone else who might still be in touch with him?"

"Sorry, but that's just it. I called up the only other person I know who used to know him, and she hadn't heard from him in years. Listen, is he in somebody's will? Did they leave him some money?"

"Well, not exactly. It's something of sentimental value—it might mean a lot to David, if I can find him."

"Well, I'm sorry I can't be any more help."

I thank him for calling. Then I look up Amy Miller, who's listed under her maiden name, Rejikowski, in Evanston. What the heck. I know Mark already talked to her, but maybe I should check with her, just to be sure.

"Hello, my name is Emily Hawk, and I'm—"

"Who?"

"Emily Hawk, Ma'am. I'm trying to locate David Miller."

"Whoever you are, I know you're just doing your job, but really, I can't help you. I'm sorry he hasn't paid his bill, but I have no idea where he is."

"I'm not a bill collector, Ma'am. I'm just trying to find him. Or at least find out more about him."

"Nina!" I hear her shout. Then, into the mouthpiece, in a quiet tone, "Sorry, my daughter's making a mess."

"Your daughter?" I hadn't thought of that.

"You seem surprised. How did you know David, exactly?" She asks with curiosity, not skepticism.

"I didn't. But a friend of mine did. His name is Paul."

"Paul." She pauses. I hear muffled talking. Then: "I've just sent Nina into the other room to play. This Paul. Is he by any chance an artist?"

So she knows. Knows something, anyway.

"Yes." I hesitate, not knowing how much to say. "I'd like to talk with you about David sometime, if you wouldn't mind. This is just a personal request."

"Well," she says after a pause. "Maybe we should. I know he knew a Paul, and that he's an artist. That's all I know. You say Paul's a friend of yours?"

"Yes."

"And how long has it been since Paul's seen him?"

"A long time. About five years."

"Oh." Like air being let out of a tire. "I thought maybe he saw him after, after we split up."

"How long ago was that?"

"Oh, a good three years. To tell you the truth, I don't know where David went. He was living in one of those hotels in Uptown, but then they tore it down. I'd get money orders from him every now and then for Nina. He had a friend who was going to fix up a building, I don't know where. Maybe David went there."

"Do you remember the friend's name?"

"Sorry."

"I'd still like to find out more about David. Would you be willing to meet with me sometime?"

After some juggling of calendars, we set a date for the following week.

"What do you know, Mango?" I say afterwards. "Things just might be looking up."

Mango sits on top of the dining table, watching me. When the phone rings, she jumps.

"Emily? Eric."

"Yeah?" I'm about to say I'm sorry I didn't make it yesterday; I'll come down this afternoon.

"He just died."

"What?"

"His sister stayed here all night. Said he never seemed to come out of it. Never spoke to her or seemed to know she was there. It was like he was sleeping, and then he just drew in a real deep, long breath, and died."

A Journey

Zee and I drive past blocks of abandoned cars, huge brick apartment complexes with rotting wooden window frames, vacant lots with garbage cans and more abandoned cars. Not many people out, despite the warm weather. Every now and then we spot an air conditioner poking out a window.

I realize I'm now *in* one of those neighborhoods that Catherine and I used to watch from the windows of the train. She lives just a few miles west of here, a few miles that might as well be Lake Michigan or the Amazon River.

Zee parks and we get out. The alderman's car is already there. He and an assistant are waiting for us.

I notice some men standing in a vacant lot. One of them sips something from a paper bag. I imagine them sleeping in the abandoned cars nearby. And I'm sad. And not at all afraid. So much energy, so much exhaustion, in fearing what is human. What humans, in their stupidity and arrogance, have created and caused. Starvation, poverty, crime, violence. How did these things come about? How did people come to be living in buildings worse than this brick building Zee is marching up to, a building with all its windows boarded up? David Miller could be somewhere in a building like this or in a lot standing with a group of homeless guys. Lots of abandoned buildings, all over the city. I walk next to Zee; we go around to a side door that's been pulled off.

Inside the stairwell it's dark. The alderman's assistant carries a flashlight. He's a young man, tall and thin, with a military-erect carriage. The flashlight looks incongruous with his dark suit, white shirt, and narrow tie. His skin has the sheen of satin.

In the light from his flashlight I see even more graffiti on the inside walls. Looks like bold, black pitchforks. Some circular symbol sprayed over them. The floor we're walking on feels spongy, like it might give way at any moment. I try not to think about rats and roaches and spiders. I try to keep up with Zee, matching my steps to hers.

At the top of the stairs we walk past doorways to what were once apartments. Old newspapers are scattered on the floor, crumpled, yellowed. The floor is wooden, incredibly worn, scratched. There's a smell like dirty socks.

"Well, this is it," says the alderman, sweeping his arm out in a circle as though to clear away cobwebs in front of him. "First floor will house an office and community rooms. This floor will be dormitory rooms."

Zee walks around the room, unafraid of corners and what might be in them. She looks at the ceilings, the torn up walls.

She folds her arms decisively and nods at the alderman.

"Yes," she says. "I can see it. We can do it."

"It needs a lot of work," the alderman says. "Of course, the budget doesn't allow for everything."

"I know. The contractors will do major repairs first. Then the residents will pitch in. Right, Emily?"

"Right. I've got a welder and a carpenter who have volunteered to donate their time." Cass and Jenny.

We head back downstairs.

"So when do you think we can open?" Zee asks the alderman.

He smiles. "If everybody in this keeps their promises, before election day."

"By then we'll need more than three times this space." Her electrified hair is etched by shafts of sunlight shooting down from the western sky. Fiona's shelter on the north side just can't accommodate enough of the women who need help.

"It's a step in the right direction, at least."

"The future, Emily, the future," Zee tells me as she drives back toward the loop. "Got to keep heading there. I know you just went to another funeral. That's why I brought you along today. I need you to stick with me, OK?"

"Sure."

She reaches over and pats my shoulder.

Bikes

"So, how was Michigan?" I ask while I'm spotting Cass in her basement. She's doing bench presses. I was supposed to meet Amy Rejikowski Miller today, but I called and canceled after Paul's funeral.

"Not bad," she says. Then pauses, concentrating on lifting.

"I just ignore the controversial stuff, you know. Whatever that was this year." Another pause. I barely touch the bar as she pushes it up again. I just help guide it. "You should have come, Hawk. Rosalie was disappointed you didn't."

"That's nice of her," I manage. "But I'll just bet she had no shortage of admirers there."

Cass finishes her set and catches her breath, chuckling too. "Well, she *did* meet someone in the kitchen clean up crew one night."

Cass doesn't mention whether Rosalie and this woman got together that night. In her tent. Or mine.

When I don't laugh or ask any questions, Cass looks at me like she knows what I'm thinking.

"Listen, Emily, you need to forget that Catherine woman. And if you'd ever bother to show any interest, I bet Rosalie would be happy to do more than borrow your tent."

It's my turn to use the bench.

"I know what you need," Cass tells me. I don't dare argue, since I'm lying on the weight bench and she's standing over me. I'll need her to take the bar away from me after I finish. Up, down. Up, down. Toward the ceiling, I'm thinking *sky*, then back down toward the chest. "You need to get your mind on something else for a while." I finish, and she takes the bar.

"Like what?"

"Like motorcycles. Remember how we used to talk about getting bikes? We start on Tuesday. I'll pick you up. Wear jeans, a long-sleeved shirt, boots, gloves."

"*What* are you talking about?" Cass used to talk about getting a bike, and I told her I'd be too afraid to drive one.

"The motorcycle safety course. Over by Northeastern. Don't worry. I'll pick you up. We'll do it together."

"Oh, yeah?" Has she gone insane? Has she forgotten I'm afraid of them?

"Well, just come the first night at least. They'll just show movies and stuff. I promise, they won't make you ride one unless you want to. Besides, it's good stuff about safety to know even if you just ride a bicycle."

"Right," I say. But I haven't got anything better to do on Tuesday.

Friction Point

"The course is free, so what's not to like?" Rosalie asks. Cass has brought her along. "You don't mind, do you, Emily?" Rosalie asked when I got into Cass and Nor's car. Not at all, I reassure her. I hardly know what I mind anymore. I mind not having Catherine in my life, but I try to put her out of my mind.

The first night we watch films about helmets and about the bike's parts. We each take home a handbook. Cass already knows everything about bikes. Tuesdays are her night off, and she says she has a ball. Rosalie and I are both nervous.

"It's just like a car," Cass says the following week. "You just let out the clutch slowly while you give it some gas. Then you go."

"Right. I guess I'm just not used to shifting with the toe of my boot."

"One down, three up. No problem."

"Right. Easy as pie."

"*Friction point,*" Rosalie says, grinning. "I like that. You just have to find the exact point where the clutch and the throttle mesh perfectly—they release all that pent-up energy and—"

"Oh, enough already! You have a one-track mind!" But we all laugh. It's good. Cass was right. The course is fun.

It's scary too. The first night we try the bikes, I'm slower than the others. The instructor, a friendly guy about average height and build, takes me aside and works with me until my balance improves. My problem is, I keep stalling the bike. I can't quite seem to coordinate my left hand on the clutch and my right on the throttle. Friction point isn't so easy for me to find. If you can just get the hang of first gear, you've got it, everyone tells me.

"You're afraid of the throttle, Em," Cass tells me after watching me screw it up a dozen times. "Don't be so afraid of the gas. Don't clutch quite so hard. You panic, then you clutch too hard."

Rosalie picks it up quick, but a few minutes before the end of our fourth class she's parking her Honda and it goes down. She goes down too. Next thing I know, I've dumped mine and have run over there. Cass already is kneeling down, helping her out.

"Rosalie, are you all right?"

She looks at me as if she's just awakened out of a dream.

"I think I just passed out for a minute, that's all. No big deal, really."

Cass wraps an arm around Rosalie and walks her over to the cycle shed. Rosalie takes her helmet off. I follow. I want to reach for her, hug her.

The instructor calls me back over to pick up my bike.

"Don't do that again, Emily," he says. I nod. I hardly notice the bike as I pick it up and start it. I let the clutch out, the throttle. It surges ahead, smoothly going forward, the power underneath me carrying me down the pavement. I do my circles, then my beginner's figure eight. When class is over, Cass and Rosalie congratulate me.

"You did it, Emily!"

I shrug.

"Rosalie, are you sure you're all right? I was worried. But I guess I didn't know what to do."

"Don't worry, Em. I'm fine. Cass just stayed with me a minute to be sure. But hey, she didn't have the teacher on her case."

Rosalie throws her arms around me then and gives me a hug.

And it's OK.

After that, she drops out of class, but she still comes every week to watch Cass and me. Rosalie prefers her bicycle. Cass and I finish the course together, ignoring the male jerk who started greeting us every week with "here comes Salt and Pepper!"

Cass buys a Kawasaki, and I buy a used Honda Nighthawk. "Has to be a Hawk, Emily," Cass tells me. "Besides, I think they're sexy. I like a chunkier bike for me, but for you it's perfect. Got your name right on it, in red letters. What more could you ask?"

So I'm Hawk riding a Hawk now, 400cc, and I like it. I still use CTA most of the time, but for fun I bring the bike. "Don't you just wish that woman could see you now, Emily?!" Cass joked the other day. "Bet she'd have a shit fit."

Catherine told me she didn't like motorcycles. She couldn't imagine why people would risk their lives riding them.

As summer turns into fall, I like to buckle up my gear and head out of the city for the open road. I go with Cass or alone, or with Rosalie. Rosalie likes to ride on the back while I drive. I go south on I-55, down past Joliet, and get off the interstate and take country roads. I go up to Wisconsin, too. Pretty country up there. I ride and think. The cycle vibrates under me, steady and powerful. The wind rushes past, a loud, drumming noise, and I feel like I'm flying. Nothing but a helmet and a jacket between me and the air. The air touching me, caressing me. The wind singing in my ears. I can go anywhere. I'm feeling my power.

Mercedes is still alive, still fighting. She might beat the odds. When I ride the Hawk out into the wilderness, past fields of shorn corn and drying wildflowers, I think she'll win. The wind tells me she'll win.

I like it when Rosalie comes with me on a Saturday or Sunday. She wraps her arms around my waist and snuggles into my back. I like that. I like it a lot. "Just what I need," she tells me, when we stop at rest stops, "a celibate motorcycle mama." I grin. I'm not afraid of Rosalie anymore. I'm not afraid I'll seduce her or be seduced by her.

"This is the future," I tell myself.

Openings

Naywa would stay another hour, but I tell her it's time for us to stop. She's been in our office an hour already, helping us work on a study of employment opportunities for Asians. I've been helping her with her English. She is a slender Chinese woman whose English is nearly textbook perfect but who doesn't believe me when I tell her how good it is. She always wants to do better.

Her brother was killed in Tiananmen Square. Now, when she and her husband call her parents, her father tells her that yes, the government is right to crack down. There was no massacre. Her brother's death was an accident, that is all. Soldiers only fired when they were attacked. Naywa mustn't believe western propaganda.

Zee and I want to help Naywa stay in the U.S. after she finishes her graduate program in sociology, but it doesn't look good. The U.S. government tells her she has to find an employer that will hire her at a salary of at least $25,000. The employer must look at a large pool of applications and select Naywa over all the Americans, and then must complete a form assuring the U.S. government that Naywa must be allowed to stay in the country because she has unique abilities essential to the position. The date is rapidly approaching.

"Is there anything I can do?"

"I don't think so. I'm going to keep trying, that is all. I have to. I have no choice. But, Miss Hawk, why do they make it so hard?"

"I don't know, Naywa. I wish I knew."

She stands to go. "Enjoy the opening," she tells me.

"Thanks. Have a good weekend."

"OK. Thanks for all your help."

I start to tell her it's nothing, but just wave her on.

I gather my things.

"Going already?" Zee asks. I nod. I know she's pleased with the work Jenny and Cass have been doing on the west side shelter for homeless women.

Outside, the sky is a crisp autumn blue, and I can see the Sears Tower, which will not be called the Sears Tower any longer but something else. It's hard to keep track of things in this city.

My job has done its work for me this fall; I become immersed in helping people like Naywa and Rafik find their way around. They read voraciously, embracing this strange language, this confusing culture. Many of my clients like me because they are romantics like me, people without skins, touched and altered by flashes of beauty and pain wherever they occur. These people come to the world with open hearts. I take extra time with them. Life will not be easy for them, but passion does not escape them and therefore they are lucky. And even their wounds will remind them that they are alive. They will not die, as Thoreau said, without having lived. As I suck in deep breaths of chilly October air, I zip up my leather jacket, adjust my helmet, pull on my gloves, and climb on my motorcycle. My new toy. I've got my Hawk, I've got Zee, I've got my clients, I've got Cass and Nora and Rosalie and Barry and Mark Berger and all the other people who are there for me and who need me there for them.

The opening is in Wicker Park. I park the bike. It's a group show, paintings, prints, drawings, sketches, photographs by people with AIDS (PWAs). Some dead, some alive. Laura couldn't make it, but I'll call her this weekend and tell her all about it. When she left after the funeral a few weeks ago, I told her I'd be sure to notice how they hung his work and what the lighting was like. Paul had already selected the pieces he wanted for this show. Paul's sister Betty has shipped the rest of the art, except for a few pieces she wanted, to Laura.

Several smaller groups of people are milling around, holding plastic cups of wine or sparkling water. I walk through the gallery first. I want to look at the art. The paintings range from male nudes to disturbing visions to abstract geometrics. The prints are campy, wild combinations of blue and yellow and red. The photographs show scenes of Chicago. Shadows on buildings. Stairwells. Predictable stuff.

Paul is represented by four pieces—a violent surrealistic landscape; a print showing textures of fabric swatches, a gold chain, a fishing lure, and a lambda charm; a self-portrait in pen and ink; and a portrait of David Miller. It's titled, simply, "Portrait of David." Seeing the drawing up close, I notice that Paul has somehow indicated a mysterious quality. The eyebrows and the eyes draw you in, but it seems as though they're looking right past you, beyond you into something you can't see. The fine, high forehead and classical lines—good cheekbones, an aquiline nose, a beautifully defined chin—all suggest a timeless elegance. The mustache is slender and neatly trimmed; the light hair is fine and seems to lie lightly on the head. There's an intelligence, a reserve, and yet a wistfulness about the face. Paul has put more detail into this drawing than into anything I've ever seen by him. The crosshatching is more thorough, the shading more carefully managed. Every mark seems more precisely executed, as though the artist knew his subject better than he knew himself.

When Eric and a few other friends arrive, I stay and chat for awhile. We talk about Paul and about Laura. It's not long before I feel like there's nothing more to say.

"Boy, that fellow was handsome," Eric says, nodding at the drawing of David.

"Yeah. The one Paul wanted to find, and that I never found. Got as far as his parents. They hung up on me. Dead end. I got the feeling they didn't know where he was and didn't care."

Then we're all silent a minute. I wonder if everyone is thinking what I'm thinking: that Paul's parents were pretty much that way, too. Only Betty came through at the end. She's back in St. Louis now. Trying to go on with her life. Like all of us. I decide not to tell them about Amy Miller, now Amy Rejikowski. The point is, I still haven't found David. It's time to leave.

I'm a few feet from the open door of the gallery, blocked by a cluster of new, well-dressed arrivals, when I see her. She's looking straight at me. Our eyes meet. A bolt of electricity shoots through my heart, my lungs, stinging and jarring me, throwing me slightly off balance. She's stunning. She's wearing white. A white silk blouse. At least I think it's silk. A strand of pearls. A black linen skirt. A matching jacket draped over her arm. She sees me, and a shadow falls across her face. She's on Patrick's arm. Both of them tall and elegant. He begins to move on to the next photograph. He doesn't see that she's looking at me. She takes a step to keep up with him, but nearly stumbles. Then he notices. Catherine never stumbles. He sees me. She turns to him. It looks as though he's asking her a question. She says something to him. He takes her arm more firmly and leads her past the next photograph and out of my view.

Catherine. I'm shaking at the mere sight of her. It's been how long–two months? Three? And she and Patrick dressed to the nines. Me in my leather jacket and black cowboy boots. Probably Patrick was making some derogatory remark about what kind of lesbian I am. Probably she was shocked to see my gear. Relieved she didn't stay with me. Relieved to know she's not with *that* kind of a lesbian. Bull dyke. Bull dagger. Dyke. I am what I am. Yep. She was definitely out of your league, Hawk. Whatever possessed the two of you to think you could be compatible? Who would have thought she'd be at this show? She doesn't know anyone with AIDS. Maybe Patrick does. Maybe they just have an hour to fill before a play begins.

Dammit, but Catherine's a stunning woman. And especially in white. She can wear white like nobody else I know. Makes it look easy. Easy to be so fresh, bright, clean. When I wear white whatever I touch finds it and stains it. Coffee. No, Emily, white and motorcycle grease just won't do. That's what it boils down to: logistics.

I wonder if she'll look at Paul's work. If she'll remember anything I ever said about him. Will she study the portrait of David Miller? Will she notice–it strikes me like cymbals being struck inside my head–how much of a resemblance he bears to her? Both of them classic. Lovely in their bones.

Uptown

"Shit, Cass, it's cold out here. We'll finish this thing just in time." We're building a shed in back of the house to store the bikes in for the winter. I've told Cass Thanksgiving weekend's my limit. Today we'll finish the shed, and I'll say goodbye to the Hawk for the winter. We could get our first snow, a light one, before Sunday.

Later, we're tired and hungry. The bikes nestle against each other like sisters in bed together. We eat a quiet meal of salad, rice and beans, and Nora's cornbread. We have pumpkin pie for dessert. Rosalie's having Thanksgiving dinner with her parents.

"You still interested in finding David Miller, or is that best left alone?" Cass asks me over pumpkin pie.

"Why do you ask?"

"Cause I gotta know."

I study her face a minute. As usual, I can't tell a thing. Cass can be unreadable when she wants. So I think about it. Would it make any difference to find him now? What would be the point? Does Cass know something?

"Sure, I guess I'd still want to find him. Why not? I could still talk to him, tell him what Paul wanted him to know."

"You sure?"

"Sure."

"All right. I had to ask. I got something for you, Em. And you ain't gonna like it. It isn't pretty. It's from my old days, you know? The 'what it was like' times."

"Oh." From the times when she drank. Did drugs, maybe.

"Ran into Herbie. My old connection. He's trying to get clear, he really is. I feel for him."

"What she means, Emily, is she's sponsoring him. He calls her every day." Nora smiles, like she's proud of Cass.

Cass shrugs. "So anyhow, Herbie, well, he knows lots of people. I mean, *lots* of people, Em. But most of them he knows through, you know, the business."

"Cass, are you trying to tell me that he knew David Miller? That David was into drugs?"

She looks at me evenly. "A real wino. Still is, Em. Still is."

"Where?"

"Right here. Chicago. Our fine city."

"Do you have an address?"

"Yep. But I'm only gonna give it to you on one condition."

"What?"

"You're not going alone. If you decide to go after him, I'm going with you."

"What about calling him? Maybe I can call first."

"Hah." She turns to Nora. "This girl don't know shit about the life." She grins at me.

"Wait a minute. How do you even know it's the same David Miller?"

"Well, it might not be. But he sounds like the same. Herbie said he's a white dude, blond. Mustache. Mid-thirties. Used to have a wife. A baby too, maybe. Talks about some damned white artist. When he's loaded."

"Paul. He talks about Paul." I'm mumbling to myself.

Nora insists we take her car, because it's newer and more reliable than Cass's, has the best pickup if we need to speed up to escape the terrible criminals that await us.

We pick up Herbie at a detox center up on Kenmore and then go to Wilson. I think of Bonnie's block in Bucktown, how the gangs took over at night. In summertime, the little kids would play in the streets and open the water hydrants. Bonnie wouldn't have water for a bath or a shower for days. She learned to save it in pots and pans. Finally, Bonnie moved. And I was glad. I realize now how glad I am. How nice it is not to worry about her safety. And if she's living with her new lover–not so new anymore–then I'm glad too. So long as she's safe.

Cass parks and we get out. I'm wearing my leather jacket and a pullover cap. I pull on gloves.

"Whoo-ee, it's getting cold," Herbie announces.

I notice some men warming their hands over a fire in a large garbage can. This is their Thanksgiving. Smoke rises lazily from the chimney of a two-flat nearby. Right here, in this vacant lot, used to be the transient hotel David lived in. Why didn't it occur to me before that he just stayed in the same neighborhood? Zee has told me that people who are disoriented or depressed sometimes do that. When the building is gone, they just stay and live on the streets.

Herbie walks up to the men. Five of them. They're bundled in overcoats and hats; I can't tell what they look like. You can't even tell the race of the men with their backs to us. But Herbie seems to know what he's doing. Cass and I hang back, listening.

"It's Herbie, man. You know. I'm over in the detox now. Whyn't you come on with me?"

"Leave me alone, Herbie."

Herbie motions us over. Cass nudges me, her arm reassuring me too.

"David?" He looks thinner, older than his pictures, but the bones are the same. The knit cap covers his blond hair. The forehead, at least. His nose looks like it's been broken. Not recently, but sometime since the pictures and the portrait. No mustache. Stubble all over his face.

"My name's Emily Hawk. David, I'm just here to deliver a message. It's from Paul Cameron. You remember him?"

I wait for what seems like a very long time. David doesn't move. He sounds like he's having trouble breathing. A cold. Bronchitis, maybe. Asthma. Then he starts walking away from the fire, away from the men.

He motions me over. Cass and I follow.

"What about Paul?"

"Paul didn't want to tell you himself because he thought you wouldn't want to talk with him. He asked me just to tell you how sorry he was about what happened. He said he was really hurt when you left, that he said horrible things. And he wanted me to tell you that he regretted it. He didn't hate you."

I wait. David needs a shave, I think. Needs a shave and a bath and some food. He stands there shivering, looking like the saddest person I've ever seen.

"Is that all he wanted you to tell me? Is that it? Nothing else?"

"That's all. He didn't expect a reply. Just wanted you to know that he, well, he loved you. Still did. Never stopped. For some reason, he wanted you to know that."

David nods his head weakly, not meeting my eyes.

"Do you think he'd want to see me, after all this time?" He's looking at me now. "Would you take me to see him? I mean, I could get cleaned up. I wouldn't want him to see me like this. Or maybe he doesn't want to see me."

He's looking directly at me now. I can't look away. He reaches and tugs at my sleeve. "What? What?"

"David, Paul's dead."

Letting Go

"The point is, you did what you could," Fiona says. Cass has put up with my blabbering all week about David Miller. She says not to worry, that Herbie's going to help David, get him into the detox center. But I can't help the crying and the need to talk about it. Again and again. So I come to Fiona.

"Maybe, maybe not. Maybe if I'd found him when Paul was still alive, he would have been able to see him and then—"

"And then what? Can you let go of torturing yourself, Emily? You're not God. You can't save him if he doesn't want to save himself. And you kept your promise to Paul. Don't you think you should give yourself a pat on the back for that? Have you told yourself anything *kind* lately?"

It's cold, it's December, and I have a cold. I blow my nose into one of Fiona's ever-plentiful tissues.

She's saying the same things Laura said. Barry said. Let it go. You did a good thing. Now let God handle it. I know they're all right. But maybe it wasn't a good thing. Maybe it was meddling. Maybe I only brought David more pain, when he's had plenty. The balm of forgiveness can be a sweet, healing blessing, but sometimes I think it arrives too late.

"I don't know whether I should tell his ex-wife about seeing him or not."

"Do you think she'd want to know? And do you think there would be any harm to anyone in telling her?"

"I'm not sure. I don't know her at all."

"Trust your instincts, Emily. You can figure that one out."

I sit for awhile. I know Fiona's right about that one too.

"You said you'd seen Catherine. Do you want to tell me more?"

I crumple up the tissue. I look away from Fiona, at a bland framed poster on the wall.

"I saw her. She saw me. At the opening. We didn't speak."

"And?"

"And, it, it, well, it was a shock. I looked at her, and I still felt it. Everything."

"Felt what?"

"Felt like I'm still in love with her. But of course that's crazy. We're not at all alike. She's this stunning, well-dressed woman, and there I was in my leather jacket."

"So? Sometimes you're well dressed too."

"Yeah. Sometimes." I'm crying again. "Fiona, I really want to call her, but I–I just know I shouldn't. But I can't help thinking about it. I want to see her again. Maybe we could at least talk about what happened. Or maybe that would just be more pain."

"It might be painful," Fiona says. "But does that mean it wouldn't be worthwhile?"

Damn. Fiona forces me to think. "But, let's say I did call, let's say she didn't hang up on me. Maybe I'd just blow it. Maybe it would just turn out to be a big mess. I feel like I've made a mess of everything." Paul felt like he'd made a mess of everything. David felt like he had. They didn't talk. "Fiona, I'm scared. I'm scared that there might just be one chance that we did love each other, and that if I don't try to find out about that, someday I'll wind up feeling just like Paul. Only then it will be too late."

I wait for Fiona to say something. She just looks at me, rocking gently in her chair.

"Well?"

"Well, what?"

"Why don't you say something?"

"What do you want me to say?"

"Anything."

"OK. I'll say something. You said you're afraid you'll wind up feeling like Paul. Only then it will be too late. Right?"

"Right. That's what I said. What do you think?"

"I don't think anything. Only you can know how you feel. So you tell me how you feel. I think it's pretty clear. Now, I think that you can probably draw some conclusions from the way you feel."

"Like what? Like should I call her? You think I should act on those feelings, right? But what if they're crazy? What if I'm really wrong? What if it's all in my head?"

"What if it is? What's the worst that can happen, Emily?"

"Well, she could yell at me. Hang up. Be cold. Distant."

"So? Is that the worst?"

I think about it a minute. "Yeah. I guess so."

"So? Can you survive that?"

"Yeah. I guess so."

"So?"

"So. So what? You think I should call her?"

"I think you should do what you need to do to take care of yourself. I'll support you in whatever decision you make."

"Dammit, why do you always say shit like that?!"

"Because I've already told you everything I can. When you were in here a couple of months ago you were convinced she had rejected you because she hadn't called you after she left. But *you* were the one who had told her not to call you. If anybody's going to call anybody, you've always known it isn't going to be Catherine. So if you think you might be ready to call her, then that's what you'll do. If you're not ready, you won't. I'll support you either way."

Foolish Pride

It's pride, that's all it is. I'm pacing my apartment. I've just had dinner and washed the dishes. I've put George's picture back in a photo album. I'm packed and ready for my trip home to see Mom and Eddie and Marianne and the kids for Christmas. So why can't I just sit down for one minute, make one very brief phone call to say that I've been thinking about Catherine. Missing her. Wondering how she is. What she's doing for the holidays. Damned foolish pride. The hawk who wants to soar too high. Really just chicken. Really a pigeon. Am I so proud I'd rather be miserable, thinking that I'm worse than I am? That's the most insidious form of pride. The pride that tells me I'm just too awful and have been the author of deeds beyond forgiving. Like a hawk preying on people. Is that what I do? As though any of my puny, pigeon deeds could have such power. Come on, Emily. So you were stupid. So you said the wrong things. If she thinks that, so be it. Worth a try. Dear Goddess, if I am killed in a plane crash, I do not want Catherine to think I really never wanted to see her again. I'd rather she think *she* chose not to see me again, not that it was mutual. If that's what she wants, so be it. She can stay in her marriage of convenience with Patrick and go places with him and not have to worry about messy intimacy. Or. Or. She might be dating someone.

If she is, she is.

There's no one who would be better for her than I am.

Sure, Emily. After the way you treated her the last time she saw you.

Well. There's nobody who's willing to learn more than I am. Nobody who would be more devoted.

And what about the differences? The music festival? She isn't going to change. Not likely.

So if I want to go, I'll go. Alone or with friends. I was stupid. I wanted to show her off. As though that would impress my friends. So other women could look and see us together and be envious of me. Whoa, look at that Emily and her lover. What a catch! More foolish pride. Nothing to do with love. Nothing whatsoever. What did Catherine want? What did I want? I can fly on my own. Why do I need her to fly with me?

I don't. I want to fly to her sometimes, pause in that arc of flight, find a point of reference. The point of return that defines all flight. Otherwise, it's all just a whirling through meaningless space. Space without definition.

But none of this is what I want to say. None of this makes it easier to pick up the telephone.

But I do. And I don't dial Barry's number. Or Laura's. Or Fiona's. I dial hers.

It rings. Oh, no, what if it's not her machine? What if she's home?

"Hello?"

"Catherine? It's Emily. I hope it's all right to call. I mean, I hope it's not a bad time. I mean, I hope you don't mind."

"I don't mind." Her voice is sweet. "I'm surprised. I just got home. It was my night for tutoring after work." She doesn't sound irritated.

"I've been wanting to call you."

"Uh-huh." Her tone is encouraging. It says she understands.

"I just couldn't get up the nerve. I felt bad about what happened. I didn't want you to leave that day. I said everything just opposite of what I meant. I don't know why."

"Uh-huh." She pauses. I think she's lighting a cigarette.

"I've wanted to call you too, but I didn't dare. Then, when I saw you at that opening, I could hardly stand it. I told Patrick I wanted to go and talk to you, but I was terrified. I just had to collect myself. Then, a few minutes later, I burst into tears. Right there at the gallery."

"You did?"

"Uh-huh. I wrote you notes. Five or six times. On cards. I'd find just the right card, and I'd write in it asking you to call me. But I just couldn't mail them."

"But aren't you angry with me?"

"I was. But mostly I was hurt. I felt like you didn't give me a chance. I felt like you thought I'd flunked Lesbianism 101 or something. Like I wasn't good enough for you." Her voice wavers.

"Oh, Catherine." The tears are coming now, salty tears. I can't bear it that I've hurt her. I want to be in the same room with her, alone with her. I want to put my arms around her and hold her, tenderly. "None of that stuff matters. I just didn't explain it. I made you think it was more of an absolute than it is with me."

"I'm so glad you called."

I savor this. I savor her voice, her words. I'm tasting my tears, but my heart is soaring.

"I miss you," I tell her. "Would you be willing to get together sometime?"

"Yes. But I'm going to my mother's for the holidays. Maybe after Christmas. Do you have plans for New Year's?"

"No. I'm going to see my mother too. But I'll be back for New Year's. Shall I call you when I get back?"

"Please do."

There, I tell Mango after I've put the receiver back in its cradle, that wasn't so hard after all. And she doesn't hate me. And she was glad I called. Glad! Shouldn't have waited so long.

I put on a Deidre McCalla tape and set up the ironing board. Good time to catch up on all my cotton shirts and wool slacks. One less chore to do when I come back.

When I've heard both sides of the Deidre tape, I continue ironing shirts in silence. The silence is peaceful, like a steady stream of warm water washing over my nerves. Suddenly, the door buzzer goes off like about ten alarm clocks all at once. Mango jumps off the table and runs into the bedroom. I go to the buzzer and push the "talk" button.

"Who is it?"

"It's me, Catherine. May I come in?"

Catherine! How? What? I punch the buzzer. She must have left Oak Park right after we talked.

At my apartment door, she's breathless both from the stairs and from the same reason I'm breathless.

"Well, now *I'm* surprised. Come in."

"I'm surprised, too." She's shaking. I help her take off her coat. I hang it in my hall closet.

"Can I get you anything? Water? I can put on some tea."

She follows me to the kitchen. "Tea would be fine."

"Sit down, Catherine. There–just move those newspapers over." I've left the day's papers scattered across my table.

"I've never done anything like this. I don't know why I'm here. I just had to see you. After we talked, I just couldn't bear waiting until New Year's to see you. Emily, I've, I've wanted so much to see you." She's hunched forward, shaking. She's crying again. I turn the flame on under the teakettle and walk over to her. I lean down and wrap my arms around her. I just hold her like that. For a long time. When her body quiets, her breathing settles down, she turns in the chair, and we hug, awkwardly. But it feels good. It feels like the most natural position in the world, she sitting in the chair, and me squatting next to her. The teakettle whistles, and we laugh. Shyly. Nervously. I go and take care of the tea.

"What's this?" There's a package on the table. I hadn't even noticed it when she came in the door with it.

"It's for you. I–I bought it some time ago, thinking I'd just surprise you with it. But then, well."

"Yeah. I know. I screwed up."

"No. We both did. Or neither of us did. Oh, I don't know. Anyway, I wanted to bring it to you tonight, for a, for a Christmas present. Since I won't see you 'til New Year's."

I just stare at it. It's wrapped in white paper with a lavender ribbon and bow.

"Open it, Emily."

She's watching me. I open it. Inside the box about the size of a coffeemaker is a carved wooden hawk. The wings are raised and slightly spread. The beak is finely polished ebony, and the eyes look like onyx. The bird itself is a heavy, dark wood, maybe mahogany. I set it on the table. Perched on its wooden base, the hawk looks like it's poised, ready to fly. Its eyes are watching the air, looking for prey or simply testing the wind, scanning tree leaves or grass or water for signs of the wind's presence.

"It's beautiful," I say.

"Yes, it is, isn't it." Catherine looks from the bird to me. "And so are you."

She's already standing up, opening her arms to me by the time I whisper, "May I kiss you?" We kiss tentatively at first, as if we have never kissed before, as if we're both testing our lips, our tongues, our mouths, carefully. We gently draw away. My heart is pounding.

"Here, have a cup of tea before it's cold."

After the tea, Catherine looks at her watch.

"Almost time for the news."

"Is it that late?"

"Yes. I should be going."

I watch her eyes.

"You have to work tomorrow?"

"Yes."

There wasn't any planning to this. She hasn't brought any clothes. I walk her to the door.

"Catherine, thanks for coming. Thank you for the hawk. I can hardly wait until New Year's."

"Me either." She leans down and hugs me again.

"I feel bad about your driving all the way in and having to turn around and drive all the way back this late."

"Don't. Don't think anything of it. I wanted to come. I don't mind."

"If you knew how I've missed you–"

"I've missed you, too. What I meant to say, Emily, was that I needed to come tonight. I needed to do this. When I saw your friend Paul's work at the show, and realized he had died, it was all I could do not to send you a card. But I didn't want you to think I was taking advantage. I didn't want to act simply out of my need. But Emily, I just knew I couldn't live the next ten years of my life the way I lived the last ten years. All those wasted years pining after Elaine, after love I couldn't have. And then I had you, and then I couldn't have you either. If you hadn't called, I don't know what I would have done.

I've just been miserable. And I would have gone on being miserable."

I hug her again. She holds me tightly. No holding back. Long after we part, long after I've closed the door after her, I feel warm. From my center, from the heart. I feel as though I'm surrounded by soft feathers. Cushioned by them. So this is what happiness is like, I think. This is what it is.

Snow Person

"I'm glad you got in touch with me," Amy Rejikowski says. I called her just before Christmas. Now it's January. We're sitting on a bench in a snow-covered park in Evanston. Nina is building a snow person with another little girl. Nina has blond, curly hair. She celebrated her fourth birthday last summer. Amy has told me of David's difficulty accepting his homosexuality. "I didn't know any of this at the time, but he told me later. He loved Paul, but he was scared. We were already having problems, but he came back and wanted to make it work. And we did manage to stay together for a couple more years. We had Nina. But I knew he wasn't happy. Not really."

"Look, Mommy!" Nina shouts at us. "Arms!" She has found two dead branches to put into the snow person.

"I knew because he started drinking more and more. He was just making himself go through the motions of our life together. Except for Nina. He loved her. But something was wrong. And then he lost his job because of the drinking. Things got worse and worse. Finally I asked him to go into treatment or leave. He left."

"He's in treatment now," I tell her.

"Has he mentioned me or Nina?"

"He talks to his friend Herbie about Nina. And apparently he's mentioned you. Herbie thinks it might take some time."

"Even though it was the drinking that made me ask him to leave, I know that's not the real problem. I don't want to get back together with him. I just want him to be happy."

"Would you want to see him again?"

"I'd like to think we could be friends. I'd like to think that someday—I mean, if he could stay sober—he could spend time with Nina. My parents help out a lot, but it would be good for her if she could have him too. He was great with her when he wasn't messed up."

"What about his parents? Are you in touch with them at all?"

Amy sighs. "Well, the Millers are a bit odd, as you found out when you called them. They don't want to have anything to do with me. They think I could have kept David straight if I'd been a better wife, even though they blame him. It's a no-win situation. They do acknowledge Nina and sometimes send her presents, but that's about it. Of course, they live so far away it doesn't really matter."

"Look, Mommy!" Nina shouts. "It's a real snow person! And it's smiling!"

The snow person has three leaves planted in its face, making a mouth, smiling.

Warmth

We have an agreement, Catherine and I. We spend Sunday nights together, and either Saturday or Friday. But one night every weekend I visit other friends or go to the coffeehouse if I feel like it, and she plans something else. Usually she goes to a show with Patrick. There have been nights of snuggling during January and February, some Sundays spent staying in and staying warm together. Even in the dead of winter, I feel warmer these days. My chest is lighter, stronger; something moves more freely inside. In my dreams it's always summer, and I do a lot of swimming. One of them recurs. We're at the beach, Catherine and I, and I'm swimming out, far from shore. I take big, broad breast strokes. My arms are wings. I'm soaring on them, buoyed by the vast liquid space. The water's currents are gentle but strong, moving back and forth, with me, against me. I'm at home in this powerful, uncontained, undefined force that moves wherever it will, regardless of me. I swim and swim, taking deep pleasure in my body's motion. Catherine lies on the shore, soaking up heat from the sun and from the sand beneath her, packed firm by recent rains. I know I will turn soon, and head back for shore, back to Catherine. But I take my time. I can swim out as far as I want, testing the cold waters, and always come back to Catherine, who will warm me.

The Quilt

By March David's in a halfway house. We meet for breakfast one Saturday. He looks better. His face has more color. He's put on a little weight. When we shake hands, his grip is steady.

"Good to see you," I say.

"You too." He smiles. "I hope I'm not so scary to look at this time."

Great, Emily, I tell myself. He must have noticed just exactly how terrified I was that day. Cass grins.

We go to a church basement where people are making panels to add to the NAMES quilt. Several other people are working quietly on panels. A few men and two women. They all look up, and some give us smiles of welcome, before returning quietly to their stitching. The NAMES quilt has grown so big it can't be shown in its entirety anymore, but Cass tells us that people will continue to make panels in their own communities, as long as people keep dying.

I work on stitching some panels together while David picks out materials for Paul's panel. Cass and I enjoy watching David sew swatches of different fabric. He adds sequins. Cass leaves early to stop by a print shop and pick up flyers for a demonstration.

"I'll see you later, Emily. Or maybe I won't for awhile—ever since you got back together with what's-her-name, it's hard as hell to catch you!" She pretends to slug my shoulder.

"Give my love to Nor."

"Sure thing. Listen, ask Miss Catherine or whatever when she'd like to come to dinner."

"OK." She might just say yes.

The panel David makes is simple. The panel itself is made of two pieces of fabric, one half yellow, the other brown. On top of it are swatches of red and gray. A border of blue sequins. Paul's name in black letters.

"It wasn't Paul," he says calmly, in his raspy voice. "It was me. I didn't want to leave. But I just didn't have the guts to stay. I ran as fast as I could right back to my wife. I really thought I could just *make* myself straight, you know."

I nod, encouraging him.

"I was wrong, of course. But then I just felt too terrible about how I'd handled everything. Paul, Amy, and then Nina."

Silent now, David looks as though he's in pain.

"One day at a time," I say. "Remember, Paul didn't want you to torture yourself over him." David nods, still in pain.

When he's finished the panel later that afternoon, I ask him to come to my apartment before he goes back to the halfway house.

"This is something that Laura and Paul's sister both agreed you should have." I show him the portrait. David's lower jaw drops.

"Haven't you ever seen it before?"

It's a moment before he answers. "I remember he kept saying he wanted to do one, kept asking me to take a day and just sit for him. I never did. He must have done it after I left."

"Do you like it?"

"Like it? Like it? It's Paul. I mean, it's the way Paul must have seen me. It's a lot more flattering than the real thing."

"I'm not so sure about that."

He stares at me. "You're nice, Emily. But even if I ever did look like that, I sure don't anymore."

It's true that he's developed some wrinkles.

"Maybe right this minute, today, you think that way. And maybe you're right. But Paul didn't just make you up. He saw something in you, and he loved it, and he tried to get it down on that paper. The question is, can you see it?"

"I don't know. I've heard that stuff about lovers mirroring each other. Your lover reflects you back to yourself. Only more beautiful."

"Except it's *not* more beautiful. You're assuming there's a reality that isn't beautiful." I stroke Mango's head. She's sitting right next to the wooden hawk on top of my lower bookcase. She's almost exactly the same size as the hawk.

"But some things *aren't.* Aren't pretty."

I know he's seen them. "Some things aren't," I agree. "Sometimes we make things ugly, make ourselves ugly. The truth is that we *are* beautiful, but sometimes we close our hearts, and without our hearts our eyes can't see. Paul loved you. He opened his heart and saw you, David. And he didn't lie about what he saw."

We study the portrait for a while. Such careful precision. Painstaking. Yet somehow it looks effortless.

Tears are rolling down David's still beautiful face.

"It helped," he tells me, "what you told me that day. I thought to myself, if Paul didn't hate me, then he wouldn't want to see me like this, and if Paul were alive, I wouldn't want him to see me like this. So I decided. I decided to stop staying in all that hate. All that guilt. It has to stop somewhere."

We wrap the portrait in brown paper, and he takes it with him. He needs those eyes, I think. The loving vision Paul has left him.

Seesaw

When the ice has melted for the third time, Catherine and I decide it might really be spring. On a cold, bright Saturday we load up her car with a thermos of coffee and a couple of overnight bags. Soon we're on the highway. Catherine sets her cruise control. She knows exactly how long this trip will take, exactly how many miles. She's told her mother when we will arrive.

"Amy Rejikowski," she says, after I've told her the latest news: David has been to see Amy and Nina and expects to visit Nina once a week. "I had no idea."

"I never told you her maiden name."

"She was a year ahead of me in high school. Had a part in one of the school plays. Patrick knew her too. So she wound up in Evanston and has a little girl."

I watch the soggy fields, the buildings we pass. From time to time Catherine turns to smile at me. I smile back. I do not reach out to touch her. Instead, I turn back to the window and study the landscape. When we reach Rockford, we drive through a neighborhood, past a school, then a small park.

"Catherine," I say suddenly. "Stop. Stop the car. Please."

She turns into the park. "What? What is it, Emily?"

"Just park here. Just for a minute. I have to get out."

She doesn't argue. She parks. I slide out of my seatbelt and snap my down vest over my shirt. I don't look back at her. I head right over to the swings and sit down in one and start swinging. After a few minutes, I hear a car door slam. Catherine comes over to the swings.

"What on earth? Have you lost your mind?"

"Nope. Just felt like swinging. Come on. It's fun."

"Oh, you. Emily, I swear sometimes I think you're five years old." But she's smiling. She stands there watching me for a minute more, then comes over and sits in the swing beside me. "I've never been much good at this. And besides, I'm too tall for these swings. These were meant for little people. Not fair, shorty."

"OK," I say, watching my breath mist in the air. I gradually wind the swing down, waiting until it's almost stopped before jumping off. "Let's try this instead."

I walk over to the wooden seesaw. It's got a good coat of paint on it, and there's no ice, no water left from the ice. I sit down. The other end bolts up into the air.

"Come on," I say.

"I don't know if I can."

"Sure you can. Just hop on."

"Besides, don't we have to be the same weight or something for it to work?"

"You may be taller than me, but I've got some meat on these bones. Try it and see."

She looks skeptical. But then she gradually reaches for the seesaw, swings one leg over it, and sits. I begin to rise.

"Hold on. Like this."

I take the bar in my hands and use it for leverage. I go back down, Catherine goes up. Then she gets the hang of it. The wooden board lowers me to the ground. Almost. Then it's lifting me back up. Then I come down, and she goes up. We balance. We keep rocking. Up, down. Catherine, me. My side of the seesaw touches the ground. Just for a second, a brief kiss. Then it sends me back up into the air. The sweet, sweet air.

Karen Lee Osborne received her Ph.D. in English from the University of Denver, where she was a member of the Graduate Writing Program. She has taught English and Creative Writing at several universities and currently teaches in the English department at Columbia College in Chicago. She was a Fulbright lecturer in American literature at Tbilisi State University in the Georgian SSR.

Her work has appeared in numerous periodicals and anthologies, including *New Chicago Stories* (City Stoop Press, 1990). Her first novel, *Carlyle Simpson,* was published by Academy Chicago in 1986; it won first prize from Friends of American Writers and the Chicago Foundation for Literature Award.